HANDS ACROSS THE SEA

Pauline Gilchrist

RP
Resource Productions

First Published by Resource Productions in 2008

Copyright © Pauline Gilchrist, 2008

All rights of Pauline Gilchrist to be identified as the author of this work have been asserted in accordance with the Copyright, Designs and Patents Act 1988.

All rights reserved. No part of this book may be reproduced in any form, by photocopying or by any electronic or mechanical means, including information storage or retrieval systems, without permission in writing from both the copyright

owner and the publisher of this book.

Conditions of sale. This book is sold subject to the condition that it shall not, by way of trade or otherwise be lent, re-sold, hired out or otherwise circulated, without the author's prior consent in any form or binding or cover than that in which it is published, and without a similar condition including this condition being imposed on the purchaser.

Discounts on bulk quantities of this book are available. For details, contact Resource Productions.

Tel: +44 1274 829003

79 – 79A Norman Lane

Bradford

BD2 2JX

Email: sue.filio@resourceproductions.com

British Library Cataloguing in Publication data

A catalogue record for this book is available from the British Library

Gilchrist, Pauline

I. Title: Hands across the sea

ISBN: 978-0-9556435-8-3

Printed and bound in Great Britain by CPI Antony Rowe, Eastbourne

Acknowledgements

I would like to thank my wonderful family for giving me the inspiration to write this.

A true love story in every sense of the word. It proves that no matter what problems are put in front of you they can be overcome. The path of true love never runs smooth and this book shows that.

I would also like to thank my dearest husband, my tower of strength, my best friend. Not forgetting the people of Indonesia whom I have never met but hope to some day.

The list of people I would thank would be endless but heartfelt thanks go to my friends Sue and Tony who have encouraged me to do this. I hope you enjoyed the roller coaster ride with me.

I would also like to thank Maureen Zablocka for painstakingly reading the proof and editing it. Any remaining mistakes are mine and my publisher's!

To my children, may they be as happy as their parents

Chapter 1

It is another cold winter morning in Dundee. The wind is blowing and there is a frost on the ground. I thank my lucky stars that we have central heating in our house, not like when I was a little girl. I recall the days in the kitchen on winter mornings and watching the breath as it left my body in a stream of condensation.

I look at the clock and think Patricia will be up soon, so I had better shower before she gets up as she tends to stay there for ages, and if I have not showered by the time she wakes it knocks the sequence all to pot for rest of the day. So I head for the bathroom followed by my lovely husband, I shower while he shaves and does his teeth, then he follows into the shower as I do my teeth.

As we leave the bathroom Patricia arrives, her usual bleary eyed self. It's not worth speaking to her as I get no sense until she has had breakfast, so we just nod and acknowledge each others existence.

James and I dress and leave for work, bracing ourselves against the cold wind as we defrost the car. I hate this time of year; it is cold and still dark, roll on summer. We head off for work and James drops me off in the town; we kiss each other good bye and arrange to meet as usual by the bank in the city centre at 5 o'clock so he can take me home. From there on in it was a typical day, nothing much to say really. Started work at

8 am had lunch at twelve then went to meet James at 5 pm.

We got home, opened the mail that had been delivered earlier in the day and I began the dinner.
'What's for dinner tonight', James shouted from the lounge?
'Your favourite, steak pie, mashed potatoes and vegetables' I shouted back. 'It will be ready about 6.30, in time for Patricia getting in from work'.

'Hi Mum, hi Dad', Patricia yells as she runs in from the cold, I don't like the cold but she hates it. 'It is brass monkeys out there!' she exclaims. Maybe she should put on more clothes I think to myself. Patricia works in a ladies fashion shop in the town as the manager and has to be the icon of fashion, but as the shop is so hot she wears skimpy fashion clothes which don't keep the cold out. She will learn I smirk to myself.

We sit down for dinner and have our usual 'how was your day' chat. Everyone was getting their tuppence worth in. Patricia had had a bad day. 'I am so bored there these days, I can do the job standing on my head', she announced, 'and there is no challenge now'. I need a change! You know, I saw an advert in Cosmo today for shop assistants on cruise ships'. 'Oh' James and I said together, raising our eyebrows a little. We have been on a few cruises ourselves and although it looks glamorous to the passengers we are not convinced it is the same for the staff. 'Is that not a step in the wrong direction? From manager to shop assistant' I venture. 'I know' says Patricia 'it was just an idea. It is probably just the winter blues and I got caught up in the dream', she smiles weakly.

'However, on reflection you are young enough, only 23 and it could be a laugh, spread your wings so to speak', I said. 'Or get your feet wet!' James pipes in and we all laughed.

'You know if you are not happy where you are then why not give it a go. You can always send in an application, get more information and take it from there. If you like what you find out then go for it. You always said ever since you were a little girl that you wanted to travel. Maybe this is your opportunity. As far as we know that when the ships are in port, the shops are shut, something to do with the duty free thing or something, therefore maybe the days are your own to do as you like, that way you would be able to see some of the world'.

We were all getting caught up in the excitement bantering ideas around the table. Maybe we should all put in applications we said, what a laugh that would be!

'Anyway', she says 'it was just a dream I had over lunch and probably won't do anything about it. I will be fine once the weather warms up a bit, I just hate winter'.

Life went on as normal, working all week and looking forward to the weekends just like any other normal family. Our son's partner was expecting a baby in April, so all our energies were being concentrated in that area, preparing to be grandparents. Not something we had banked on this early on but exciting none the less. James, Patricia and the parents knew the sex of the unborn babe but I asked not to be told as it would spoil the 'surprise'. I spent my time buying baby clothes and blankets in cream, a nice neutral colour.

Then one day as usual we arrived home from work, checked the mail delivered that day and there was a big envelope addressed to Patricia from a cruise company! 'Well, well, well', I thought to myself, 'she seems to have taken us at our word and made enquiries into that job she was speaking about'. I ran through to the lounge where James, as always, was watching the evening news. 'Look at this I exclaimed!' He took the letter from my hands and looked at it with great interest. 'Wow!' He said, 'I never thought she would do anything about it, did you?'
'No, but you know what she is like, she gets something in her head and won't rest until she has explored it'.
'I know, I will put it by her dinner plate and see what she does. See what reaction she has'.

That night Patricia bounded in as usual and greeted us with 'Hi Mum, hi Dad'. It is now February and still as cold and she is still as scantily clad. Maybe she won't ever learn! We sat at the table with bated breath and waited for her reaction. She sat down, and looked at the envelope....

'Well', we both said in perfect harmony. 'Oh my goodness', she said, I never thought I would hear from them, I sent the slip from Cosmo away a couple of weeks ago'. Inside the envelope was an application form.

'Are you going to fill it in?'

'Well in for a penny' she said, 'likelihood I won't hear anymore but, well why not. Mum you are good at this sort of thing; you will help me won't you?'

'Of course, filling in forms is what I am good at; I do it all day at work'.

That night after dinner and the house tidied up again we set to work. It asks for black ink, so if you want to stand a chance then complete it in black, don't give them any excuse to ditch it before they read it. I scanned the form on my PC and we used that as a template. Once we were happy with everything she lifted the information and copied it onto the original. She then promptly put it in an envelope and asked me to post it on the way to work in the morning. As all good mothers I did what she wanted and posted her application.

Before we knew where we were there was a reply to her application, the cruise line seemed quite keen. No wonder, a manager with lots of retail experience, chances are, they would grab her.

*Dear Miss Gilmour you are invited to an interview on the 18th March in Edinburgh......*The look on her face was priceless. So the dye had been cast. We decided to make a day of it in Edinburgh. Patricia could go for her interview, which was an all day event and James and I would spend the day shopping, after all the 18th of March is my birthday!

We dropped her off at the hotel in plenty of time, she looked great, a funky diva but with an air of sophistication. We all had our mobile phones and agreed that she would call when it was all over, and we would go back and get her. So off we set to the shops, leaving a somewhat nervous daughter behind. I wondered what treat my darling James was going to buy me for my birthday. As it turns out I was as nervous as her, and all I could think about was how the interview was going. However I did get a lovely pair of black shoes with a heel to die for and matching bag, so not a total loss. We went for coffee and cake and waited for the call. It was now 4 pm and she had been there since 10 am so we assumed all was going well. Then the call came. We headed off to the hotel to pick her up and get the low down on what had happened.

All the way home in the car was question after question, getting all the information from her. It all seemed quite exciting. Although the wages were poor, she would have her board and lodgings supplied and therefore the wages were for her to do with as she pleased. They had told her that they pay for her flights, and every ship had a doctor, so if she was ever sick it would be ok, in the case of serious illness they would fly her to the nearest hospital and eventually home, so that was a weight off our minds. We were right about the shops being closed whilst in port, so she would have some time to see the places the ship visited. Her main concern was 'what if I get the job and they send me away before the baby comes?'

'Not likely', I said, 'the baby is due in six weeks and I doubt if it would happen as quickly as that'. So, we played the waiting game, every day waiting to get home and check the post to see if anything had arrived. I was told I had to call her at work if a letter arrived.

Then one day it arrived, was it *'I am pleased to tell you that you have been successful'* or the other, *'sorry but…'.* I was on the phone in a shot, 'Patricia', I said all excited, 'it's here.' I will leave it on the table for you', although secretly hoping she would ask me to open it, which she did. My hands trembled as I fumbled to open the large white envelope; James stood over and kept saying 'come on come on, hurry it up!' I grasped the contents and scoured the first few lines; it was a *'you have been successful'* letter. I screamed the news down the phone just to hear her cheer with delight. The letter said that they would be in touch in the next few weeks with dates, and an itinerary.

That night she bounded through the door, no 'Hi Mum, hi Dad' just 'where is the letter!' She read it over and over again taking it all in. 'Oh my God', she said, 'could this possibly be the start of something new and exciting? Am I doing the right thing? Will I accept when the offer comes through? Should I hand in my resignation now?' A hundred and one questions came from her mouth. 'Stay calm', I said, 'the letter says *'do not tender your resignation at this time as you will be given plenty time…'* when they give you your itinerary'.

'True, true', she said and then read the letter again. 'I have read this letter several times and there are things I have to do before I get my details'.

'Oh, like what?'

'I have to be passed fit to work on a ship and have to get a specific doctor to pass me. I will get that arranged, and I also have to have an American Visa as this is an American company. It is going to cost me though as these things don't come cheap, I have to go to London for the Visa. Fancy a trip Mum?'

So she arranged an appointment with the doctor and sent away her Visa application.

I was at work when I got a call from my son, 'Louise has gone into labour', he said, 'and I am going to be a Daddy. Can you come up and keep us company as Louise doesn't want to go to the hospital too soon?'

Not bad I thought, only one week late, not like me with Patricia two whole weeks and then I had to be induced. 'Great son, I will let Dad know and be there as soon as we can.'

What a relief I thought to myself, Patricia will see her new niece or nephew before she goes. We were somewhat worried that she may miss the big event as things had been moving so quickly.

We all went to our son's house to keep them company

and make sure Louise was ok. By the time all three of us got there Louise was well on the way with her labour so we didn't actually stay very long. Louise had a bath and as soon as I made sure she was ok we left and my son took her to hospital. I waited by the phone for the news. The night dragged on and on, James and Patricia went to bed as they had to go out of town for her doctor's appointment for her seaworthiness medical the next day. So I sat there all night waiting patiently. I called the hospital several times for updates, and was told Louise is doing well but not nearly ready to deliver. By 8 am still nothing, so I was marched off to bed to get some sleep as I was told my new grandchild would not want to see his grandma with bags under her eyes. So I did as I was told, although sleep was the last thing on my mind. I must have nodded off for an hour or so though, as I heard Patricia and James return from the doctor. I got up and headed down stairs, in a bit of a daze but desperate to know how she got on.

'It all went well and I have been passed fit so that is one thing out the way. How about Louise any news yet?'

'No nothing, I don't think that baby wants to come out!'

I made tea and coffee and just sat down when the phone went!

'It's a boy! said a tearful Josh, 'and he is beautiful.'

'It's a boy,' I exclaimed!

'Yes we know,' said James and Patricia, 'we have known all the time remember?' and they laughed at me in unison.

'When can we see him,' I said through tears of joy and relief.

'They are just tidying Louise up and checking Cameron over then they will move them to the ward, so you can come up about 7 pm.
'Cameron,' I said, 'he has a name and it's Cameron.' I was tickled pink, or maybe it should have been blue!

We ran upstairs, changed and then ran to the local supermarket, grabbed some flowers for Louise and a blue outfit. It was strange knowing what to buy this time. We then hurried to the hospital to welcome the newest member of the family, Cameron. There he was, a beautiful baby boy, he looked just like his Daddy, dark hair and lovely dark brown eyes and perfect in every way. The new Mummy and Daddy looked exhausted and no wonder, that was a long labour but nothing could cloud their happiness and pride.

Three weeks later Patricia and I went off to London to get her Visa, it was hard for me leaving the baby but I did. We set off on the train, Dundee to London a six hour journey. We pulled out of the station, and as we did I waved to my colleagues in the office block where I worked as it overlooked the station. No one was there to return my wave, but that was ok, it was done with a hint of sarcasm anyway. We then headed over the Tay Bridge and we looked at the seals on the sand banks in the river. We were armed with lunch and drinks to keep us going, and magazines which we swapped throughout the journey. We had been in London together in the November before this cruising thing began, so we were prepared and travelled light, no point taking as much luggage as we did last time, as it came home unused. We arrived in Kings Cross, and this time saved the price of a taxi and took the tube to Bayswater... Again, keeping to the same location as before, as we knew it was nice. The tube journey was uneventful, which was good. I was advised to look straight ahead and not to make eye contact with anyone, and to keep my bag over my shoulder. London is a tricky place, and these precautions can save a whole heap of trouble. Patricia had been to London several times and knows all the ins and outs. It was strange taking instructions from her instead of the other way around but I was glad she did. I have a bad sense of direction but she knew exactly where we were going so I was happy to let her lead the way. She moves with ease and speed so I had to jog to keep up with her, not wanting to lose sight of her. She thought this was hysterical, her leading me. We checked into our hotel, it was clean and tidy, which was good as we got a bargain package and were somewhat apprehensive in case it was not nice. We dumped our bags in the hotel room and left to go exploring. We had bought an all day tube ticket so we headed back to the main shopping area of Oxford Street. Patricia and I went on a shopping spree whilst we were there, and managed to find a newborn Manchester United football strip for Cameron. We knew Daddy would be impressed with that as he had been a fan of theirs since he was a boy himself. Patricia could shop for Britain so we used our time roaming around and taking in the fashions there. We then headed back to Bayswater and went for dinner. It was great spending girly time with each other.

We had a nice pasta meal and then went back to the hotel. Next day Patricia went to the American Embassy to get her Visa. She had to do this by herself as security at the American Embassy is somewhat strict. So I waited with her in the queue until the security guard moved me on. There was a big queue and Patricia being a sociable girl got chatting with the people who were also waiting in line. I went and did some shopping and sight seeing, but did not go too far as I have a dreadful sense of direction and was afraid I would get lost. I could see the headlines now.

'New Scottish Grandmother Gets Lost In London'. I smiled at the thought. I waited for her text to let me know that she was finished, so we could arrange a place to meet. About 4 o'clock the text came through and we met up again in Oxford Street, like I said I don't go much off the beaten track. Taking advantage of the late shopping Patricia couldn't resist another look around the shops. She bought some bits and pieces and we decided to go to a Chinese restaurant for dinner. What a disaster that was. Everyone's meals looked delicious but ours arrived and looked somewhat anaemic compared to others. We looked at each other and neither of us would admit that we were not impressed. The majority of the meal was left; we paid the bill and headed for the nearest shop that sold chocolate. We bought some supplies and went back to the hotel, watched TV and ate sweets a bit like a pyjama party. My feet were too sore to do much else as I had walked all day. I was not brave enough to get the tube on my own.

We headed for home the next day, on the train home Patricia told me that she was staying with her friend overnight the next night so they could catch up on what had happened in London, the Visa etc. Her friend Kaz had travelled about a bit so she is keen to hear the entire goings on

Another day at the office, after all the excitement of London I spent the day telling all my colleagues of my antics. Then another strange phone call, I was asked to go down stairs as Patricia wanted to see me. I went down to see her and she asked me the strangest question.

'Hi Mum, which number plate do you like best, this one or that one?'

'What a strange question,' I said, 'why ask me that, you don't drive and don't have a car'.

'Well,' she said all in a quiver, 'I do now; I just passed my driving test!'

'Wow you kept that quiet, I didn't know you were taking lessons'.

'I know,' she said, 'I have been taking lessons for ages and it has been hard keeping it a secret, but I did it', then she burst out laughing.

'All you need now is a car then!'

'I know Josh wants to sell his as he wants a four door car because of the baby. Why don't you see if you can buy his off him and he can buy another for the family?'

'Good idea Mum, I will speak to him tonight.'

She called Josh that night and it was arranged that she would buy his car for the amount that was outstanding on his loan and he would buy another that was more suitable.

She was now mobile, a taste of freedom! As all mothers I was concerned about her driving alone for the first few weeks but I need not have worried as she is a very confident driver. It was good for us too as we were no longer a taxi service!

It has been a whirlwind and no mistake, then the bolt came out the blue, the phone goes again. This time Patricia says, 'Mum I am off to Seattle on the 17th June and going to cruise Alaska!'

Chapter 2

Oh my, the 17th June, the day before James's birthday! That will upset him, his little girl not here to help celebrate his birthday. You see James and Patricia have a special father-daughter bond. They are so similar, the same nature, temperament, outlook on life, she looks like me and that is where the similarity ends. Patricia and I are great friends as well as mother and daughter, but her Dad is her hero. That will be hard for them both, separated on a special occasion.

I phoned James at work to tell him the news; there was a deathly silence at the other end.
'Are you ok?' I asked.
'Shocked,' he replied, 'I never thought she would actually do it. I thought that it was a fantasy and would never come to be, as it were.'

We discussed it at length and decided she was a big girl and that she should do what she wanted, not that we had any chance of stopping her once she had made her mind up. Like I said, just like her Dad!

That night over dinner we all talked about the up and coming adventure, which after all was going to be a great experience. Going to travel, see the world, and getting paid for it. It sounded ideal, but a bit scary. The next thing was to get everything organised.

Next day she tendered her resignation at work. That was it, the adventure had begun. Patricia posted notices at work advising everyone that she was leaving and having a leaving party at one of the pubs in town, the date and venue already arranged. Then she had to do the mundane things like chose court shoes, the one bit of uniform that was not supplied. Court shoes indeed! Patricia the icon of fashion in black or navy court shoes! She owns more shoes than Imelda Marcos her father would say, and he was pretty near to the truth, sandals, shoes, high heels, flat shoes, boots all colours and styles, but court shoes, not on your life. Then there was her wardrobe to sort out, what would she take? She was going to Alaska so should it be bikinis or woolly jumpers? Or hot pants or jeans?

'Take an assortment' I said, 'that way you can't go wrong.'

She agreed with me and began to choose what was hot and what was not.

'You can take lots of stuff with you, you have a huge luggage allowance and your dainty size 8 clothes won't take up much room.'

'Good point,' she said.

So the pile of clothes on the bedroom floor increased. That's my girl! Her bedroom was never tidy and today was no exception, she had clothes, shoes, lotions and potions scattered all over the place including medicines like headache tablets, cold remedies.

'Better to be safe than sorry,' she said.

So the days passed and the dreaded day got closer. It is

hard to think of your little girl becoming an adult and making decisions, life changing decisions, leaving home and going so far away. I mean Alaska! The bonus was this was going to be her training ship and then the ship would leave from Vancouver instead of Seattle. My sister lives in Vancouver so if it all goes wrong I have a contact close by to help. '*Over protective mother!*' I hear you say; well I guess you are right.

The tickets arrived in the post. Flight details, hotel details, instructions of what she has to do when she arrives in Seattle. Now it is real, everything in place nothing left to think about, it was under way and under control.

It is Saturday night and we have on our glad rags, we are off to the pub for Patricia's farewell night. Lots of people were there to wish her well. Gifts were given to her, drinks aplenty, lots of hugs and kisses and a few tears, but a good night had by all.

'I didn't realise I was so popular,' said Patricia.
'Of course you are Patricia,' says James 'and I a lovely, witty, beautiful girl, you will be missed by many, but not as much as by Mum and I.'
The tears rolled down my face as I realised my little girl was now a woman and all grown up.
'Hey, Mum you know I am only going to be gone for six months, I am coming back you know. If you are feeling flush you and Dad should come over and do a cruise

and I can see you then and you can also visit Aunty Carol. Then you won't miss me as much eh?'

'Now you are talking,' I said. 'That could be good, I haven't seen Carol for years, so we could kill two birds with one stone. Alaska is meant to be beautiful too, so a cruise there would be wonderful.'

My wheels were beginning to move, I smiled at her and she laughed as she said she could hear the wheels whirring.

On the 16th June we had an early birthday dinner for James so Patricia could help celebrate. All the family were there, James and I, Patricia, Josh, Louise and Cameron. We spent the evening on edge knowing that a goodbye was looming. We did the birthday cake and candles, but no gifts. We decided that they could wait until James' birthday on the 18th, something to look forward to after the day at the airport.

Well the time came for Josh to say goodbye to his sister. I hate goodbyes so I hid in the kitchen until I thought it was over. As I walked out into the hall they were still hugging each other and I choked back the tears again, this was becoming a habit. Only a few months earlier my son had left home to live with Louise that was hard and now I was watching my daughter leave home too. What happened to my children? They are all grown up now, was I redundant?

Patricia said her farewells and gave Cameron a baby hug and kiss and took another picture of him on her mobile phone so she could keep him with her. He slept through it all and was unaware that his only aunty was going away for six months. What a difference she will see in him when she gets home. Here I am looking forward to her coming home and she is not even away yet!

I spent the rest of the evening tidying up the house and keeping busy. I was dreading the next day. I spent a dreadful night, as did James, unable to sleep, tossing and turning in harmony but not saying a word. Our world was about to change!

Chapter 3

We all get up, it is only 3 am but we had to be at the airport three hours before take off and it takes an hour and a half to get there. We are all bleary eyed due to lack of sleep, I had my usual coffee but no nicotine as we had stopped smoking before Cameron appeared, not wanting to pollute him with our smoke. I could kill for a cigarette today but I am strong. I can do this without a cigarette. James is feeling the same and we just look at each other knowing what the other is thinking. Patricia is quiet too, full of apprehension, fear, excitement, uncertainty, but like her Dad putting on a good show.

We check and double check the tickets, passport, visa, luggage, money and instructions. I have read them so often that I know what she will be doing at every step of the way. Then it is time, we pick up the entire luggage and put them in the back of the car, everyone strapped in and James starts the engine, this is it, the beginning of Patricia's adventure. We try to make polite chit chat in the car but it was strained. We are all feeling the same. Patricia was feeling somewhat unwell. It was that time of the month and she had cramps and a head cold so she was a bit miserable. All that on top of the nervousness did not bode for a happy journey. I kept thinking to myself that she will be back for Christmas and that this is good for her but it didn't help the heaviness in my heart or the nauseated feeling I had in the pit of my stomach.

'Exit 29 for the airport,' I announced, and the car began to turn left, slowing down as we reach the terminal.

'You two jump out here with the luggage,' said James 'and I will park the car. I will meet you inside in a few minutes.'

'OK,' so Patricia and I grab the luggage, hand luggage and my handbag and head into the terminal. 'We will wait here for Dad by the coke machine and we will all go to the check in together.'

'Yeah, whatever!' she said.

I could tell by this response that she was feeling awful. I told her to take some painkillers for the cramps and she would feel better, knowing that this was only part of the problem. At least it was one thing less for her to contend with. I watch as James enters the airport, the normal spring in his step is missing. His smile is weak as he approaches us. He is trying so hard to be cool and calm but inside he is a wreck. He has to stay strong or we will all collapse in a heap of tears. It can't be easy being a man. Showing on the outside that you are cool and calm, in control when inside you feel someone has torn out your heart and jumped on it.

We head off to the check in desk, dragging two large suit cases behind us and Patricia with her hand luggage containing all the documentation she needs. We walk up to the desk with her, James picks up the heavy luggage and places it on the conveyor belt to be weighed, then we step aside. James looks at me and says,

'I don't know how she is going to manage all that stuff at the other end. There is nothing of her and that stuff weighs a ton.'

'She is strong she will manage, and if push comes to shove she will bat her eyelids at some unsuspecting gentleman and hope he will help her,' I joked.

'True, true,' he replied, 'and she knows how to bat her eyelids, she has been doing that to me for 23 years, and it works every time.'

We laugh.

'What you two laughing at?' says the little voice behind us. We turn to see Patricia with a puzzled look on her face.

'We were just saying.....' my voice tapers off as I look at her and realise she is bagless.

'That's it,' she says 'all booked in and the flight is on time, I have to be at the gate in an hour. So, anyone for a cup of coffee?' The paracetamol has obviously kicked in and she is feeling a bit better. That's a blessing.

We head for the coffee shop and order two mocachinos and a black coffee for James.

'I can't stand all that carry on with coffee,' he said, 'whipped cream and blenders, chocolate powder, what ever happened to plain old fashioned coffee?' He is back on form, having a bit of a moan about being ripped off with the prices. 'We should have gone to the burger bar, the coffee is cheaper there and you get more of it.' Patricia and I look at each other then skywards as we have heard this conversation so many times before, and we titter amongst ourselves. James looks at us and laughs too knowing that we are making fun of him.

That was a good ice breaker as we all start to relax a bit and the conversation flows more freely. We all love to people watch in places like this, so the fun begins.
'Look at what she is wearing,'
'Honestly who wears black with navy?'
'Those shoes, is there a special shop for shoes like that, you never see them in the high street!' The comments flew between us, we know sarcasm is the lowest form of wit but it made us laugh which helped release the tension. The time was passing too quickly, but in a way it was good, we were spending our last hour laughing.

Then the moment came, we had all secretly been watching the clock knowing the goodbye was to come, the inevitable tears.
'Well,' I said taking a deep breath, 'I suppose it is time, you don't want to keep the pilot waiting.'

We all stood up, the silence was deafening, as we started the walk towards the departure area. My legs were like lead weights and I knew the others felt the same. So, we got to the bottom of the ramp that lead to passport control, already the tears were falling down my cheeks like burning rivers, and I hadn't said a word. I watched as James took her in his arms and held her close, whispering to each other words of love, encouragement and comfort. Then she turned to me, her tear stained face looked at me and we fell into each others arms and sobbed. I nestled her close to me like I did when she was a little girl, cradled her head in my hand and whispered to her, 'You will be fine.'

She whispered back, 'I am scared.'

'I know honey.' I said through stifled sobs, 'You are strong and it is what you have wanted to do for a long time, travel and see the world. Remember, we are just at the end of the phone if you need us and you can always email us, we will email you and you can check every time you find an internet café.'

I looked at her and said goodbye then showered her with kisses. She turned to look at her hero once more, but James was crying.

'I can't do this,' she sobbed.

'OK then let's take you home, I will pay the cruise company for the flights.'

'Oh Mum, if I go home I will never know what I have missed, I have to do it although it hurts so much.'

'I know honey,' her Dad and I said in chorus 'all we want is to keep you safe as always.'

We stood still, braced ourselves and let her go. Patricia started the climb up the ramp, wiping tears away from her blue eyes with the sleeve of her jacket just as she used to as a girl. She turned several times as we waved frantically to her. We watched until she was out of sight, all the way through the stream of other passengers who were obviously heading for holidays they were full of excitement unknowing that we were standing there in a state of turmoil. Then she was gone. James and I stood on the spot and hugged each other close sobbing as we did so.

'She will be OK, whispered James.

'I know, I know,' I replied, 'but this is so hard. I feel someone has taken my heart and thrown it on the floor and stamped on it.'

I could barely breathe, my chest was tight and my face swollen and blotchy. We continued to look up the ramp, secretly hoping she was going to run down and ask to be taken home, but it didn't happen. We regained our composure and headed for the car, our hands full of soggy tissues.

We reached the car, got in and sat in silence. A few minutes passed and we made sure we were both ok before we started our journey home.

'Yes let's go, no point sitting here.'

We were no sooner out of the car park when my mobile phone beeped, it's a text message. The message is from Patricia it read.

'I am sitting in the toilets and can't stop crying. I am scared. I love you both xx.'

James said, 'Who's it from?'

I can't tell him as I am crying again, the tears stinging my eyes. I am trying to text back but making too many mistakes as I can't see. Composure regained again, I reply to her and tell her we love her too and it is natural to be scared. The texts continue for a while and the last one read, *'I am about to board now. Love you x.'* I replied quickly hoping she gets it before she gets on the plane, before I lose contact with her. Once on the plane her mobile will be off and she will be more alone than ever. *'We love you I said, keep in touch, we are with you every step of the way xx.'* I press send.

'I hope she gets it,' I said to James but as I look at him the tears are cascading down his face.

'I can't do anything to help.' He is driving and on the motorway so he can't pull over. He wipes his face with his hand and tries to focus. I am watching the road now and making sure we don't collide with anything. He is ok now, he has stopped crying then I start again, this went on all the way home, when one was crying the other watched the road, how we didn't have an accident I don't know.

We pulled up at the house and walked through the front door; the house was quiet and felt empty. What now? More coffee, I seem to have been living on this for weeks now. I made tea for James and a coffee for me. I logged onto a website that tracks flights and saw that the flight left on time and that its status was 'in flight'. 'Ah well, she has gone,' and I say a silent prayer that she gets there safely. I head upstairs and straight into Patricia's bedroom. It is as untidy as ever which makes me smile. Nothing daunted I begin to tidy up, change the bed linen and collect all the dirty laundry. By the time I get downstairs James is sound asleep in the armchair. So I get going with the laundry. I can't settle, my mind is reeling and soft tears keep appearing. I pick up her dressing gown and before I put it in the machine I hug it close, it's like getting a hug back from her. Then I place it in the machine and press the button. Her clothes start going round and round, a bit like my head.

Back to the computer, I know her flight is not due in for hours but I check anyway. The status read still 'in flight'.
James wakens and wonders where I am. I have gone into the garden, the sun is still shining and I am looking skywards.
The voice behind me says, 'It's no use, you can't see her you know.'
'I know,' I said and begin to cry again, this time sobbing uncontrollably.
'Come on, come on she is going to be ok.'
'I could kill a cigarette,' I said.
'Well you know where they are if you really want one.'
So once again I weaken and reach for the cigarettes. I stay in the garden to keep the smoke out of the house, and inhale deeply. James said 'Well? Did you enjoy that?'
I wanted to say, 'No! It was awful,' but it wasn't so I said, 'Yes it was blooming marvellous.' That was the start of my downfall as far as the dreaded weed is concerned. It only takes one they say, and they were right. Before I knew it James had a cigarette too that was it, all our hard work gone in an instant.

The day drew to a close, and for the umpteenth time I checked the flight status, this time it said 'on approach'.
'She is nearly there,' I said and continued to watch the screen until it said 'landed.' A sigh of relief, at least she

27

was there safe and sound. All she had to do now was get to the hotel that had been booked for her, get some rest and wait to be picked up in the morning by the cruise company and taken to her ship. It was called 'The Diamond'. We had checked it out when she first got her letter, a magnificent ship, big and grand, very posh,' as we would say.

A while later there was a text on James's phone. *'Dad there has been a cock-up at the hotel, and the people here don't seem to understand me.'* Panic!! Our little girl was in trouble and so far away that we couldn't help. What to do now? James texted her back and asked for the hotel phone number meanwhile I was on the phone to my sister, keeping her on standby in case she had to go to the rescue. I know it is a fair bit away from Vancouver to Seattle but she was the nearest person I could trust and know that she would go in a second if there was a problem. 'No problem,' says Carol, 'keep me posted. I can be there in no time at all.'

There was no reply to James' text so he decided to phone her. Problem is his phone relates to his job and is paid for by the company so long oversees calls were not permitted.

'To pot with this,' he says, 'this is an emergency.' I heard him talk to Patricia and told her to speak to the people at the hotel again and speak slowly if they are having difficulties understanding her Scottish accent. To make it clear that she was to join the cruise ship, show them her documentation and see if they know what is going on. He was stern and forceful, he had to be, poor Patricia was in a state.

'Call me back as soon as you can and let us know what is going on. Mum has Aunty Carol on standby already so if it all goes wrong there will be someone you know with you soon. Stay focused,' he said as he hung up. Yet again I was a quivering mass, tears, sobbing getting in a state.

About an hour later she called home.

'I have spoken to the man at the desk again and have sorted things out. It appears the cruise company have given me the name of one hotel but booked me into another! So, I am waiting on a courtesy bus to take me from this hotel to the other. He was actually very nice and managed to understand me. He says this happens a lot, pity the lady didn't understand what I was saying. Anyway, I will call you as soon as I get a room. Love you, you can tell Aunty Carol to stand down; the panic is over, well for the moment anyway.'

As good as her word she called back.

'I am here, the hotel is nice and I have met some other people that are joining the ship tomorrow. I am not in the mood to be sociable so I am going to bed, whether I get any sleep or not is a different kettle of fish but at least I will try. Good night guys, I will call again tomorrow if I can. I am being met at 7 am, if they get that bit right! They may go to the wrong hotel.' she gave a little laugh.

'OK baby, get some rest and stay safe.'

The phone receiver was returned to the cradle. That's it for sure this time, panic over. Well, until morning!

So we retired to bed and tried to sleep, but again our minds were going over the events of the day. Another restless night spent in the Gilmour house.

The next day was uneventful, no phone calls from our girl. We have to assume that she was picked up and away to the ship. Now we wait patiently for her to contact us as we know as previous cruisers ourselves that mobile phones don't work when at sea. We check our emails regularly but nothing. There are still tears but not as bad as yesterday. Josh came over with Louise and Cameron. It was nice to see them and the baby kept me amused. Their visit eased the tension and we told them all about the antics of the day before.
'Don't worry guys,' said Josh, 'she will be back before you know it, meantime you can do all the babysitting, that will keep you busy.'

A few days later we got the call we had been waiting for.
'Hi guys, it's me! Sorry I haven't phoned before but it has been crazy here. I am in training this week so a lot of my day is spent in a class room. Blimey I have been in retail for years and they think I need training! The ship is beautiful and so big; I need training in how to get around this thing. I have met some nice people and some not so nice but that's life, right?'
It was good to hear from her, this time she was happy and sounded less strained, that was a blessing.
'I had to wait and get a phone card for the satellite link thing which has taken me a few days that is why I

haven't phoned earlier.'

There is a delay in her talking and us hearing and vice versa due to the satellite.

'It's hard to get used to Mum, they have given me a uniform. It is grotesque! Navy! It only fits where it touches so I will have to get it taken in! The boutiques are lovely so bright and big. I think I am going to like it here so don't worry.'

'What about the accommodation, what is it like?'

'Well, actually, it is quite nice. We have been put in passenger's quarters as there is no room in the staff section. Apparently this is par for the course while training as this may not be the ship I will be on for my contract. I will find out on Friday. I hope it is this one as it is really, really nice. I will let you know as soon as I know, ok?'

'Yes sure,' I said, 'just keep me posted, and drop me an email or something if you can.'

'Sorry Mum no can do, there are internet facilities on board but I am not entitled to use them yet as a trainee. Once I have been allocated a ship properly I will be able to email. I am not allowed off the ship either so no internet cafes for me. I have seen some lovely sights from the ship though during breaks. I had better go as I only bought a $10 card as I may not be here next week. Love you.'

'Love you to,' James and I shout down the phone, the line went dead.

'Well it was good to hear her hun?' said James.

'Yes, she seems quite happy and content, maybe now we can relax knowing she is ok.'

'Yes he agrees I am happier now.'
'Yes me too.'

As good as her word Patricia phones a few days later. 'Hello!! Just a quick call as I don't have much credit left on this card, $10 doesn't seem to go far. I just wanted to let you know I have been given my next ship. I hope you are sitting down before I tell you.'
'Oh oh don't think I like the sound of this' I think to myself.
'Well I am heading off to Auckland, New Zealand!! I am going to be working in the Pacific!'
'What!' New Zealand! Lord above even further away!' I exclaimed
'Yeah another nightmare flight ahead of me. There are a few of us going so at least I won't be travelling alone. I have heard mixed reports about the ship I am going to but it is known as a fun ship so I am looking forward to it. This one is lovely but very up market, just not me. So I fly out on Friday and join my new ship on Monday. Apparently this ship goes to places like Fiji, Tonga, Australia and New Zealand of course. I can't believe my luck and I thought I was going to be working in the Mediterranean. I will let you know my flight details as soon as I get them. I will be able to text you when I get back to Seattle. Got to go and pack again. I miss you guys, give Cameron a baby kiss from me and tell Josh and Louise I said hi. My money is running out so I will say bye before I get cut off.'
'Bye!' we both scream down the phone having barely

got a word in edge ways.

'Blimey couldn't get further away,' I said.

'No, she couldn't could she,' says James.

'Are you ok?' James and I said together.

'We agreed we would both be alright.'

'I will be happier when she has landed in New Zealand.'

I do hate it when people are travelling you hear so many disaster stories. I can never relax until I know they are safe and sound.

'Back to the PC again,' says James. 'Monitoring more flights then,' he chuckled.

'You can laugh,' says I, 'but you are right. As soon as I know those details I will be watching'. Always watching!

'I know I am such an old mother hen I look out for my family all the time, but that is who I am.'

The next day the post fell through the letter box. I was so excited to see a letter from America. I ripped it open; it was a card from Patricia. It had on it a mermaid with a green glittery tail. I opened it to see her writing and read it carefully. The card said,

'Hi guys, I am just writing to say thank you. Thank you for being you. I want to say sorry for being so silly when I got to Seattle, crying like a baby. I can't believe I did that, but it was good to call you and know there was someone just on the other end of the phone for me. It was like you were with me, guiding me as usual. I am so lucky to have such smashing parents. I know I don't say I love you very often but I do, I love you both

very much. So please keep this card to remind you. I don't think I will be on this ship when I have finished my training but I will phone you and let you know. I may even have called by the time you get this.'

Once again the tears rolled down my cheeks. I was getting used to her not being here and the words in the card reopened the wounds of my aching heart. She was never one for saying anything like that face to face so the words echoed and I felt the love in every letter on the card. I did notice however that her spelling had not improved but who cares about spelling when the words came from her heart. James came down the stairs to catch me wiping the tears.

'Oh no! What now?'

I passed the card to him. He read the words and I noted the single tear roll down his cheek. 'She really knows how to get to us doesn't she?'

'Yeah, I sighed, 'lovely though.'

I placed the card on the fridge and held it there with a magnet, that way I could read it whenever I wanted.

'Any other mail,' asked James.

'Oh heaven yes, there is something here for you.'

He looked at the envelope.

'Oh great,' he said 'it is our flight tickets.'

We were going to Spain for two weeks.

'Can't believe the flight times, they are really good'. 'This is just what we need, two weeks soaking up the Spanish sun, relaxing, fine wine, and nice food'. 'Just what the doctor ordered.'

Next day there was an email for me.

'Hi Mum and Dad,' it says, 'a friend here has let me use her internet time so I can send you this. Here are my flight details. She was to be flying to Auckland on Saturday. She gave me all the details and reminded me of the time difference.'

Chapter 4

Well it is Saturday so I am spending the day at home doing house work and watching the PC from time to time monitoring Patricia's flight. The day passes slowly but at least the house is ship-shape you might say; everything in its place, clean and shiny. I have even done the ironing. At least I won't have to do anything tomorrow which is good. That means I can spend time with Cameron when Josh and Louise bring him over. We are making it a weekly ritual, they come over on a Sunday and we all have dinner together. I love it you can't beat the giggle of a baby and the smell of baby wipes and powder. They stay late enough to let me bath him. I would be lost without that little boy, he makes my heart sing. A baby's love is unconditional and his big brown eyes look up at me with such trust. We have a strong bond Cameron and I.

The PC tells me that the flight has landed, another sigh if relief. *'That's good I think to myself.'* I will wait for the next phone call and news of her new ship. It is Sunday afternoon and everyone is here, as good as her word Patricia phones. Great, she can have a word with Josh and Louise too. She is twelve hours ahead of us so it is 1 am Monday morning to her.
'Hi,' she says, she sounds tired but I put that down to jet lag again.
'Hello baby, how are things your end?'
'Fine Mum, fine' she said. 'My new ship is called *'The Destiny'*. It is only small, well small compared to the

Diamond. It is not as fancy either which is just fine by me. It is actually in dry dock just now getting some repairs done. It will be there for a week or so. We are making sure all the stock is there and stuff like that. People are nice enough too, so all is all going well.'

'How was the flight?' I ask.

'Yeah, it was ok; actually there were three of us so we had a laugh not to mention a few drinks.'

'I wonder why they sent you there if the ship is in dry dock, you could have had another week on the Diamond, that way you could have got off and seen Alaska!'

'There was no room Mum,' she explains, 'there were more staff arriving as I left. It seems to be popular as a training ship. Builds up expectations then you are moved to a ship like this one,' she jokes. 'Is Josh there?'

'Yes,' I said, 'and Louise.'

So I pass the phone over to her brother who talks to her as only he can. For brother and sister they get on really well. I recall the day Cameron was born, as she saw him pushing the cot to the ward, their eyes locked and they spoke volumes without saying a word. Not like now they are chatting away like mad. James is waiting patiently for his turn to speak to his little girl. Josh looks at his Dad and realises. He breaks the flow of conversation and passes the phone to James. They catch up, he makes sure she is ok then hangs up. So we spend the next hour reliving the ten minute conversation. We

discussed the phone call, putting the picture together of her new life. She seems fine we all agree, quite chipper.

Josh says 'Yeah she seems to have made friends quite quickly.'
'I am glad; I don't like the thought of her being so far away on her own.' James and I just look at each other, welcome to the club!

Our working week passed as normal, nothing much going on. We are preparing for our holiday. Making sure we have Euros, the laundry is done and I have put the clothes that are ready for packing on Patricia's bed. I don't want to pack them too early.

Sunday again and like last week the family are round and I am preparing lunch. The phone goes, its Patricia.
'Ha ha,' she laughs down the phone, 'I knew I would get you all again.'
'You sound happy,' says James.
'Well we are down town having a couple of drinks. I just wanted to let you know that we are sailing to Sydney tomorrow, taking the ship to its new location. I think it is a test or something to make sure it is ok after all the repairs and stuff. So I will be at sea for a couple of days so back to the lack of contact,' she giggles.
We both giggle,
'Had a few have we?' I ask her.
'Just one or two,' she says.
'So you are off to Australia eh? You are certainly getting around.'
'Yeah not bad in just a few weeks, can't complain. The ship is ready for sea so they say, so they are moving it

to the first port of call in Sydney and prepare to take on passengers. We are to be there for a couple of days before the first cruise. That way they have time to correct any small upsets and we will start to stock the shops properly.'

'Great, it is all coming together now then, passengers and the like?'

'So far I haven't done much except find my way around the ship and made friends. My cabin mate is nice she is from Romania. There are people here from all over the world UK, America, Canada, Philippines, Italy, Indonesia, very multi-national. Anyway I had better go as we have to be back on board by 2 am. Just like when I was younger isn't it? Telling me when I have to be home! I will call again from OZ next time. Byeeeeeee!' she bellows and then she is gone again.

She is obviously getting used to being away from home now which is good. James and I are getting used to the quiet too, and the house always being tidy. Well apart from the mess a baby leaves behind, but I don't mind that. We tidy away the towel and nappies then head upstairs to pack for our holiday. We leave on Friday for two weeks of relaxation. It has been a strange few weeks emotions all over the place so we are looking forward to spending some time away, although I will miss Cameron, my little angel.

We spend the rest of the week preparing for our holiday making sure everything is in order. There had been a couple of emails from Patricia telling us of the antics she had while transferring to Australia. It all seems like fun, boy I wish I had as much fun at work. She is ready for action and for taking on passengers; she is looking forward to it as she says the honeymoon period is nearing a close.

Friday is here and we are heading back to the airport, seems like only yesterday that we were there with Patricia. On the way James noticed that there were lots of metal fences in the fields as we drive along.
'They are for the G8 Summit that is being held in Gleneagles soon,' he announced. It is all part of the security, to keep people at bay, making sure no one could get near the place. To be expected I supposed.'

We get to the airport and check in. Our luggage is taken and we head for the bar this time. We are on holiday now so no coffee, a little drink or two before we head off. We look around and we can still vividly see the drama that had unfurled just a few weeks before. I look around to see if there is anyone saying goodbye to loved ones and I do. I know what they are going through the pain they are feeling. There is a family leaving, it looks like Mum, Dad and two young children about 4 and 6 years old. They are saying goodbye to what I assume is the girl's parents. Oh boy I thought, what we went through was bad but to say goodbye to grandchildren too must be even more heart breaking. I can say that now being a reasonably new grandmother. My heart goes out to them.

I order a Bacardi and coke and James has a pint of beer. We sit there enjoying each others company and discuss what we will do whilst away. I am a great sun lover so I just want to sit by the side of a pool and soak up some sun, James wants to explore so we agree that we will do a bit of both. That sounds fair, we clink glasses, cheers we exclaim and begin to laugh.

The flight was uneventful. Typical aircraft food and as

usual not enough leg room but the flight is not too long so we we're ok. The door to the plane opens and we let the eager passengers off first. There are always those who can't wait to get off, always in a hurry, why I don't know, they still have to wait for luggage. So we wait for a few minutes and head to the door. The heat hits us like opening an oven door.
'Whoo hoo,' says I, 'bring it on' and I giggle. James just looks at me and smiles.

We get to our apartment within an hour and a half of landing so that was good. We book in and are taken to our rooms. I wait patiently until the man leaves having put our luggage by the side of the bed. As soon as he leaves I run round like something possessed, checking the bathroom, the view and how the air conditioning works. I like the sun but I don't like my room to be over hot or I can't sleep. That done we unpack then again head to the bar, this time we have a drink by the pool soaking up some sunshine before the sun goes down for the day.

The holiday unfolded at a nice pace, and the sun shone every day. We did try and explore but it was so hot that we did not get very far. We did try to find the beginning of the cable car, but as it was up hill it was not the best idea in that heat. We headed for the beach instead and went walking hand in hand with the waves lapping at our ankles. It was heaven. The sun was heating our shoulders and the sea cooling our feet.

Next day was my day so we spent it by the pool. I just want to lie there and read my book.
'We can then go to the poolside bar for lunch, then James you can chose where we will go for dinner tonight.'
'Great, I like the sound of that, and I think I know where

we will go tonight. There was a small place in one of the side streets called the *Blue Lantern* that looked quite nice I think we will go there.'
'OK that's that sorted. Grab the towels James; I have the books, lotions and hats here.'
We headed down to the pool and chose a nice spot where there was a nice canopy in case it got too hot but close enough to the pool so we didn't burn our feet en route. This is my idea of a holiday, peace, quiet, sun, good company and a good book. Yes not a bad combination, James agreed.

We were lying there minding our own business when all of a sudden my mobile started to jingle the little tune I have when I receive a message. It read...
Have you seen the news? There have been bombings in London! Not sure what has happened yet something about a bus.
It was from Josh.
'Oh my God!'
James sat bolt upright, he could tell from my voice that there was something seriously wrong.
'What is it?'
'Josh has just told me that there have been bombings in London! It is something to do with a bus!'
I asked the man next to me if he had heard anything in the news.
'No! But hold on my apartment is just over there, I will go and check the news and find out what is going on.'
I text back and tell Josh that we had not heard anything but we were trying to find out. The chap came back and told us about the bombings. It was hard to believe, boy it is close to home. We all spent the rest of the day discussing the situation as the majority of the other holiday makers were from the UK.

Sad I know, but I had to check my emails whilst away.

The place we were staying had internet access so I allowed myself a few Euros to check what was going on with Patricia. There was only the one and it was about the bombing in London. She said she saw it on the news and she was in tears.

'I sat there watching it with my hand across my mouth and found myself wondering what I would have done if it had happened in Scotland and me being all this way away. It wasn't worth thinking about as it upset me so much. I love you guys so much' she said.

There was no talk of ship life.

Well I suppose all good things must come to an end, it was time to go home. We got up in the morning and had breakfast. James came through and said.

'My back hurts.'

'Must have been the way you were laying,' I said and continued to clear the table.

'This isn't funny,' he said, 'this is sore.'

I looked out some pain killers and gave them to James with a glass of bottled water that I had kept in the fridge, so we had some cold water to take to the airport. He stood on the balcony overlooking the pool. I massaged the small of his back trying to help.

'Stop! Please that isn't helping.'

'OK,' I went to the bathroom and soaked a hand towel in cold water and another in hot water and took them to James, who to be honest didn't look well. I spent some time applying the towels alternatively hoping to ease the pain. Nothing seemed to help. One way or the other we had a plane to catch.

'Look,' I said, 'I will take the luggage down to the reception and book us out. Give me ten minutes and follow me down.'

'Yeah, OK,' he said through clenched teeth.

I dragged the luggage to the lift and waited patiently. That is the worst thing about everyone booking out at the same time; the lift was always full by the time it got to our floor. Finally I got in and handed in our keys to the receptionist. I waited downstairs for James. He was never coming, I was starting to worry. Where is he? I told myself to stop being silly and that he would likely have to wait for a space in the lift too. Thirty minutes later he arrived looking grey and barely able to stand up straight.

'Oh my word James what the heck are we going to do with you.'

'Just get me home,' he said.

Easier said than done I thought. I managed to get him and the luggage to the front door and hailed a taxi.

'Aerpuerto por favour,' I said in my best Spanish.

The driver was very kind and helped James into the taxi. He avoided the bumps and holes in the road obviously realising that James was in considerable pain. We pulled up at the airport and he helped James out of the car and me with the luggage.

'Gracias, muchas gracias,' I said and gave him a hearty tip. Not all men would have done that. I got hold of a trolley and put the luggage on, I propped James against the trolley and told him not to move until I came back, I went in and found out that the flight was on time and what check in we had to go to. I went back and collected my poor James. He is the only person I have ever seen that was going home grey and not tanned.

I supplied more painkillers and kept James as comfortable as I could. Poor soul couldn't sit, or stand still for too long so he kept taking the luggage for a walk. Leaning on the trolley seemed to help. We got checked in and went through to the duty free. I deposited him in one of the cafeterias as I wanted to get a toy for Cameron. There was a shop not far from there so I could keep an eye on James at all times.

The flight home was a nightmare. James was in so much pain. He spent the entire flight with his head on the back of the seat in front. I put him on the end seat with me in the middle. Fortunately the chap next to me didn't move for the duration of the flight which was a Godsend as I don't think James could have moved to let him out.

We got out of the airport and waited for the bus to come and pick us up and take us to the car. I was dreading driving home. I dislike motorway driving but knew James couldn't do it. Yet another knight in shining armour came to our rescue. A bus driver who was not from the company we had used said,
'Look mate, I will take you to the car park, you really don't need to be standing there waiting.'
We got to the car and James said, 'look, I will drive. The drivers seat has a lumber support so that may help and it will keep my mind occupied if I drive.'
'I don't think that is a good idea. I know I don't like driving but it will be safer if I do, don't you think?'
We agreed that he would give it a go and if he couldn't manage then I would drive home. As it happens he made it, but when we got home I had to ask Josh to come up and help me get his Dad out of the car. Josh was there within minutes; thank goodness he only lived down the road. We got James into the house and the luggage put in the hall. Josh headed home and said he would pop in tomorrow.
'Sure son thanks.'

Well things went from bad to worse. I ended up having to call a doctor during the night; He came and gave James some strong pain killers and some Diazepam to relax the muscles. They seemed to help a little. So we got a little sleep but I was conscious of every move that James made. Next day was not much better; I made sure James took the tablets left by the doctor. I made some lunch and made sure that James ate as I don't like the idea of tablets on an empty stomach. He went to the back door to have a cigarette, on the way back he said he felt ill. The next thing I knew he was about to faint so I grabbed a chair from the kitchen and sat him down. We were in between the kitchen and the hall. I grabbed the phone that was in the hall and called the emergency doctor. James was losing consciousness and not making much sense, his speech was slurred. I explained all this to the nurse on the phone. She told me that she was going to send an ambulance but I had to stay on the phone.

'OK, will do.' I had to hold James on the chair or he would have fallen to the floor. Fortunately my bag was still in the hall so I got hold of my mobile and called Josh.

'Get here quick son,' I shouted down the phone. 'I need your help now!

James by this time was grey and clammy; I was convinced he had had a stroke. Josh burst through the front door. He looked at his Dad and then up to me. I shrugged my shoulders and continued to hold James to stop him falling. I kept thinking how do I tell Patricia that her Dad was dead? Her hero gone forever and she was not here? Josh was kneeling at his father's feet and speaking to him. Somehow he began to come around, thankfully. Maybe it had been the fact that Josh had left the door open and there was a nice cool breeze blowing. Then we heard the siren. The ambulance was here, thank goodness. The paramedics were great, had everything under control. They put James in the ambulance and I said we would follow. Josh drove to the hospital following the ambulance.

It turns out that James had popped a disc and the pain had been so unbearable that he collapsed. A couple of hours later he was sent home having had Morphine. The doctor told him to continue with the painkillers and

Diazepam and bed rest for a few days.

'You scared the living day lights out of me,' I said, 'I thought I had lost you there.'

'Me to,' said Josh, 'I have never seen anything like that before and Dad, I hope I never do again.'

'Sorry but I had no control over it, I wasn't too keen on it myself you know!'

I was to return to work the next day but I couldn't leave James, he needed help to get out of bed and other things besides. I called in and explained the situation.

'I will keep you posted.' I told my boss.

We took the doctors advice and kept James in bed for a while only getting up to use the bathroom .Then one day I started to cry, for no reason, but I couldn't stop. This went on for a few days so I told the doctor.

'I am not surprised,' he said, 'you have been through the mill and now that James is on the mend you are beginning to buckle.'

He told me that he was going to keep me off work for a while to recharge my batteries. I told Josh and the rest of the family that Patricia was not to know that her Dad was sick and that I was off work too as she would just worry and that is not good when she is so far away. So that is what we did, she was totally unaware there was trouble at home.

Chapter 5

The emails and phone calls continued at regular intervals from Patricia, the ship was now taking passengers and she was always full of stories and details of places she had seen. Most of the stories revolved around the crew bar.
'This is where the staff hangs out when they have finished work.'
Drink was cheap and it was time away from everything.
'It is not easy you know, this ship is my home, my work place and my social life. This is all there is, so the crew bar is the only place to unwind. We have some laughs here and I get to meet staff from all over the ship not just the 'shoppies' as we like to be called. So here there are florists, photographers, waiters, hairdressers and girls from the spa, the only people not here are the officers as they have there own place, which is great as this is our space.'

When we chatted it was always kept light and airy so she would not catch on that things were not as she left them. I usually told her tales about Cameron that took the heat of me and my crying at the drop of a hat.
'You really must send me pictures of him as I am missing so much.'
'No problem,' I said, 'I will email you some for now and post some to you.'
'That would be great,' she said, 'I can put them on my wall, the cabin needs a touch of home. There is not much room in staff cabins not like on the Diamond when I was in a passenger cabin. So it would be nice to make it feel more homely. I will look forward to getting photos soon.'
I admitted to her that I had found a web site that showed the camera view from the ship so I could actually see where she was, granted only the ports but it was good. I

felt like a nosey neighbour sneaking a peek through the blinds, we both had a laugh at that idea.

'Mum' she said, 'you are sad!'

I felt the hairs on the back of my neck stand on end, had I given something away, had she picked up on my situation? I took a deep breath.

'Sad? What do you mean sad?'

'You are sad, that you are spending time finding web sites so that you can keep an eye on me!'

Phew!

'Yes I suppose so but you know me' and we laughed again.

I got away with it I thought to myself, what a relief.

'I was thinking of buying a cam-corder here on the ship, so Dad can you please convert the amount of Oz dollars into pounds and tell me if it is worth it.'

She gave her Dad details of the make and model so he could check it out

'By the way we got your letter and photos; it must be amazing sitting there with Sydney Opera House in the back ground. Who would ever have thought that? You are lucky lass,' I said.

She agreed, 'Yes so far so good, I have seen some amazing places. The weather is nice but not hot, but I have to remember that it is not summer here although it is August. Typically it improves when I head for home about Christmas.'

James is well on the mend. I have been taking him to see a physiotherapist for a few weeks and it seems to be working.

'The physiotherapists are all ladies,' he said 'and all tiny but they seem to know what they are doing.'

At the next appointment he came out looking a bit worse for wear.

'What the heck happened to you?'

'I got a new physiotherapist today, his name is George!

He has hands like spades. I thought he was going to break me in half; he is a giant and not necessarily a gentle giant. He did say that he can sort me out once and for all so we will see.'

The next day he could hardly walk.

'He has given me new exercises to do to before I see him again.'

'That I would like to see, look at the state of you.' I thought to myself

However two weeks later he was as good as new. George had managed to manipulate the disc back into place; he was as good as his word. Obviously the ladies were not quite strong enough but George and his spade-like hands had sorted the problem.

James returned to work leaving me at home to get my act together. It was easier now that I was on my own and not having to nurse my beloved husband.

I got a strange email from one of Patricia's friends her name is Mel, she wanted to know if I had a contact address for Patricia as her birthday was approaching and she wanted to send a birthday card. It mentioned a waiter that Patricia had been talking about.

'I think things are looking romantic there don't you think?' Mel obviously thought that we knew about the waiter.

Strange I thought, she had not mentioned anyone to James or me only that she had bought the cam-corder she had been speaking about. That is not like her, she normally tells us all about her boyfriends, not that there had been many. I will ask her the next time she calls.

Saturday arrives and the phone rang.

'Hey baby how are things with you?'

'All good here Mum, I am getting used to the way of life

on board. I need a favour though. Can you please send me some new underwear? I put the stuff in the machine and it chewed up three of my bras. Don't spend too much on them just in case it happens again and besides it they may get lost in the post.'

'Sure no problem, I will get that done for you tomorrow and post it on Monday. You should get them not next turn around day but the one after.'

Turns around days are the ones where the passengers get off and the new ones arrive, the ship is restocked and made ready for the next cruise. We chatted about this and that but I noticed no mention of any waiter so I decided to bite the bullet and ask outright.

'Ahhhhhhh!' she said. 'Mel has been telling tales out of school eh? He is not my boyfriend; he is a friend who is a male.'

'Oh yes, does this friend have a name?'

'Of course, he has a name it is Kayvan.'

'Kayvan? That is an unusual name, where is he from?'

'He is Indonesian; he is so funny he makes me laugh all the time. I don't actually see that much of him to be honest as he works till midnight. We meet in the crew bar and chat that's all, no romance.'

'Oh, I was just curious that's all.'

'Yes, you looking for an on board romance Mum, it isn't worth it as I am only here till December.'

'Fair comment, I agreed with her!'

'By the way here is some news for you, I have been asked to perform in a dance to celebrate Indonesia Independence Day. I have been practising for a while, it is a national dance and I have to dress as a Princess. It is so cool, very traditional and a crown of fresh flowers in my hair. I am dreading it but looking forward to it to. I will get someone to video it for me on my new cam-corder. That way you will see it when I get home.'

A few weeks later Patricia announced that she and

51

Kayvan were an item. What happened to 'only there till Christmas' then?

'Ah well we really like each other and…….well what the heck what will be will be. You would love him Mum if you ever met him. He is so kind, considerate, and thoughtful; he treats me like a princess not like some of the other guys I have gone out with.'

That was it………….Kayvan is all she spoke about.

had another bridge to cross; it was going to be Patricia's 24th birthday in three weeks. I had bought her a CD, some of her favourite sweets and had had a t-shirt made for her. It has a picture of Cameron on it with the words *Have you met my aunty*? I also sent an email to her friends telling them that if they wanted to send cards or anything to get them to me and I would include them in my parcel. As it turns out it was a great success lots of her friends handed in cards and gifts so she would be delighted when she got them all. I parcelled up all the gifts and cards and took it to the post office. I hoped I had timed it right so she had it before her birthday. We were dreading her birthday; it would be the first one since the day she was born that we wouldn't all be together.

The day eventually arrived and we decided to keep ourselves busy and hope it would pass as quickly and as painless as possible. The phone rang!!

'Hi guys……..'

'Hey baby, HAPPY BIRTHDAY we yelled down the phone.'

'Thanks guys and thanks for the gifts. I was good and didn't open the parcel until this morning. I love the tee-shirt I have it on. I don't have long but had to tell you the news!!'

Oh no she is going to tell us she is pregnant, wouldn't that be it all?

'Have you seen the news?'

'No?' we said in unison, we were sharing the receiver so we didn't miss any part of her conversation on such a special day.
'You won't believe this but the ship has run aground, it is on the beach.'
'What!'
'Yeah we were out and about on the Isle of Pines. We decided to make a day of it for my birthday, so we hired some buggies and went driving round the island. On the way back we were coming down hill and I said.
'What time is it as the ship isn't there? Have we missed it? 'No we are early, we don't have to be on board till 5 pm and it is only 3 pm now' my friend said
'What do you mean the ship is not there?' my friend asked
'Well put it this way, it isn't where we left it'! We got down to the beach and there was the ship on the beach. The people that were on couldn't get off and the people who were off could not get on! It is amazing there are news helicopters all over the place. Got to go I don't want to miss any of the action. I will phone again soon promise. Byeeee!'

Well that was it the rest of the day was spent searching TV channels for news hoping to see some of the antics. I was at my best searching the internet especially Australian news channels. It was bizarre but it was a great way to pass the day, it added zing to what we thought was going to be an awful day. We couldn't find anything anywhere but it was fun looking. The next day we did find it in an Australian newspaper. So it was true. It turns out the ship had become unmoored and ran adrift. That will be a birthday she will never forget that's for sure.

News was coming though, in her latest call, that Patricia was not happy with her manager. He was not as skilled as her and was picking her brains with regards merchandising and staff control.

'That is not what I am here for,' she said, 'I thought I left all that responsibility back home, I wanted away from all that but it seems to be following me.'

'Well remember he is being paid for his skills and you are not.'

'Exactly Mum so I am going to ask for a promotion.'

'You go girl, nothing ventured nothing gained! How is Kayvan,' I asked?

'He is wonderful; we spend every minute we can together. My cabin mate Beth has been great, when he comes to my cabin she goes out so we have lots of quality time to be a couple, you can't do that in the crew bar. Thing is every morning Kayvan brings me a bag of chocolate muffins fresh from the bakery on board, they are delicious only thing is I am putting on lots of weight. I was in the shower yesterday and got the fright of my life. I thought someone else was in the shower with me, I looked down and saw this fat leg then I realised it was mine! So another favour, can you send me some size 12 navy trousers. The ones you get for uniform are awful so please send me nice ones you know the kind I mean.'

'Yes I know I will get on to that for you. I can't believe you are a size 12; you have never been that big.'

'It is good too Mum, everyone is saying how good I look, and I have curves. Now I actually look healthy.' 'Muffins and cheap drinks at the bar, no wonder you are putting on weight, but that is not a bad thing.' Although all the clothes you have here won't fit when you get home. Just an excuse to buy new ones I suppose.'

'I don't know about that, I have seen so much poverty here, it put things into perspective, I don't need to spend all that money on things I use once then cast aside. I never told you did I, on my birthday Kayvan woke me at one minute past twelve and gave me lovely flowers and sang happy birthday to me, he is such a romantic. I forgot to mention it when I called on my birthday there was so much going on due to the ship being on the beach.'

'What about the dance for Independence Day? You never mentioned it.'

'Oh what a laugh, I was dressed in traditional Indonesian dress with the crown of fresh flowers in my hair. However despite all the practice at strange hours we still made a few mistakes. It didn't help when I got a dose of the giggles. I have it on video for you so you can see it in full. I have made a few people unhappy though as some of the Indonesian girls on board thought they should have got the part. What was I to do, they asked me and I said yes, it never entered my head to pass it on to an Indonesian girl... oops!'

'We can't wait to see it, it sounds interesting.'

'We are in *Mystery Island* tomorrow and I am so excited as Kayvan has got the day off so we are spending the whole day together. He doesn't get many days off. The hours are long and we just grab time together when we can. He waits on tables from 6 am until 11 or 12 pm with just an hour off here and there and nine times out of ten I am at work if we are at sea so spending the whole day together is a novelty. The other day a lady came up to me in the shop and asked if my name was Patricia? When I said 'yes,' she said.

'Ahhh so you are Kayvan's girl then?'

'He had been telling all his guests about me and they were intrigued. When she walked away I saw her confirming with another passenger that I was the Patricia, Kayvan had been talking about. Well it seemed to cause an epidemic because there were several people checking me out after that. I wonder if that is my fifteen minutes of fame as Andy Warhol mentioned. It didn't make me any money, if it was, but it sure embarrassed the life out of me. Kayvan is such a sweetheart, the passengers love him. He is so attentive and polite and makes them feel on top of the world. Pity they don't recall how great he is when it comes to tipping though. Funny how he seems to slip their minds then! It is such a shame as the wages are not great and they depend on the tips to help boost their income. Anyway I had better go as my credit is running low and I want to call Josh, so take care, love ya, bye.'

It makes me laugh how she could go from chat, chat, chat, and then all of a sudden it was *'love ya, bye!'*
'Well this Kayvan chap has certainly made an impression, James, what do you think?'
'Emmmm, well you know, he certainly takes up most of her conversation these days I am a bit worried about the fact that they are maybe getting too close and come Christmas she will end up with a broken heart.'
That was the last thing any of us wanted for her.
'I do tend to agree with you but she is sensible so I am sure she has it covered.'

We had spent the last few weeks decorating some of the house. It needed cheering up so we set about picking nice bright colours, bought some new furniture and carpets. Patricia will be surprised when she comes home. I had always been afraid of putting colour on the wall and plumped for pastel shades, not this time, the lounge was now red and pale pink and we followed the same colours into the kitchen, and a nice deep pile red carpet. The bed room was bright yellow; it looked sunny all the time even on the gloomiest of days. I had done a fair bit of the decoration as I did not want James climbing and over stretching in case he hurt his back again. I wouldn't want to go through that and sure he wouldn't either, so he was happy to let me do it as long as he was there to make sure I didn't make a mess of it.

One night we were sitting watching a DVD that I had

rented when my mobile rang. It was a text message. 'Who on earth is sending me a text at this time?' Low and behold it was Patricia. She said she was on wharf duty and bored so thought she would text as she knew we would still be awake. I had to laugh she was a nut case. I texted her back and told her so. Then I had a thought, wait a minute if she is on wharf duty that means the ships camera could maybe pick her up on the wharf side. I logged on to my favourite site and low and behold there was the wharf. Granted there were quite a few people about and a few lorries but that was to be expected. I text her again and said.

'Hey there I am looking at the wharf, what are you wearing let me know and I will see if I can see you.'

That was all I needed to say to James, He ran up stairs and logged on to the PC whilst I was on the laptop in the kitchen. We were both looking at the same site. A reply came back almost immediately.

'I am wearing a bright yellow jacket I don't think you could miss me.'

This started a text frenzy which went like this.

'Are you beside a large white lorry?' Send.

'No but I can see one.'

'OK get next to that and gave me a wave.' Send.

'Hold on there are two lorries here now, which one do you want be to be beside.'

'The one beside the large blue bollard.' Send.

'OK, I am there now and waving, feeling rather silly, can you see me.'

All the time I was shouting upstairs letting James know what was going on. I stared at the screen and saw this little yellow dot and knew that the little dot was her. I started to cry. Wow wasn't technology wonderful? There is my little girl on the other side of the planet and I can see her. James was shouting.

'I can see her; I can see her can you?' James was yelling

57

'Yes,' I screamed through the tears.'
'Hey are you crying,' he said?
'Yes, I'm afraid so.' I sobbed
'Don't worry I am to.' We started to laugh. I text her to tell her that we could see her and she replied.
'Well that's good but I am not waving anymore I am getting some strange looks.

I found out later that on wharf duty she had to help receive the cargo that was being brought on for the next cruise. She had to deal with the lorry drivers and it was them that were giving her the funny looks. She had told them what she was doing and one guy said'.
'You should have said I would have waved to them too.'
This part of the job came with the promotion she had got. Not quite assistant manager but a step up which increased her salary. Her boss had recognised that she had potential and that she helped him considerably and put her forward for more responsibilities and money. OK he was not the best manager but at least recognised her abilities.

Chapter 6

'Wow it is getting cold out there,' I said as I ran in the front door from work. I had returned to work a few weeks earlier, fully recovered and back to my old self. Patricia never did find out. November certainly brings the wind chill factor with it.
'Sure does,' says James as he turned and locked the door. 'We aren't going anywhere tonight are we?
'Heaven knows, I am going to stay here and enjoy watching television in the warmth.'
'I will give Josh a call later and see if he has any ideas about a present for his birthday.'
Patricia was so organised before she left, that she had left gifts and cards for Louise and Josh for their birthdays. It had been Louise's 21st birthday a few weeks ago and Patricia had left a card with £21 in it for her. She had left a CD for Josh; it was *The Red Hot Chilli Peppers*, his favourite.
I made dinner and tidied up again, not that it took much these days with just the two of us in the house. I called Josh and caught up on my beautiful Cameron's progress.
'As for your birthday son, what would you like this year?'
'Dunno really, I can't think of anything.'
'Nothing new there son' I laughed. 'What about a new football shirt?'
'Yeah that sounds good Mum, but can I have the Manchester United away top?'
'OK, I will have a look about and see if I can find it in town, if not there is always my mighty internet facility!'
'Yeah Mum, there is no stopping you when it comes to searching for anything is there?'

As it happens I found the top in the sports shop in town so I didn't have to use my magical keyboard skills this time. Well now I have that sorted I can concentrate on

Christmas shopping. This is the first Christmas in years where I can go to toy shops.

James sighed, 'I have a feeling you will be spending a lot of time there. Can I come too?'

We laughed so hard as we knew that we were going to spoil Cameron, he was our first grandchild after all.

'I will have to think about Patricia and gifts too, what do I get for her? Clothes are out of the question as I don't know what size she is going to come back.'

'Ah well I have been meaning to tell you something but couldn't find the right time so I guess this is as good a time as any. Patricia phoned the other night, the night you were out with your friend.'

'And, what's up' I asked?

'Well nothing's up exactly but she did tell me that she may not be home for Christmas.'

'What! Are you kidding me?'

'No, sorry babe, I am not joking. Apparently, if her replacement doesn't arrive she won't be allowed to leave. The way the dates work out if she doesn't get off on the 17th then she will have to do the next cruise which takes them over Christmas, then it may be a month before they can let her go. She was told that it is quite common for people not to turn up at that time of year. She did not want to tell you because she knew you would get upset.'

'Upset! I am not upset.' Who am I kidding?

'Don't worry it is only a maybe, but I would hold buying her anything just now.'

'Don't be ridiculous,' I said, I have to get stuff now in case I have to send it to her, I can't have her there and nothing for Christmas. Bother! Not being here for James, Louise, and Josh's birthdays' were bad enough not to mention her own but Christmas, this was never in the equation. Especially this Christmas, Josh is going to propose to Louise on Christmas day. I even have the ring hiding in my drawer upstairs. Josh had even asked

me to help with the proposal as it were.'
When they were children I used to hold back one gift and hide it somewhere in the house. I made up cryptic clues for them and one clue led to the next and the next until they found the present. So Josh wanted to do this to Louise, starting in the lounge and finishing at the top of the tree in the lounge so going full circle as it were .I had been down to the house and noted all the places where I was going to hide the clues. Now I was annoyed not upset.

I got on the computer straight away and sent an e mail to Patricia to let her know that I had heard the news. I told her I would be gutted if she wasn't here for Christmas but if that's how it has to be then there is nothing we can do about it. I told her I understood which I did. But I didn't have to like it. I called Josh to tell him the news.
'I know,' he said, 'I got an email from her the other day. I told her that I would not propose to Louise until she got home. Christmas would have been good but Valentines Day would be OK too. Louise was not expecting anything so she won't be disappointed. I couldn't and wouldn't do that. I want my sis there to share in my happiness.'
That bond is stronger than ever I thought to myself.
What a lovely gesture, putting his life on hold until his sis got home. Surely she would be home for February!

Right, what can I buy her that is small and light but that she would want? *What about more underwear or nightwear?* Yes, that sounds good. I try to keep things light as postage to Australia from the UK is expensive. I will have to try and time it right that is the only thing. I don't know when she will find out if she is getting home or not and I have to make sure it gets to her in time.

Josh's birthday was great; he loved the football top and other gifts from the family. He got his first *Happy Birthday Daddy* card and that tickled him pink. We had a birthday tea here for him and the cake as usual; you can't have a birthday without cake. There were the five of us but we knew there should have been six but we were all used to the idea of her not being around so it all went smoothly, no tears .He loved the CD from Patricia, 'As organized as ever wasn't she Mum, or did you get the CD and said it was from her?'
'No not at all, she had it all sorted out before she left in June. Not like you son, I bet you haven't even thought about Christmas yet?'
'Nope you are right Mum; I will sort that out at the last minute as usual.'
We winked at each other without Louise catching sight of us; we didn't want to give anything away about the possible engagement and the ring that laid nestled amongst my T shirts.

'I thought Patricia would have phoned today,' said Josh. No sooner were the words out of his mouth when the phone rang.
'You better get that son, if it is her she will want to speak to you.'
'Yo bro! Happy birthday!' I heard as he picked up the phone. I knew she wouldn't forget and would call if she could. Sometimes the satellite link was down and she couldn't make calls.
They chatted for a while and he said, 'I had better pass the phone to Mum she is lurking about in the back ground.' He shot me a glance and a wicked grin.
'I think Dad actually would like a word.' Usually we try to split the call but the past few have been all me and I am feeling guilty.
James took the phone, 'Hey babe how are things?' which really was all he said, the rest was listening. I hate

that because I don't know what is being said and when I ask James when he hangs up he has forgotten half of the conversation.
'OK babe will let you go, take care, love you. Bye.'
'Well! What was she saying?'
'I will give you one guess and one guess only,' said James.
'Let me think, was it Kayvan?'
'Yep that's about the size of it, Kayvan this and Kayvan that I couldn't get a word in.'
It was great to hear her so happy but I feared the worst. 'Never mind she may be there a bit longer now, and the romance may fritter away I thought'
'She was also saying that she feels guilty and upset that she is missing out on Cameron's growing up and you should send more photographs of him.'

No sooner said than done, I went straight to the PC and looked out some recent photos of Cameron that I could send to her. Then I had a brainwave. James is a great one for gadgets and a few weeks earlier he had bought a system that could manipulate pictures. So I dug it out and began to tinker with it. I realised that I could cut her out of a picture and add it to a picture of Cameron. So I spent some time doing just that, adding her to pictures and adding Cameron to some of hers. That way it looked like she was actually there. I copied them into an email and sent them to her. That will get her going I thought to myself.

Now into December and the Christmas preparations are well under way. Lots of toys and clothes bought for Cameron, and wrapped, cards written and surprises hidden. On the table in the lounge was a small pile of underwear and a nice night dress for Patricia. I had brought a box home from work and was going to pack it away and get it posted in the morning. I checked my emails as usual and there were two from Patricia. The first one was just what I wanted to hear. She was getting home on the 17th as originally planned. Her replacement had arrived a week early for some reason. So she will be here for Christmas. The second which was sent later in the day were her flight details; she will be arriving in Glasgow on the 19th at 12.25.

'So can you do me another favour, I am going to need a job when I get home so could you see my friend and see if she has any Christmas work going. If so tell her I will start on the 21st. Keep me posted.'

The email continued however. It was all about Kayvan and how she was going to miss him. What would she do without him? Would she ever see him again? I could tell by the tone of the email that she was upset. There is nothing I can do and I felt so helpless. There is lots of advice and love a mother can give but when it comes to affairs of the heart there is nothing I can say or do that is going to ease this pain. I replied to the email and consoled her as best as I could, I told her that a family that loves her will be waiting at the airport and there will be lots of hugs and kisses. I reminded her that there will be one little fella dying to meet her. Cameron would be 8 months old and she would see such a change from the baby she knew. I didn't know what else to say so I left it open and waited for the reply.

A few days passed and nothing, no email no phone call.
'She must have it bad,' I said to James, 'we haven't heard for a few days, I hope she is OK.'
'Mmmmm,' said James in his usual concerned tone, 'I just had a feeling this would happen, I said that to you didn't I?
'Yes dear you did, you know her inside and out.'
I called Josh, 'have you heard from your sister recently?'
'No, nothing.'
'Oh dear, this is going to be awful, I can't even pick up a

phone to call her and make sure she is ok. What next?'

At last, an email. Again not what I expected, she was saying that the reason she hadn't been in touch is that she had been arranging with her friend Kelly to go to Thailand in February. She had decided that she was unsure of doing another contract on the ship but she still wanted to see the world so Thailand was on the cards.
'Then I am going to Indonesia.'
So the plan was to go to Thailand with her friend for a few weeks then onto Indonesia on her own and her friend would fly back to the UK.
'I am going to meet Kayvan's family. He gets off the ship in February so I will head there after my trip to Thailand and I will be there for his birthday on the 8th of March. At least that way I know I will see him again, so saying goodbye on the quay won't be so hard. Now you know why I am just looking for Christmas work, I don't want anything permanent, don't worry,' she said, *'I will be home for your birthday and Cameron's first birthday I wouldn't miss that for anything. See you soon, love ya Moi! Xx'*
This was her latest signing off rather than her name she would say 'Moi'.

Thailand, Indonesia, is this girl trying to drive us crazy. It was bad enough letting her go to the ship, at least we knew she would be safe, but two young girls travelling Thailand then her moving on to Indonesia alone. What could we do? Nothing! Absolutely nothing! James and I discussed it in great detail and had to admit although we were not exactly pleased about it we had to admire her courage. Anyway she was coming home and that's what counts.

The 19th loomed and I thought it would be a good idea if we all went to the airport to meet her. So we arranged a

people carrier with a baby seat so we could all go in the one vehicle that way we could all catch up with her stories on the way home and she could see Cameron. That may help take the sting out of her journey and the goodbye she had gone through. Just for a laugh I bought five Santa hats and advised the family that we would all wear them at the airport for her arrival. That will cause a laugh, I thought. Josh was not over impressed with my brainstorm.
'Yeah whatever,' he said 'and if you think you are going to catch me wearing one of those you can think again.'
'Well we will see,' I said and just left it at that.

The day arrived, the day Patricia was coming home. I had just heard that Patricia was to start work in the department store on the 21st and for about eight weeks, perfect. I will tell her when I see her. Josh Louise and Cameron arrived early. We made sure Cameron was fed and his nappy changed ready for the trip to the airport. We piled in the car; made sure everyone was comfortable and set off. This time there was a buzz of excitement in the car not like the day we took Patricia through six months ago. I had checked the internet as usual before we left and it read in flight and also on time, I found that amazing that she can come from the other side of the world and be on time.

We got to the airport, and all went to spend a penny. We wanted to make sure we didn't have to leave just at the time when she was due to walk through those doors. We were there all of five minutes when the information board told us that her flight had landed. The anticipation was building. I pulled out the Santa hats and asked everyone to put them on. Josh looked at me, giving me one of his looks; he took the hat out of my hand and said, 'I will put it on but not until the last minute.'
I laughed, 'That's one to me then!'

We put our hats on, including Cameron even though it was too big for him; he looked as sweet as a nut, whereas we just looked nuts! We waited patiently; there were so many people, so many faces. Then the flight crew came out, I had said to James 'where do you think she is?' The captain obviously heard me, leaned over and said, 'That there were still people waiting for luggage.' That put my mind at rest; it had crossed my mind that she didn't get on the flight. A further thirty minutes past, Cameron was getting restless, not easy entertaining a baby in confined spaces. Then, the door opened, and there under a baseball cap was Patricia. I ran like the wind, past security men, grabbed her and hugged her close. Closely followed by James who cuddled her for what seemed like an eternity.

She started to laugh when she realised we had on Santa hats.

'You are crazy do you know that!'

Then I said, 'not as crazy as this.'

I stood to one side to reveal Josh, Louise and Cameron all wearing Santa hats and Cameron holding a balloon that simply said '*Welcome Home!*'

I gave her the once over and noticed she had gained some weight and for the first time in her life looked curvy. She suited the look; she looked more like a woman now! I made a comment and she just smiled at me.

'You look more like me than ever now, I was never as skinny as you were before you left home' I laughed

'What took you so long sis?'

'They have lost one of my suit cases; I am not pleased I can tell you as it is the one full of all my souvenirs.'

'It's not like I can go back and get them again, chances of me going there again are slim. It's not like I have just been to Spain and lost a donkey. Well I just gave then a hard time. They said they are confident that they will get it to me if not tomorrow then the next day. Pity, help them if they don't!'

The journey home was good, all full of chat and news. Patricia was amazed at the size of her nephew; she kept pulling funny faces at him.
'Look at the size of his eyes and oh my word he has teeth!'
I was right it was a good idea to bring him. I told her about the job and she seemed pleased although she looked so tired that I think the 21st is maybe a bit early. It was her idea so she must know what she is doing.

We got home and Patricia was amazed at the new look.
'Wow, colour eh, what possessed you? Not a pastel to be seen. It looks good.'
I made a meal for us all'
'I am not really hungry,' she said, 'I am whacked I could sleep for a week and no mistake. It will be good to get back to a decent sized bed, which is the only thing that has kept me going the past day or so. Oh and seeing you guys too of course.'
'Look,' said Josh, 'we will head off, it is getting on for bath time for Cameron and you need some rest. I will catch up with you soon. It's good to see you sis,' he reached over and kissed her on the cheek, and she returned it with a hug.
'Sure bro, see ya soon; here baby a kiss from your aunty.'
That left the three of us; well that is the three of us and the phone. It seemed to ring constantly with her friends trying to catch up. I ended up saying that she had gone to bed and would call them back tomorrow.
She wandered around the house looking lost.
'You ok,' I asked her.
'Yeah Mum, I am ok just tired I guess. Mum'
'Yes pet,' I replied.
'I miss him!

'I know baby, it's not easy is it?'
She started to cry and I joined her.
'What are you crying for,' she said.
'I don't like to see you sad and there is nothing I can do.'
'Just being here helps Mum, thanks.'
'Look off you go to bed, get some rest and we will talk tomorrow.'

The next day Patricia came down the stairs looking somewhat tousled. Not exactly what I would call rested. I was hoping a night in her own bed would help but it appeared not.
'Hi babe, welcome home again,' and I gave her a hug, she looked like she needed one.
'Morning Mum,' she said through a sleepy stifled yawn.
'It is good to be home, although it looks so different, it feels the same.'
'Well that's good isn't it?'
'Yeah I guess so.'
'Come on have some breakfast, I bought your favourite cereal, the one with the chocolate pieces.'
'Great.' she said although no enthusiasm.
She removed a bowl form the cupboard and milk form the fridge. She sat at the table looking lost, sad, and not comfortable.
'You ok?'
'Yeah I am just over tired that's all, I will be better tomorrow.'
'You had better be you start your new job tomorrow; I think it is a bit early but you know best.'
She looked up at me and smiled.
'I didn't think I would be this tired maybe I should have thought it through better. All I know is that I am going away again soon and need spending money. How about later on we go to town, I need to get some clothes that fit and want to see Jenny to see what hours she wants me to work.'

'Of course, are you sure you are up for it.'
'Not really but the sooner I get myself back on UK time the better. I just hope I don't see anyone I know I am not really in the mood to be sociable.'
That was as plain as the nose on her face, I could see she was trying hard to be her old self but it just wasn't happening.
'OK, go and have a shower when you have finished breakfast and squeeze into something then we will go to town; I know Dad would like that too. He has missed you so much, we all have.'
I left her to finish breakfast and alone with her thoughts.

A while later we all went to town, it was looking as pathetic as ever, the Christmas lights were the same as the ones they had when I was a girl. You would think they would change them occasionally I thought. There was the odd token different one but nothing that stood out and said, *'Hey look at me I am new!'* The tree in the city square was nice enough but that was as good as it got. I don't actually think Patricia even noticed. We went and got some new jeans and some tops. The strange thing was that she went to the cheaper jean stores and not the designer ones that she used to frequent on a regular basis.
I made the comment and she replied, 'I will tell you this, when you have seen such poverty as I have it brings it home to you just how lucky you are. I don't need to spend £50 plus on jeans these at £15 are ample.'
Wow she actually got the message; I had been telling her that for years. Then we went to the bank. She had lots of different foreign currencies that she wanted converted and put into her account. . All the money went into her savings account. She was the saver in the family, ever since she started work she would put part of her wage into this account and would not take any out unless absolutely necessary. She had managed to save

a fair bit in seven years, quite a nice little nest egg.

Then we popped in to see Jenny, Patricia had a quick chat with her and confirmed that she would be there tomorrow. Jenny was a sensible girl and gave her hours to cover the lunchtime period.
'That way you don't have to be up early,' she laughed. 'I will increase your hours next week but thought it best to break you in gently.'
'Thanks you are a good mate.'
'Now I have to get some shopping at the supermarket so we will head there next.'
As we wandered around the supermarket I could see her failing fast.
'Look,' I said, 'let's head home I can get this stuff later.'
James just followed around looking lost too, he was feeling her pain.

We got home and decided to watch TV for a while before I made dinner. She was fighting sleep; her eyes were staring but not taking anything in.
'Look,' I said, 'go have a shower, I will make dinner then you should get off to bed.'
'Hummm, yes sounds like a good idea.'
So off she went to the bathroom armed with her cosy dressing gown and pyjamas. That gave James and me a chance to talk.
'She looks dreadful,' I said.
'Yes, she is exhausted I don't know what possessed her to get a job so early on, she should have waited a week or so. She has never mentioned Kayvan, I wonder if I should speak to her about it or let it lie. I don't want her to think she is going through this and no one caring.'
'Don't be silly,' said James, 'she know we care, she has never been one to show her emotions, it will come out in time just let it be for now.'
Wise words, I thought to myself, so headed to the

kitchen to prepare dinner.
Dinner was quiet, not much being said at all.
'I think I will head for bed now guys,' she said and headed for the kitchen door. Just then the phone rang.
'Likelihood that will be for you Patricia.' said James
'Mum can you answer it I am not in the mood to chat.'
'OK, no problem.' I ran through the lounge and grabbed the phone. A familiar sound rung in my ears, well actually there was no sound at all. That is what happened when she used to call from the ship, there was always a pause before you heard her. A strange voice said.
'Hello, can I talk to Patricia please?' The accent was pleasant and polite.
'Sure hold on a second I will get her.'
I realised this was Kayvan and she would not want to miss this call.
'Patricia!!!' I bellowed up stairs, 'I think you'll want to take this call!'
I heard her pick up the phone in her room so I hung up.

A few minutes later she bounded down the stairs.
'That was Kayvan,' she said, it was the first sign of the girl I knew.
'He was making sure I got home OK, and told me how much he was missing me. I never thought he would call me as it is expensive and he doesn't have much time, but he asked if he could have ten minutes to use the phone. The Maitre D let him have the time to make the call. He didn't have to, you know, but he did! It was so hard leaving him behind. I have never cried that much before, and that includes Glasgow airport and Seattle. We had been quiet with each other for a few days as we knew that I was going soon. We were preparing ourselves I suppose. The day I left we held onto each other on the quay side not wanting to part. We were both crying, sobbing. I knew I had to get on the plane and the

bus was waiting to take me and the other staff that was going home to the airport. We held each other for the longest time, kissing and consoling each other. It was awful. I got on the bus and waved until I couldn't see him anymore. I cried all the way to the airport. Will I see him again, well now you know why I am working tomorrow, the more I can earn the better my chances are of seeing him in Indonesia.'
We put our arms around her and told her that we know how she felt and that she should do what she has to do.
'Why does my heart ache like this?'
'I hate to tell you this but I think you are in love,' I said.
'Love!' she said. 'It hurts I didn't think it would hurt and certainly not like this'
'Well it does, and it is a great feeling really, it shows you how much you care for him.'
At that she said, 'thanks again guys.' turned on her heels and went back to bed.

The tears that filled her eyes whilst she told that story convinced me that they would meet again and the sooner the better.

About an hour later the door bell rang. Who could this be, we were not expecting visitors and it is too late for Josh he would have the baby in bed by now surely. That makes me think there is a problem, if ever the door goes or the phone rings late in the evening there is usually a problem.
'Honestly,' said James, 'you are such a worrier, for heavens sake open the door.'
I opened the door and to my surprise was a gentleman from a carrier service.
'I believe this is yours,' he said and handed over a large black suitcase.
'Fantastic,' I said, it is not mine, but my daughter's.
'Where was it?'

'Apparently it never left Dubai airport. Sorry for the inconvenience.'
'As long as it is here she will be pleased, thanks.'
I half expected Patricia to come down again but as it happens she was sound asleep.
'That will be a nice surprise for her tomorrow,' said James.
'Another problem solved then,' I said.
The next morning Patricia came downstairs and saw her suitcase sitting there. 'Thank goodness' she said. 'I really thought I wasn't going to see that again'
She put the combination into the lock and checked frantically the contents of the case.
'Phew they are all in one piece.'
There were all sorts of things that she had picked up on her travels. Photos of her and Kayvan seemed to be the most valuable possession.
'This is him, isn't he hot!'
'Very nice young man,' I said.
He was good looking and had a big broad smile, with a hint of cheekiness. I could see what attracted her to him. She took the photo in her hand and kissed it gently, held it to her chest as a hug, then placed it on the table.
'I can go to work a happy bunny now,' she said.
She got herself ready to go to work, nicely dressed and make up applied discreetly.
'I am not exactly looking forward to this,' she said in monotonous tone, but it has to be done. The thought of Christmas shoppers is a daunting task especially when I am not fully compos mentis. At least it is only for a few hours. I really must try and get back onto UK time as quickly as possible. This is doing my head in I can tell you, I know I am awake but my body is still asleep.'
'Don't worry a few days and you will be as right as rain. Tell you what why don't we watch your video footage tonight, that may help keep you awake as you will have to tell us where you are and who is who.'

'That sounds good,' she said her tone picking up a bit; 'it's a date.'

I spent the day doing finishing touches to gifts, tying ribbons and writing labels. Then I worked on the clues for Josh so his proposal would go smoothly. There was to be an engagement after all, now that Patricia was home. Exciting times I thought. I had bought them a clock for the lounge, it was the one thing they didn't have. It used to drive me crazy when I was babysitting not knowing what the time was. I wrapped it in silver paper with congratulations written on it, I didn't want it to get muddled with the Christmas presents. They were wrapped in red and gold so the engagement present stuck out like a sore thumb. I was going to keep it aside when delivering the gifts on Christmas day, after all she may not say yes! I doubted that very much, but stranger things have happened. I walked myself through the clues, making sure they were in the right order; it wouldn't work if they were out of sequence. *'Yep, it all worked I thought to myself.'* I can't wait to see her face.

The day passed nicely, I love this time of year, so full of happiness, good will to all men as it were. I was looking forward to spending the evening watching the video and seeing all the places Patricia had visited, the people she worked with, the ship the whole lot.

After dinner we set up the cam-corder and prepared to be dazzled by the exotic places.
'I will start from the beginning and talk you through it.'
'Great,' James and I made ourselves comfortable on the couch and opened a bottle of wine.
'None for me thanks,' said Patricia, 'I need to be alert,' she smiled.
'This is Sydney,' the picture was great but the quality of filming not so great, we saw a lot of the pavement as

she had obviously forgot to turn it off whilst walking. 'That is Raquel she worked in the spa and that is me with Karen she worked in the spa too.'

The commentary went on like this throughout the evening. Then we saw the rest of the crew who were sitting on deck, granted they all had on sweaters as it was cool. They all stuck out their tongues and made rude gestures as people do. Some were hiding as not comfortable being on camera.

'Look like a lively bunch,' I said.

'Yeah they are crazy.'

The images changed to wonderful islands with wonderful names like Vanuatu, Noumea, Nuku'alofa, Suva, seeing the people of these islands in native dress, signing and dancing to entertain the tourists was amazing and beautiful. Then she changed discs and this is the one I wanted to see most. It was the dance to celebrate Indonesia Independence Day.

There she was dressed in a beautiful outfit. It consisted of a yellow tee-shirt covered with a small green jacket with very ornate green and gold sleeves, and over that was a heavy orange and gold collar which made her shoulders look like the peaks of a mountain. The skirt which had been wrapped around her several times was as ornate as the sleeves in the jacket. It was secured with a lovely red, purple and gold cummerbund. In her hair were gorgeous white flowers held in a golden crown and down the side of her face were red tassels. Her make up was done to give her the look of an Indonesian with almond shaped eyes and just above her nose were four red stones making a diamond shape with a clear stone in the centre.

'Wow,' we said you looked beautiful. Every inch a princess and no mistake' we said.

'It was so funny,' she said, 'as they tied the skirt so tight I could hardly walk let alone dance. Keep watching and you will see what I mean.'

We watched eagerly at the whole show.
'Which one of these guys is Kayvan?' I asked?
'Him! Him!' she said pointing to the screen but every time she pointed he had moved. '
Then I spotted him, I watched more intently now, trying to get an idea of who Kayvan was. He danced with her and the rest of the cast. Every time they looked at each other I could actually see the affection. There were the odd glances between them that seemed to speak without a word being said. I glanced over at Patricia who was obviously reliving the whole thing in her head, a feint smile across her face. At the end of the show the crowd stood and applauded and the dance team took their bows. The Captain then congratulated them, on their performance.

'I have lots of photos too but I will leave them for another day,' she said. 'I think I will turn in for the night.' 'OK babe, sweet dreams.'
How could you not have sweet dreams, I thought having seen all these places, and experienced all that? I was hoping that maybe seeing Kayvan would help ease the anguish she was going through, or would it maybe make it worse. She will tell me soon enough no doubt, once she has her head around it all.

Christmas morning arrived all the gifts under the tree as always. It seemed strange Josh not being here. Normally the pair of them would come down and open presents together, but not this year. Josh had his own little boy who would need Daddy's help opening presents.
'This is different isn't it? Right? Let's have breakfast first this year then we can open gifts after that.'
Then out of the blue Patricia said, 'you know what I would like to do?'
'No babe, what?'

'I want to go to church.'
We had not been to church for a long time so this was a comment that stopped me in my tracks.
'What a lovely idea, yes lets go.'
We dressed warmly and headed to the church down the road. Mass was at 10.30 am. This was the best Mass as it was the children's service. We prayed and sang Christmas Carols. Before the end of the service the priest invited all the children to come and sit in front of the holy alter.
'Now,' he explained, 'as you know this is Jesus' birthday, and you all have received nice presents but the baby Jesus hasn't. So I think it would be nice for you all to sing Happy Birthday to the baby Jesus.'
The children gathered around the manger and began to sing Happy Birthday. Well before I knew it there were tears running down my cheeks. Patricia looked at me as if I were mad.
'What was all that about,' she said as we left the church?
'I just think it was a lovely thing to do, all these kids singing happy birthday to a baby in a manger.'
'I must admit,' she said, 'I did have a lump in my throat too.'

When we got home, the smell as we opened the door was terrific; James announced that the duck was nearly ready. We had decided that as we were all going to Josh and Louise for dinner that we would all contribute something rather than them having the whole expense. We were taking home made soup, duck and trifle. Louise's parents were taking prawns, chicken and cheesecake. Josh and Louise were supplying the vegetables and the electricity.

'Present time I think!'
'Yes let's open them now,' came the chorus from the kitchen.

We sat in the lounge and took it in turns to open a present, making it last longer.

'You first James, then Patricia, then me, we will keep it in that order till they are all opened. OK?'

James opened the first and uncovered a sweater, then Patricia who had got a bottle of *Provocative Woman* perfume then me I got a lovely handbag in tan leather. This continued for an hour or so. I then picked up all the paper and ribbons and placed them carefully in the bin making sure I hadn't picked up any small objects.

Then we headed down the road to Josh and Louise's house armed with the food for the day and more gifts for them and Louise's parents. Lifting the presents out the car I made sure that the silver wrapped clock remained in the boot. Don't want to give it away now after all this planning. I also left the card which said 'Merry Christmas to our son and his Fiancé.' We walked in and wished everyone a merry Christmas and handed over their gifts. I looked at Josh who nodded at me to confirm that all the clues were hidden in the correct places ready for the big event. There was a lot of general chit chat about who got what and from whom.

'What about you Louise what did you get from Josh.'

'Ah! He is such a romantic,' she said sarcastically; 'he gave me a new toaster.'

'Oh dear,' I exclaimed, 'that was nice of him.'

Just then Josh appeared with the first clue.

'As if I would just give you that,' he said and winked across at me.

He handed her the piece of paper which read.

'You have to go find your real present so this is clue number 1. This one will lead to the next and so on until you find it.'

She looked somewhat puzzled by the whole thing.

'Trust me,' he said, 'follow the clues and you will get a nice surprise.'

She didn't look convinced but decided to play along.

First clue led her to the kitchen; the next was the bedroom, then the dining room. She was up and down stairs like a yo-yo which added to the fun. The last clue led her to the star on the top of the tree. Behind this was a scroll of paper tied with a golden ribbon. She reached up and unrolled the scroll, it read:

'This is it, no more games or mask but now there is a question that Josh has to ask!'

Then when she turned around there was Josh on one knee, ring in hand and said.

'Will you marry me?'

Well I have never seen anyone blush so much in my life. She covered her face with the last clue. Josh gently took her hand and looked at her, smiled and asked the question again.

'Will you marry me?'

'Of course I will marry you, silly.'

The ring is lovely; it has three diamonds in an unusual twist on a yellow gold band. Cheers rang through the house, and champagne was popped. We all drank and toasted the newly engaged couple. I ran down to the car and gave them their engagement present, card and Christmas card. Hugs and kisses all round and yes, a tear or two. I looked over at Patricia, afraid that this may upset her but if it did she was putting on a brave show, she was laughing and congratulating them with the rest of us. Poor little Cameron didn't know what was going on; all he knew is that there were lots of toys and people in his house. He seemed quite content playing with the box that his Winnie the Pooh sit-and-ride toy came in. Typical, the toy being ignored but playing with the box it came in.

It was a great day everyone liked their presents, a double celebration and Patricia telling stories of ship life. Dinner was a success too, everyone cleared their plates and Cameron sat in his high chair with a paper hat on, an ideal photo opportunity. We all stayed until Cameron had his bath and went to bed, helped to tidy up then headed home. We had to walk home in the cold due to the alcohol that we had drunk over the course of the day. We would go for the car later on tomorrow. It was a nice walk home with the frost glistening and all the houses had Christmas lights in the windows, on chimneys, walls and even in trees in the gardens. It was very festive and the odd person shouting 'Merry Christmas' to us as we walked home, the three of us linked in to each other.

When we got home the phone rang I thought it was likely Josh but no, it was Kayvan.
'Merry Christmas,' he said. 'Thank you for the gifts.'
Patricia told me that she had left gifts for him with her friend Beth to give him on Christmas day.
'I know he is Muslim and doesn't celebrate Christmas but I do and he is so special I had to give him presents.'
She had also left notes with Beth to give to him at regular intervals; she wanted to remind him that although she was far away he was always in her heart.
'Beth has been great,' he said, 'looking out for me and keeping me company when I am down. I miss you babe more than you can imagine. I am counting the days until I see you again. The ship isn't the same now that you have gone. I wish I could spend Christmas with you and your family. I have put all the photos that you had in your cabin on my wall. It makes me feel close to you. I look at them all the time and I know you are safe with your family and I am happy about that but my heart is empty.'
James and I left the room to let her have the conversation in private. That way she could say what she wanted to say without thinking that we were listening.

Once she hung up she came through to the kitchen.
'I hate this,' she said. 'His calls are always limited due to

the time and cost and I can't call him.

'Yes we know that's how we felt when you were away. Does he have an email address; can you keep in touch that way?'

'Yes of course he does but it is not the same is it? I email him two maybe three times a day.'

'I put my arm around her shoulder and gave her a squeeze. This is going to be hard for you but at least you have a line of communication.'

So the emails continued, as did the odd phone call. Whenever he phoned she would run up stairs to take it in the privacy of her room. Sometimes however he misjudged the time difference and the phone would ring at all hours of the night.

One day she told me that she had received an email from Beth.

It said, *'I am sending this to you as a warning, I know you are going to Indonesia soon but be warned Kayvan keeps talking about marriage! I thought you should be prepared.'* The comment was made and dismissed as quickly. It was never mentioned again.

New Year came and went, nothing exciting, Christmas is great but New Year is boring, nothing but drunken bums hounding everyone. Besides we had an engagement party to go to. Louise and Josh had arranged a party for all family and friends to celebrate their engagement. They thought that later in January would be a good time to have it after all the festivities of Christmas and New Year. Louise's Mum and I had spent the day of the party preparing food, and nibbles to take to the bar where the party was to be held. We had such a laugh dancing and drinking all night. James didn't dance as his back was a bit sore and rather than risk another episode of bed rest he avoided the dance floor. I ended up dancing with Josh's friends, I think I scared them. I had not danced for such a long time that it was hard for me to sit down, so if

I didn't have a partner to dance with I just grabbed another friend, it did cause a riot of laughter. At the end of the evening Josh was encouraged to make a speech to thank everyone for coming and for the gifts received. Well he did stand up and say something but he was so drunk it was hard to decipher what he was saying. We did manage to pick out thank you but that was about it!

Chapter 7

We head into February at a rate of knots. Patricia had booked her flights to Thailand. The plan is that she and Kelly would go to Dubai for three nights then on to Thailand, back packing for two weeks. Then Kelly would head for home and Patricia would spend three days in Singapore, from there she would fly to Jakarta to meet Kayvan.
'She really knows how to worry me doesn't she?' I said.
'Yes,' said James, 'Thailand was bad enough but three days in Singapore all on her own!'
That is the worst bit as far as I am concerned.
'They say Singapore is a very safe city, she will be fine.'
'Yeah! You sound as convinced as me.'
So again back to the airport we go, this time taking the two girls and their back packs. The packs were nearly as big as them. By this time Patricia had lost all the weight she had gained on the ship so she looked smaller than ever with this huge back pack on her shoulders. We made sure they were checked in OK and no problems with tickets and left them to get on with it. 'Not staying here any longer that I have to,' said James, 'I am getting sick of the sight of the place and the parking fees are astronomical. After all it's not like she is on her own this time.'
'I agree, let them get on with it.'
Again it is hugs and kisses, this time warnings to look out for each other and not to fall out.
'Let us know when you get to Dubai, take care and have fun.'
We left leaving the pair of them giggling as they went through to the duty free shops.
'That was less painful than last time,' I said, although there was a lump in my throat that would have choked a horse.
Before we got to the car my phone rang with the first text

message.
'Don't worry about me I am a big girl now and can look after myself. I am so looking forward to seeing Kayvan. Moi! X'
I replied, *'Hey I am a Mum that's my job, worrying about you guys! Say Hi to Kayvan for me x'*
That was it this time, no floods of tears, no desperate messages from the toilets. She was looking forward to seeing more exotic places, not to mention Kayvan.

Later that night a text came through telling us that they had arrived safely in Dubai and that the hotel was in the old part but nice and clean. Well that's good news, one leg of her journey over. I had to laugh when I told James that although they were carrying back packs they were actually staying in hotels, OK maybe not 5, 4 or even 3 star but hotels none the less! They had booked into one 5 star hotel in Thailand for a night as a treat in the middle of their holiday.

They spent the next few days seeing the sights of Dubai, gold shops, meeting people, enjoying the sunshine. Patricia was like me, she enjoyed the sun, and how it heated her body and turned her skin a nice shade of brown, Kelly on the other hand was not so keen on sun bathing and tended to keep covered as her fair skin burned easily. Next stop Thailand. Again I was back to plane spotting on the internet, Patricia had given me times and dates of where they were to be and when they were moving from place to place. James and I had both insisted on this before they left as a precaution as you hear so many stories of people disappearing whilst on holiday. At least this way we would be able to say where they should have been should anything have gone wrong! They arrived in Bangkok safely and had arranged to take the overnight train to their first stop. They had a few hours to spend in Bangkok before the train, so spent it wisely and had a look around. The smell there was overpowering, mostly food being cooked and the heat was stifling and unbearable.

'Never mind we will be on the train in a few hours and our adventure will begin,' said Kelly.

The next week consisted of a few days here and a few days there. The accommodation was basic to say the least. Patricia was not impressed with the outside toilets and shower but had no choice but to use them. They had only been there for two days when Patricia began to suffer from an upset stomach even thought the toilets were outside she had no choice but to keep them close as when her tummy started playing up it was like Vesuvius going off.

'This was not in the plan,' she said, 'but here we are so I have to make the most of it.'

It did not seem to matter whether she ate or not, the severe pain and diarrhoea persisted. At least they had a day in a nice hotel to look forward to with nice showers and toilet facilities. She had taken medication with her for such things happening but was told not to take them unless essential. If she was travelling from place to place fair enough, but not to take them all the time.

Before she left she found out that the ship she had been working on was to be in the area she was visiting so she had arranged to meet her old cabin mate Beth and a few others. So they were to spend the day with Patricia and Kelly at the hotel. A touch of luxury she thought for her ship mates as she knew the sort of facilities that were on the ship so a day at the hotel would be nice to spend time by the pool and sipping drinks. As it turned out Patricia stuck to bottled water as she did not want to encourage any other adverse effects by drinking alcohol. The gang met up and spent the day together as planned and it was a chance for Kelly to meet some of Patricia's ship mates.

The next few days were spent heading back to Bangkok so that Kelly could catch her flight home. They shared lots of experiences on the way, including visiting a Buddhist Monastery and a village where the people wore rings around their neck. She was told that they had a ring placed around their neck every year so there were lots of people with very long necks. Patricia had a photograph taken with a young girl who had about 8 rings around her neck. Back at Bangkok, Kelly got her flight home and Patricia got a flight to Singapore. Kelly was picked up at the airport by her friend, we were so thankful that we didn't have to go back there again to pick her up, although we did offer should she have had a problem.

Patricia landed in Singapore and headed for her hotel. This time she was on her own and had booked into a nice hotel with an inside toilet and shower this time. She was still feeling unwell but was able to get out and about without too much problem. She asked at the hotel where she could get a bus to see the sights but the man at the hotel was not very helpful. Nothing daunted she decided to go out on her own and have a walk around to see what was close to the hotel. As luck would have it she stumbled across a youth hostel and the man there gave her instructions about buses and directions and a map of the area so she could get around. She spent the next day at the zoo. This place is huge and so much to see. The day after that she spent shopping. She was waiting in the bus station when she recognised a familiar face. She could hardly believe it, there on the other side of the station was one of the waiters from the ship. She called out and the guy turned around. He was as shocked to see her as she was to see him.
'I can't believe this,' they said.
As it transpires *The Destiny* was docked in Singapore for the day so he was lucky enough to have been rostered

for a day off so took the opportunity to go on shore an do some shopping. They spent a short time catching up'

'If only I had known you were going to be here today, we could have gone shopping together. I still can't believe I am on the other side of the planet, on my own and manage to bump into someone I know. What are the chances of that?'

She told him that she was heading off to Indonesia the next day.

'You are so lucky,' he said, 'I wish it was me but I still have another month to go on my contract. I am missing my family and friends. Ten months is a long time to be away from home.'

'I understand,' she said, 'six months was long enough for me.'

She returned to the hotel, had a meal and prepared herself for the meeting with Kayvan tomorrow. The next day she headed to the airport, excited but a bit apprehensive after all she had not seen him for nearly three months, would they feel the same she thought?

At least this time the flight was short and on time. She arrived in Indonesia. She got her back pack off the carousel, heaved it onto her shoulders and headed for the door that was to take her to Kayvan. She was feeling rather nauseous but this time it was nervousness. As she walked through the door the nervousness disappeared as Kayvan ran towards her, threw his arms around her and kissed her.

'I can't believe you have come to my country,' he said.

'I told you I was coming to see you and meet your family.'

'I know,' he said, 'but I still can't believe it. I really didn't think I was ever going to see you again. Oh babe it is so good to see you, but my, you have gone skinny again.'

'Yeah sorry about that but not had muffins for breakfast everyday and I have been really sick whilst I was in

Thailand.'

'Oh no, sorry to hear about that, are you ok now?'

'Well not great but better than I was before thankfully.'

'This is my uncle, he drove me here. It is a four hour drive from my village to Jakarta so I am afraid you have another long journey ahead of you.'

Patricia shook hands with his uncle and Kayvan made formal introductions.

'He does not speak much English I am afraid so I will have to be your interpreter while you are here. My sisters speak English, don't worry you won't just have me to speak to.'

They both chuckled. They got in the car and headed to Kayvan's house. Patricia and Kayvan held hands all the way giving each other loving looks. The looks did not last for long but the hold on Kayvan's hand got tighter and tighter, even though they drive on the same side of the road in Indonesia as they do in the UK the roads are somewhat different. There are road markings but no one seems to pay any attention to them. Where there should be two lanes of traffic there seemed to be five or six, all heading in the same direction. The roads were manic, everyone vying for position, horns tooting, and as for speed limits, well no one seemed to pay attention to them. It seemed to be that as long as you were moving it was OK. It got worse as they left the city as the roads were winding and they were heading uphill. Kayvan laughed at the expression on Patricia's face.

'I love fair ground rides and roller coasters,' she said, 'but I have never experienced anything like this before.' The colour drained from her face and she spent time with her face buried in Kayvan's shoulder. *'Four hours of this,'* she thought, *'I hope I live to meet his Mum!'*

The car began to slow down and then stopped outside a lovely house.

'This is my house,' he said. 'I had it built for me whilst I was at sea. My Mum and sister live here, that way the house isn't empty when I am away at work.'

She gathered herself together and got out of the car. She was welcomed by Kayvan's family. First his Mum, quickly followed by sisters then aunts uncles cousins. They were all keen to meet her as they had heard so much about her. Neighbours seemed interested too; after all it was a white woman in their street.

She was taken in the house and made to feel very welcome. Mum seemed very interested and asked lots of questions. She seemed concerned that she was travelling alone and kept asking through Kayvan.

'Does your mother know you are here?'

'Yes, of course she knows I wouldn't be here otherwise.' This intrigued Patricia, 'why does she keep asking me the same questions,' she asked Kayvan.

'Well you see Indonesian women would not do what you have just done. The fact that you are alone frightens her. She is worried for your well being.'

She laughed; 'it must be a Mum thing.' she said.

Then the food arrived, it seemed endless, there were all sorts of things that she had never seen before, not wanting to seem rude she tried some of the food being offered. It was very spicy and it tasted quite nice but she was suspicious of what she was eating. Lots of rice and noodles, she was happy with that but some of the other stuff she was not so happy with. After eating she was taken to the bedroom and she unpacked some of her stuff and unearthed the presents she had brought from Scotland for them all. There were various things usually with a hint of tartan.

'I am tired,' she said, 'it has been a long day,' so she and Kayvan went to bed.

I knew they would be sharing a bed, nothing new there, after all they did share a bed on board *The Destiny* at

least this time it was a proper bed and not a single bunk.
'Your family seem really nice,' she said, 'and made me feel very welcome.'
'I am glad you like them,' he said, 'they have been looking forward to meeting you.'
Next morning they were woken by the sound of Kayvan's mother calling on him. It was time for prayers.
'What on earth?' Said Patricia.
'That's my Mum calling me to make sure I am awake for morning prayers.'
'Ah, OK, she looked at her watch, 'Kayvan it is only 5 am.'
'I know but that is how it is here, we pray 5 times a day.'
Kayvan got up and left Patricia in bed, 'you stay there,' said Kayvan, 'get more sleep I will be back in a while.'
'OK.'
No way was she getting up, to her it was still the middle of the night. 'More sleep,' she thought, but not a hope. The noise was echoing throughout the house and even coming from the street. She tried burying her head under the pillows but that didn't help. Kayvan went to wash before the Morning Prayer and then performed his prayer with dignity and humility.
The rest of the day was spent meeting even more family and friends.
'I have put together a plan Patricia,' said Kayvan; 'I thought I would take you to see my country. So we will move west to east stopping here and there on the way. I have family all over, so there is no problem with accommodation.'
'Wicked!' she said, 'that's sounds great. I am looking forward to that as I thought we would just be here with your Mum and sisters.'
'No, not at all, it is your first time here and I want to show off my country to you and you to my country.'
A few days later they headed off on their travels.

They went to see magnificent temples and the scenery was spectacular. Everywhere they went there were cries of what sounded like 'bulley', this is how they refer to a white person or tourist. They would flank around Patricia and admire her and comment about the shape of her nose! Her nose is like mine, turns up at the end. Then a word she knew 'Barbie!' Like the doll, tall slim and white. This amused her, and everyone wanted to take her photograph. 'Obviously tourists were not here often,' she thought, an effect of the Tsunami of December 2004.

Lots of places had not recovered from that, she saw what would have been beautiful places but had been destroyed or damaged by the tsunami and obviously no money to make repairs the so things were not as beautiful as before.

They had booked into a hotel for a night which happened to be Kayvan's birthday. So they went for something to eat and she gave him a new baseball cap that she had taken with her, somewhat funky but again with tartan inlay. There had been other things that she had bought him too.

Patricia met more of the family and they showered her with gifts. They made her feel like a princess and some even cried when she had to say goodbye.

'The weather was poor,' she told us, 'rained most of the time' but she was with Kayvan and that's what counted. The relationship was as strong as ever and being with him 24/7 gave her a better idea of who he actually was. On board was good but it was just like being girlfriend/boyfriend. This way she learned so much more about him as a person, his family, his culture and his country. She was loving it there and loving Kayvan too.

On the way back to Kayvan's home they made the journey by train, this was not great as the train was full of creepy crawlies and bugs, she spent the 12 hour journey leaping about and stifling screams. They were everywhere, crawling up the windows and coming out of the seats. 'Never again,' she kept saying, 'never again.'

Unfortunately the food was not always what she expected. 'This is a poor country,' she was told, 'and we use everything when we cook. If we have chicken we use all the chicken including the feet.'

This of course led to more tummy upset and Patricia was losing weight hand over fist which she could ill afford, she was skinny enough as it was. She could not even drink the milk, she thought that milk would help but it is not treated the same way as here in the UK so it caused more problems. She ended up living on rice and corned beef, at least this way she was getting some food.

She was disappointed that the tan she had built up in Dubai and Thailand was fading, and fast. Then the email came that spoke volumes but it was only two lines it read:

'Only a week to go here in Indo so I will see you soon before I head off to the seas! Yes that's right back on board if, and only if, I can get the same ship as Kayvan. So hopefully I will be away again in the summer.

I got a phone call from Patricia to wish me a happy birthday. As always she had been prepared before she left and had given James a present to give me and a birthday card. How thoughtful of her, she is always so organised.

Back at the village their time was spent with Kayvan's Mum and seeing sights nearer to home. They went on a boat ride and also to a water park. Patricia felt somewhat underdressed as she wore a bikini but the other girls in the family were covered from head to toe. This made her feel very uneasy.

'Not to worry,' she was told by the family, 'you are a tourist here, you are not Muslim therefore it is not a problem. Relax and enjoy your time here.'

The inevitable day was looming, the day they had to part again. The pair of them went through the silence again, the same silence as before. It was the same awful silence that was on board the ship before they parted a few months earlier. Things were getting desperate, what were they to do now?

Well it was made clear by email sent to me, it read:

'Well it's my last few days in rainy indo and it's been wicked. I've had my picture taken at least 100 times, and rubbed a good few pregnant tummies and learnt a few dirty words but it's home time. The whole 7 wks have been amazing....though Dubai does seem 1 million light years ago. I am however ship bound ... as of 20th June. I can't believe I am going to The Destiny to be with my baby. I can't believe it, I was sure I'd never go back on board but what's 6 months right. Mum and Dad – *I pray u don't read this b4 I call u in 30 seconds.'*

She was lucky we had not read the email before she called us.

'Hello there,' she said in cautious tones, 'have you read my email?'

'No, what's up?'

Then she dropped the bombshell, the fact that she was only going to be home for a short time before she would be off on her travels again.

'So I will need a job for a while could you do me a favour? I know I am always asking you to do things for me but I need your help. Can you ask about and see if anyone needs temporary staff. I need another job for a while. I thought maybe Susan. She has a coffee shop; maybe she could give me something. I just want something to give me something to do but preferably something with no responsibilities and not retail.'

'Sure,' I said, 'I will give her a call and see what she says.'
Susan is my nephew's wife so it was not a problem approaching her.
'How has it been over there,' I asked gingerly.
'Great!' she said, 'I will tell you all about it when I get home. Are you ok with me going away again?' she asked.
'Of course, it seems you just visit here now, it is not a problem. See you soon, say hello to Kayvan from us.'

'Well another shock eh James?'
'That's good though, it shows that this is not a flash in the pan romance by the sounds of it'. 'At least she will be here for your birthday this year as she doesn't leave until the 20th June.'
'That will be nice, her being here not like last year.'
Oh dear another hectic journey to Jakarta airport, I am not looking forward to that. The traffic frightens the living daylights out of me.
At the airport they spent their last hours together being silly. He was pushing her around the airport on a luggage trolley and taking photographs, sitting close together and he holding the camera at arms length trying to fit them both in. The goodbye was as painful as last time. Lots of tears but more kisses and hugs, at least this time.
'I know I am going to see you again,' he whispered in her ear. Time will pass quickly and we will be together in June.'
They embraced each other for the last time, kissed each other tenderly, and then she said, 'I have to go.'
They parted and the touch of their fingers lingered for a moment more, another brief kiss, and she was gone.

The texts began:
'Mum I miss him already and we have only been apart

for five minutes. If I could I would run back to be with him. I'm cryin! X'

'I was expecting that angel, don't worry you will be together again soon,' I replied.

'Still cryin, can't stop. Can't wait to see you guys too though. X'

'We will be there to pick you up. Back to the computer to watch your flights. See you tomorrow...x'

Next morning we knew we had to go back to the dreaded airport.
'I think we should move our bed there,' I said to James, 'we seem to spend so much time there these days.
I logged on to the computer to check the flight details and found that Patricia had emailed me, it read:
'bloody hell, I'm in Singapore, then have to stop in Colombo then Dubai ....
Will I ever get home arrgghhhh ?
c u soon xxxxxxx'
'Ah well at least she isn't crying now by the sounds of it so that is good news,' I said.
The computer said that she was now on the Dubai leg and that the flight was again on time.
'That is amazing, her flights always run on time; I bet there are not a lot of people who can say that,' said James.
So back in the car and back to the airport again. We waited patiently for her to come through those doors again. This time she arrived fully laden with all her luggage and she was wearing a sweat top that I hadn't seen before.
'That new,' I asked? 'No she said, 'it is Kayvan's. I was cold at the airport so he gave this to me.'
I looked at this skinny little girl whose eyes were dark

and shadowed.

'You look hellish,' I said.

'Thanks for that, just what I needed to hear. I told you I had been sick.'

'Well I know but didn't realize how bad it was, there is nothing of you.'

'Well at one point it was coming from both ends so anything that went in just came out again one way or the other.'

'Let's get you home, I am going to feed you up before you go again.'

Next day she was still not feeling well. I told her to get to the doctor, I was not happy with her.

'This should not be going on all this time,' I said.

So I forced her to call the doctor, he was going to see her at 9.30 am. It transpires that she had picked up a bug, it was partly to do with the food she had eaten but this bug had got a hold of her and the remedy was dreadful.

'It is also very infectious,' the doctor said, 'so take precautions.'

I made sure that things she touched were properly washed and that hands were washed at all times. I isolated her towels and clothes and made sure they were dealt with separately. She had to take eight tablets at once as a bolus dose and then every four hours after that. This went on for a few days but then she began to be terribly sick, the poor girl vomited all day. By evening she had dissolved in a pool of tears. I had had enough; I called the emergency doctor in the late evening.

'You shouldn't have to go through this,' I said.

The doctor on the phone was really good. I explained the whole situation to her. She said that if I took her down that she would give her something.

'I don't think she is able to come down,' I explained.

'Well if you come down I will give you something to give

her to get her through the night then she can see her own GP tomorrow if needs be.'

I jumped in the car and headed for the night surgery. The doctor there was waiting for me. She gave me some tablets and told me that Patricia had to put one under her tongue and let it melt. She was not to swallow it. I headed for home driving like a demon, I just hoped that I was not caught by the police I was not in the mood to be pleasant. I got home and gave the tablets to Patricia.

'Not more tablets,' she said and started to cry again.

'Look!' I screamed at her, I was getting so worried about her, 'I know it is another tablet but for heavens sake girl grow up.'

'I can't,' she sobbed, 'I am so sick of taking tablets if I swallow another I think I will die!'

'Don't be ridiculous,' I said, 'and besides you don't swallow this one, just stick it under your tongue and let it melt.'

By this time I was ready to scream myself. She was green and looked so ill.

'Mum you never shout at me.'

'No wonder Patricia I am worried sick, please just stick this tiny little tablet under your tongue, you never know it may help.'

'What if it tastes horrible,' she said?

'For the love of Pete,' I exclaimed.

Under duress she stuck the tablet under her tongue.

'Is it horrible,' I asked?

'Well actually it doesn't taste at all.'

'There you go then all that carry on for nothing. Honestly, how old are you?'

Within a few hours I watched her turn from a horrible green to a nicer healthier pink, it was amazing. A tiny tablet has made all the difference.

After that escapade her recovery was faster and she was more like her old self.

She finally got around to unpacking her bags from her travels. I was under strict instructions not to touch them, or they would have been emptied a long time ago. She had brought back lots of knick knacks that she had bought in Thailand and Indonesia. Mostly ornaments but some other things too.

'These are for my house whenever I decide to get one. It will be full of items that I have bought all over the world. You know me; I am not one to have ordinary everyday things.'

Then she handed a parcel over to me and James wrapped in brown paper.

'This is from Kayvan for you,' she said.

On the paper was written: *'Thank you for letting Patricia come to my country, this is a small gift of thanks for you.'*

I opened it up and revealed a beautiful silk banner in abstract form the colours were stunning.

'It depicts the modes of carrying things in Indonesia,' she said.

Right enough if you looked closely you could pick out cycles, yolks and ladies with things on their heads.

'It is beautiful,' I said, 'and so thoughtful.'

'It cost him a lot of money,' she said, 'money he doesn't really have to spare.'

'We will have it mounted,' said James. 'It would look great with light shining through it,' he said, 'like a stained glass window. I will see what I can do.'

James is a very handy man so I left it with him. As it happens he couldn't find a way to shine light through it without it damaging the silk so he mounted it on a board and put it on the wall.

'You must give me Kayvan's phone number so I can thank him.'

'That is expensive Mum,' she said, 'but here is his email address, send him an email.'

No sooner said than done I sent an email off to a man I had never met but felt like I knew him. I expressed my

thanks for the banner and also for looking after Patricia while she was away.
A few days later I got a reply which read:
Hi Pauline and James..
My pleasure I was look after Patricia and I'm happy with it.
Actually I wanna spent more longer with Patricia, but she need rest and she need you to. I realize our food is very different until she can't eat.
I'm afraid she got sick, didn't enjoy in Indonesia...
but I was tried my best to made her happy..!!
I wish she can enjoy it. and I'm happy to you like the gift. Send regard to, James (Dad), Josh & wife and also the baby Cameron..
with love
Kayvan
How sweet, I didn't expect him to reply. As it happens it was the start of many emails to come.

I was busting at the seams, I was desperate to ask Patricia if Kayvan had mentioned the marriage thing but with her being sick I didn't want to upset her.
Once she was feeling better my curiosity was driving me crazy so I asked the question that had been hounding me since she got home.
'Patricia,' I said coyly. 'Was the marriage thing ever mentioned?'
'Oh yes,' she said, 'practically every day. Well every day we were away from his home. He asked me several times a day in fact, he kept saying, *'hey Patricia will you marry me?'*
'And, what did you say?'
'Well,' she said, 'I just kept saying stop asking me, it has to be the right time, the right place and with a ring.'
'What did he say to that?'
'Nothing much, but it didn't stop him hounding me about it. It became a standing joke eventually.'

Chapter 8

Well the traveller returned and I had arranged for her to get a temporary job with Susan in the coffee shop. It was not for long so her hours were made up to suit any shortfall in the coffee shop staff. That was enough for her; after all she knew that she would be back to working long, hard shifts on the ship so she thought this would be a way of earning a few pounds without draining her battery. She also thought it was great as she had no responsibilities and the hours were good, maybe only 3 or 4 a day which let her get other things done before her departure in a couple of months.

James and I got talking about this guy Kayvan who had seemed to steal our daughter's heart.
'I think this is getting really serious,' I said. 'I wish we could meet this boy; the last thing I want is for her to disappear and get more involved without having met him.'
'Yes,' agreed James. 'Not an easy task though considering he lives in Indonesia.'
We spent sometime discussing what we should do if anything after all it was our daughter's welfare. So, we decided that we would approach Patricia and ask if we paid for his flights if we could bring him to the UK so we could meet him.

That night once we had all eaten; James and I approached Patricia and told her of our idea.
'Well, that sounds great but hardly likely. This is now April and I am away again in June,' she said.
Disappointed we had to agree that it would be difficult to arrange and so decided to put it down as a good idea but not necessarily practical. What a pity we thought, but she has a valid point, so we will have to wait and see what develops between them when they get back on

board.

The next day Patricia announced that she had emailed Kayvan and he had said he would be delighted to come and meet us, so if we were still keen enough to meet him then we should go ahead.

'Fantastic,' we said, 'lets get the wheels in motion; we don't have much time as we would like him to be here for at least two weeks.'

So the emails started between Patricia and Kayvan.

'We need to know how we go about this, so can you ask him how much time he needs and if we can book his flights or should he do them? We are fighting a ticking clock so we need details as soon as possible.'

Patricia came down later that night and explained that Kayvan not only needed flights but also a Visa and this could take a long time, she knew the predicament so again it looked like it was not to be.

I then received this email from Kayvan:
Hi how are you mom...?
I am doing well here and I would like to say 'thank you very much for inviting me to Scotland (Dundee) I really appreciate.' and wanted to come.
I really want to meet Patricia family .. and show to you all this is Kayvan.!!
But honestly I don't have enough money to come over coz I am build my second house...!! I was asking to travel agent today for the visa and the ticket!!
I told to Patricia this morning... (I was confused and don't know how to do...!)
I really appreciate...and once again thank you very much for inviting me..!!
Send regard to James, Josh, Louise and Cameron..
with love
Kayvan

So I sent this reply back.

Hi Kayvan, I am well thank you and glad you are to.
We would really love for you to come to Dundee and meet all of us but it seems very complicated. It is such pity. I am sure Patricia told you that we would pay for your flights and look after you while you were here. I wish we had thought of this before Patricia left Indonesia then you could have come here with her.
We will meet Kayvan one day but it looks like we will have to wait a little while.
Look after yourself and I will look after Patricia for you.
Love Mom x

I had noticed that he called me mom, so I decided to avoid more complications I would just respond to mom, it seemed nice and if things kept going at this rate I may be his mom in the future.

Well you know nothing ventured nothing gained so not daunted James and I decided that if it was within our power that we would get him over here. The emails became frantic, explaining to Kayvan that we were going to do all we could to get him here before Patricia left to go on board. We had daily emails to each other and as it turns out getting the flights was the easy part, the Visa on the other hand was more complicated. In Indonesia all applications have to be through an agent and not directly with the Embassy so this was going to slow things down to. We decided to send money to Kayvan so he could get his flights at least that part was easy. It then transpired that the Embassy needed details of our income, outgoings and letters from our employers to confirm that we were UK citizens and in full employment.
'So, that is how it has to be is it?'
It was like someone was challenging us. Well I like a good challenge so the fight was on. James and I spent a couple of days getting all the details they required and sent them off to the agent along with covering letter

advising that we were to be responsible for Kayvan during his stay and that we would meet any expenses giving him board and lodgings throughout his entire stay. There were copies of bank statements, utility bills I letters from employers, the whole works.
'Hopefully we can pull this off, we said, as we posted the letter.
As a safe guard we faxed the details to Kayvan's uncle, this way the agent would have all the information and would get the original documents in time.

We got the following email form Kayvan

Hi....
On Monday my travel agent will call me and I was booking a flight on 18 May..but if my visa finish earlier I was tell them to booking my flight near that date coz I really....wanted to meet Patricia and her family..!!
I was asking Patricia she want a romantic place for engagement .. and I don't know place in dundee..and I wish its not expensive!! ha..ha...
its so exited for me....!!
and I was receive you money and I'll pay it for my ticket.. once again thank you very, very much...
I am so lucky person coz I have pretty, nice, kind, friendly girlfriend with a lovely family...!! thank you God.. have great day to you...!!
with love
Kayvan

Well that's something I suppose at least he has the money to pay for the flight and his Visa, all we have to do now is hope he gets the Visa in time so he can have his trip to Scotland. We were getting desperate for time now, it may be a case that he is only here for one week now but at least it is better than nothing.

I also noticed the engagement part of his text and replied asking what he meant exactly, was he going to propose again this time in the right place with a ring? It turns out that this was his plan and he asked for my help. *'Wow, what an honour,'* I thought to myself. So I got to thinking where would be a romantic place here in Dundee? It would have to be different, special and somewhere Patricia would not expect anything to happen. After a great deal of deliberation I came up with the idea of the *RRS Discovery*, this is the ship that Captain Scott used for his Arctic expedition and is here in Dundee. My thinking behind this was that they met on a ship so why not use this as a nice place for a proposal. Many emails later it was decided that this was a good idea; after all they met on a ship on water so Kayvan thought this would be a great idea. I also had to mention the ring! I was told not to worry that his mother, who makes jewellery had made a ring for him to give to Patricia. He had told me that one day whilst they were in Australia that they had been looking in a jewellers shop and she had pointed out a ring that she liked, a simple solitaire, remembering this he told his mother about it and had made a ring to meet his description.

The flights were booked and the Visa in place, he was to arrive on the 6th June, so we had it all planned that he would pop the question on the 7th. That way if Patricia said yes we could have a party before she went away. As it turns out she had to join the ship on the 20th June but had to leave on the 17th the day before James' birthday so again she won't be there. That went down like a lead balloon but there was nothing we could do about that. As it turns out Kayvan was going home on the 17th so at least we only had one trip to the airport. He had arranged to be here until she left, that way getting as much value out of the money we sent. Patricia was somewhat surprised that he was staying until the last

105

minute as she had hoped for a day or two to say goodbye to friends, but after all the carry on getting the Visa realized that it was better for him to be here longer and getting our moneys worth.

In between all the secret emails between Kayvan and me things were going along well. Patricia was enjoying her job although she had been made supervisor so she had inherited some responsibilities. That was not a problem for her but she had made it perfectly clear that it was temporary. I had asked in conversation what she would do if Kayvan were to ask her to marry him while he was here, she laughed.
'Now you are being silly,' she said, 'it was just a crazy joke Mum that's all.'
'Yeah, I know that but what if…,' my voice tapering off.
'I don't know what I would say, he knows the rules, right time, right place and with a ring. If he met all criteria I would likely say yes,' she giggled.
If only she knew what we had been up to.

I spent the next little while preparing the house for our visitor making sure everything was ship shape, pardon the pun! James and I were getting quite excited about the arrival of Kayvan. Patricia as always took it in her stride. James and I are not exactly what you would say naive so we realized that Patricia and Kayvan would be sharing a bed not just the bedroom therefore we made sure that everything was OK.
Meanwhile Patricia kept asking me.
'What if he asks me again Mum, to marry him that is?'
This question was asked often and I just kept saying 'Well what if he does? What will you say?'
Knowing fine well that he was going to ask, and that he was bringing a special ring with him, and the location already chosen for the proposal.
She said, 'I will say yes, so just in case he does ask,

how about looking at wedding dresses with me?' 'Well, I suppose there is no harm looking; it could be a bit if fun too.'

Before I knew where I was we had booked appointments with bridal shops in both Glasgow and Edinburgh to co-inside with her days off. I had to take holidays but I thought what the heck, if that's what she wants to do then let's go! After all, I knew he was going to ask and she had said that she would say yes so it had to be done at some time and she was going away in June so best to do it now.

A few days later we headed to Glasgow, we had appointments in three shops so we had decided to make a day of it, a girly day and I said, 'if you pay for the train fares, then I will buy lunch.'

We arrived at the first shop and the lady was superb. She asked Patricia what kind of dress she wanted, if there was anything particular she wanted. The only stipulation she had was that she did not want a 'swoosh' at the front, everyone seems to have that and true to form Patricia didn't want to be like everyone else. So the fun began, dresses by the score and not a swoosh in sight. She had already decided that the theme of her wedding would be red and white as these are the colours of the Indonesian flag. So she tried on long dresses, ballerina style and even some with red embroidery to fit in with the theme. She looked stunning in all of them but as they all had full skirts she looked a bit lost as she is so slim. Then we went to the other shops and did the same. There were one or two that were nice but not 'IT'. They didn't make her feel special. I liked one that was typical bridal dress style but it looked exactly the same at the back as it did in the front, an exact mirror image, but she was not impressed. As a typical girly day we had not had time to eat, so lunch was out the question. So we headed back to the railway station and we ended up having a burger and fries which we had to eat at such a rate that we ended up with indigestion. The train journey home was full of chat about dresses and shoes and that although the dresses were lovely they had not hit the spot.

The following week we headed to Edinburgh, the same scenario as Glasgow. The dresses again were lovely and the one we liked was way out of any budget that we considered suitable for a one off occasion. It was long, white, with a train nearly as long as the one we had got off earlier. The train was painted with red silk roses, absolutely stunning but still not what she was looking for. The last shop! I was glad to get there, we had walked for miles and my feet were killing me but this seemed to have a dress that we both loved. It was long, white and fitted from her bust to her knees then kicked out in a fountain of taffeta, then over the top was beautiful beaded lace, but just partly covering the taffeta leaving a train behind. It shone and sparkled and she looked at me, I looked at her and we knew this is it! Even though the dress was two sizes to big and there were handfuls of material gathered at the back she looked every inch a bride and a stunning one at that. 'How about a veil,' the assistant asked?
She tried the veil but it took the look away from the ornate décor of the dress, so it was decided that there would be no veil. In the changing room Patricia whispered that she felt a fraud as she had not been proposed to and she didn't have a ring.
'I bet the assistant is wondering what we are up to,' we giggled silently.
I told the assistant that we liked the dress but that we had other places to go. That got us off the hook. It was decided though that if he was to ask and if she was to get married that was the dress she wanted. I had to agree that it was her to a 'T' so unusual and so ornate; it

almost had an Asian look to it. I had never seen a dress like it and I had been to lots of weddings in my time.

Again it was a lovely journey home, getting excited about the prospects of a wedding.

She said, 'You know that if he asks and I say yes that you will have to arrange everything while I am away, you can be my wedding co-coordinator.'

'Well that could be difficult,' I said, 'it is not my day but yours and I would never do anything without your say so.'

'Hey, Mum I trust you implicitly but you can always email me details and we could arrange a virtual wedding,'

We giggled again.

Then one weekend we went and looked at possible venues for the wedding. James, Patricia and I all went looking to see places that were not run of the mill. Patricia was adamant that it would be somewhere that no one else had used. As it was to be a civil ceremony she decided that the ceremony and reception would be in the same place.

'That way we would not need wedding cars,' she said.

'I want you to have wedding cars with nice ribbons,' said James.

This was a bit bizarre as she was not even engaged but she had a feeling that she may be before she left for the ship so it had to be done now. James and I did not mind as we knew that there was to be a proposal. We went to several hotels, none in Dundee but all within an hours drive. Typically the one she liked was the last one after we had driven for miles all day. It was a lovely hotel, only eleven rooms but so quirky. Part of it was very Scottish and some of it was very art deco. There was a whiskey bar which was decorated in tartan and the restaurant area was purple with black and white checked furniture and salt and pepper cellars. There was also a room which was hexagonal shaped filled with leather couches and a huge fireplace. In all the windows were huge vases of silk flowers. The bedrooms were amazing and the bridal suite had a lovely silver four poster bed. In the entrance hall stood a very Scottish style seat. It was high backed and covered in tartan material. At the top were what looked like deer antlers, a strange looking seat but fitted in beautifully with the quirkiness of the place. So the choice was made, this was to be the one if there was to be a wedding. It was called *The Cairn Hotel*.

Before we knew where we were the date of Kayvan's arrival was upon us. So yet again we headed to the airport. James and I were so excited and Patricia was quiet.
'Why so quiet,' I said. 'I am excited about seeing him again, and I can't wait but it has been a few months again since we last saw each other so it feels a bit daunting.'
'To be expected I suppose,' but I was keen to meet the guy who has made my daughter so happy and James felt the same.
'You do realize I will be watching him carefully,' said James, 'I am not letting just anyone take you away.'
'You know Dad,' she said, 'I know you are not even kidding, I like that. If he doesn't meet up to your requirements he has had it!'
'If this is the man for you then there nothing we could do to stop you, you are too stubborn just like me,' he bellowed out a laugh.

We arrived at the airport and headed straight to arrivals.
'His plane is approaching,' Patricia announced eagerly.
'Blimey! I hope you like him. If not you will have a stranger in your house that could be awkward.'
'Look, if you like him I am sure we will like him too, don't panic. Worst case is that we don't like him but it is only for ten days so I am sure we will cope.'
James and I paced the arrivals area like our feet were

on hot coals. Patricia sat there quietly and just looked at the door waiting for the arrival of her Kayvan. We looked at the door every time it opened hoping to see this boy. Then we realized that we didn't even know what he looked like, OK, we had seen photographs but that is not quite the same is it?

Then the doors opened, and coming through was a guy wearing a baseball cap, and a grin that was from ear to ear, almost blinding us with his lovely white teeth and skin the colour of coffee.

'That's him,' exclaimed James!

Patricia leapt to her feet and approached him, almost cat like, so cool so composed. She flung her arms around him and placed a dainty kiss on his lips. He picked her up and swung her round and round hugging her as close as he could.

She broke away and said, 'This is my Mum and Dad.'

We ventured forward to meet him. The smile on his face said it all. James held out his hand and shook Kayvan's and said, 'Well it is good to meet you at last.'

I on the other hand said, 'Is it OK if I give you a hug? We have spoken so much via email that I feel I know you already.'

'Sure!' he said and I hugged him and he said,

'I can't believe it I am here in Scotland!'

We headed for the car. I needed a cigarette and Kayvan was glad to see me reach for the lighter.

'Here let me do that for you, and his arm stretched out as quick as a flash with a lighter already ignited.'

'Thanks Kayvan,'

'No problem,' he said.

He then proceeded to light a cigarette of his own, 'I needed that,' he said, 'I haven had one for so long.'

The journey home was the usual conversation, how was your flight, bet you are tired etc. He and Patricia sat in the back holding hands and he kept giggling.

'What is so funny?' she said.

'Nothing I just can't believe I am here, in Scotland, with you and your parents.'

His spoken English is better than his written word I thought, but considering I don't know any Indonesian he is doing well.

We got home and decided to spend the afternoon in the garden. It was a beautiful day, so sunny and warm, unusual for it to be so warm at this time of year. We chatted and quizzed poor Kayvan, getting to know him and what made him tick. What a lovely lad, and so polite. I popped into the kitchen for more beer and Kayvan followed and asked if I needed any help.

'No, no just you sit down, you are our guest.'

'Thank you,' he said, 'but I used this as an excuse to speak to you. I have the ring in my bag and want to make sure I understand what you have planned about the ship thing.'

I chuckled; 'if you have the ring then you are half way there,' I said. 'We will take you out tomorrow and make sure that we take you to see the *Discovery* then you will know.'

'Sounds like a plan,' thanks mom.

'Not bad,' I thought, he is calling me mom to my face now.' I smiled gently.

As the sun began to set and it got cooler we went inside and had our dinner. Kayvan showered and disappeared for a while.

'Has Kayvan gone to bed,' I asked, 'he must be exhausted.'

'No,' she said he is praying, 'he will be back soon.'

'While he is out of the room what do you two think of him.'

'I think he is perfectly charming,' I said.

James said, 'I have to agree I can see what you see in him babe, he seems very nice.'

'Yeah and hot,' she said with a smile almost as broad as his.

Kayvan re-appeared and announced that he was going to bed as he was tired.

'OK,' we said, 'goodnight, sleep tight as we have a busy day for you tomorrow.'

He looked at me directly and laughed.

The pair of them went upstairs. James and I took the opportunity to discuss what we thought of our visitor. We agreed that he was very nice but it is early days and we will talk about it again as we get to know him. Patricia came down stairs a while later and had a chat with me.

'Mum,' she said, 'sounding somewhat perplexed, Kayvan left his suitcase open and I saw a ring box! Do you think he is going to ask me properly this time?'

'Well, I don't know,' I said, 'what if he does?'

'Well, how do you know if he is the one?'

'What a question,' I said. 'Well let me put it this way, when you parted from the ship did you think, 'Ahh well bye, or was your heart aching knowing you may not see him again?"

'Yes,' she said, 'my heart was aching.'

'So when you left him in Indonesia was your heart aching again? When you are not together do you miss him?'

'Yes to both of them Mum,' she said. '

Well without knowing the answer to your actual question it sounds to me like you love this boy but only you know the answer. There is no fanfare, or shooting arrows babe, listen to your heart and you will be fine. If he asks it is ok to say no if you are not sure.'

At that we left the conversation and I left Patricia with the thought as she turned and went off to bed.

Chapter 9

The next morning we had breakfast together and made our plans for the day.

'I think we should take Kayvan up the Law Hill' I said, 'it is a lovely starting point and he can get a panoramic view of the city, then maybe the beach as we don't know how long this weather is going to last.'

I had prompted James earlier as he knew our plan so he popped up with, 'how about we take Kayvan to see *RRS Discovery?*'

Patricia looked at me as if to say what! That is so boring! I backed James up saying that Kayvan may enjoy it is after all one of Dundee's biggest tourist attractions. Just because it is not her cup of tea it may interest Kayvan. Not to mention that although it is in our city we have never seen it properly. We had obviously seen the ship, you can't miss it, it is so big and close to where I work, but we have never done the exhibition, which is often the case when things are on your doorstep. Brow beaten she gave in and agreed that it may be worth a visit. Kayvan and I gave a huge sigh of relief.

So we headed off to the Law Hill and showed Kayvan the city pointing out places we intended to take him later including the *RRS Discovery*.

Then we headed to the beach, 'it is very pretty,' he said but enjoyed the visit to the castle more. Then we headed off to the ship, my heart racing with anticipation. Patricia was totally unaware that we were up to something. We went in and paid for the tickets to the exhibition and Patricia and I ended up having a laugh and taking silly photos. As the main point of the exhibition is the Antarctic there were lots of things that we took advantage of, like her with the models of crew of the ship and us pulling faces at them? This kept her busy and unsuspecting. Once through the exhibition you are allowed onto the ship. We all spent time appreciating how rough it must have been and Patricia and Kayvan laughed saying how the quarters there were almost like on *The Destiny*, well actually maybe Captain Scott's crew had better!!

We got to see everything there was to see and Patricia was anxious to get off.

'I am hungry,' she kept mumbling.

She kept heading upwards trying to get us off the ship. When we got back on deck James and I headed to the front of the ship as if to admire the view over the river, like we had not seen it a million times before. That was Kayvan's cue. Patricia headed for the stairs, panic!

'Patricia' Kayvan called, 'come and see this, maybe we should have had one on *The Destiny*,' and he pointed to the helm.

Patricia annoyed that she had been caught trying to escape reluctantly climbed back up the stairs. She shuffled towards him, showing to one and all that she was less than pleased. He took her hand and started moving the helm and pretending to steer the ship. James and I were still lingering and watching in secret at the goings on.

The next thing we knew, Kayvan was down on one knee and said, 'Patricia I love you, and the reason we are here is so that I can tell you something. The sea and ships brought us together. I have the ring this time and hope this is the right time and place.'

He opened a velvet red box and produced the ring his mother had made for her, and said 'Patricia will you marry me, do me the honour of being my wife'.

He stood up and Patricia threw her arms around his neck. I looked at James. 'I think that is a yes!'

We began to applaud and she looked over at us with a smile that said it all. She looked so happy, and the grin on Kayvan's face was even bigger than the one he had in the airport. We ran up and hugged the happy couple and offered our congratulations.

'OK, now let's go celebrate; we will go for a late lunch, our treat' said James.
We went to the restaurant beside the ship and ordered meals.
'OK let me see' I said.
She held her hand over the table to let me see the ring.
'It is stunning,' I said.
So plain and simple and yet stunning. It was white gold, with a single solitaire sitting proud in a beautiful mount just like the one she had seen in Australia. She took a photo of it with her phone and sent it to all her friends.
'What a show off,' I said. 'Now we will have to arrange an engagement party for you both.'
'Great idea,' she said, 'we can make it an engagement come leaving party.'
'We will get on it when we get home.'
We went and did a little shopping in the town and bought Kayvan a book with Dundonian expressions, like 'ah dinnay ken', meaning 'I don't know'.
Patricia took every advantage to show off her ring when handing over cash, just like a little girl, it made us laugh.
I had been speaking to Kayvan on the way to the shops and he said the most beautiful thing to me, he said that he had had other girlfriends but 'they are like clothes in a market, whereas Patricia is like a lovely gown, like the ones you see in shops that are so beautiful they are kept behind glass.'
I could tell that he idolized her and that he was so proud and pleased that she had agreed to marry him.
'The ring is beautiful Kayvan it must have taken your mother a long time to make it, and for it to fit perfectly was a great talent.'
'She is good at what she does,' he said, 'she had checked her out when she was in Indonesia and just knew what size to make.'
James then took over the conversation with Kayvan and that gave me a chance to speak to Patricia.

'Well, that's it, done! I take it our chat last night helped?'
'Yes Mum, thanks'.
'I have only known the boy for 24 hours but he seems lovely and I am sure he loves you, so now you will leave for the ship as an engaged couple, and I will get a move on with wedding arrangements.'

When we got home we started phoning people telling them the good news and inviting them to a party on the Saturday afternoon, we thought if the weather was to be good a BBQ would be a good idea. It was a good way for family and friends to meet Kayvan too. She sent an email to Josh who was away working off shore in the middle of the North Sea to tell him he was going to have a brother-in-law.

The next day I got up before everyone else and headed for the superstore down the road and bought them an engagement present and a card. I bought a laundry basket and basin etc, all the little things that would be useful when they get married. I bought gold confetti and filled the baskets with it. Well, you can't have an engagement without a gift and cards especially from your parents. I got home to find everyone else waiting for me.
'Come and give me a hand with this,' I said to both Patricia and Kayvan. They were delighted to get the gifts and the confetti went everywhere.
We had decided to go out and about, keeping things simple as Kayvan was still a bit jet lagged. We had planned to take him to Edinburgh and Stirling and to show him some of the scenery as Scotland is beautiful in the summer but not straight away, best to wait until he is fully alert we thought.
'We should take him to see the hotel too,' said James; 'we may even have lunch there or something, test the food so to speak.'

We went into town and put an announcement in the local paper, *'Mr. and Mrs. Gilmour are pleased to announce the engagement of their only daughter Patricia to Kayvan Augustin of Indonesia on the 7th June 2006.'*

At night Patricia was very quiet, unusually so. I thought she would be full of excitement and as high as a kite but she wasn't.

'You ok babe,' I asked'? 'Dunno,' she said. 'I feel funny'. 'Funny, what do you mean funny?'

'Weird like,' she said. 'Have I done the right thing? I know I should be on cloud nine but I'm not.'

Oh dear, alarm bells rang in my ears.

'I understand that it maybe came as a shock as it were but it had to be done as soon as he got here so we had time to arrange a party. Maybe it would have been better if he had left it until just before you went away. Look, things will be OK; you know you love him I think you are a bit frightened of making a commitment, a natural feeling.'

'Yeah Mum you are right as always I am just freaking out a bit that's all.'

Well the next day was no better, Patricia was as unhappy as the night before. Kayvan was somewhat confused about the mood Patricia was in. He came to talk to me. I explained that she was feeling a bit overpowered by the situation but advised him that it would all be OK in a day or so once she got used to the idea.

'Ok,' he said, 'I trust you mom and I will just let her have her space and hope she comes round soon.'

The mail was delivered; it was an engagement card from my brother and his wife with a gift voucher for the happy couple, as they live in England they could not make it to the BBQ.

'That's nice,' I said, 'and so quick, I guess that is so they made sure you get it before you both leave.'

Kayvan was confused about the whole thing, so I

explained our customs to him. He seemed quite delighted that family give gifts and was in awe of it all.

An hour or so later it all went so wrong. Patricia was having a really hard time dealing with all this. She and Kayvan disappeared and came back later with an announcement that the engagement was off!! Well not off exactly, just postponed! She had explained to Kayvan that she did love him but for some reason which she did not understand that she was having all these doubts. We all discussed it in great depth and advised them that it is best to deal with this now and not later. If one of the couple is not happy then it is obviously not right. There is no point in pretending. Relationships should not be based on pretence. So the ring was given back to Kayvan, the lovely ring his mother had made was back in his possession.

'Keep it,' she said, 'and bring it with you when you come to the ship.'

The lovely romantic bubble had been well and truly burst. There were tears from Patricia and she was so upset that she had let us down, and that she had hurt Kayvan.

'I have broken his heart,' she said, 'the last thing I wanted to do. You are right though Mum I do love him, I am just so afraid, afraid of the responsibility, giving up my independence. How do I know he is the one?'

'It is like I said honey, listen to your heart, it will keep you right.'

'Another thing, what will people think of me, getting engaged one day then a couple of days later calling it off.'

'They will think I am crazy, a silly girl. We even put it in the paper.'

'No babe, they will think you are brave for admitting you have made a mistake, no one will think you are silly. It is better to do it now and not leave it until he goes back to

Indonesia and tell him by email.'

My heart went out to Kayvan, here he was in a strange country with people he has just met and his world had been turned upside down. Emotions all over the place, his English is good but when you want to pour out your heart you don't want to have to think about every word before you say it, you just want to blurt it all out in a torrent of emotion and the poor lad couldn't.
He came to me to talk.
'I don't know what I have done that is so wrong,' he said.
'You have not done anything wrong,' I said keeping my voice low and even and making sure I did not use words that he did not understand. I had to make him understand that Patricia was hurting too, that she did not want to hurt him, but that she was confused.
'What you have to hang on to,' I said, 'is that she has not called it off just postponed it. She has asked you to take the ring with you when you go back on board, so it may not be final.'
'I take the blame for this,' I said, 'I thought it would be a good idea to do the proposal as soon as you got here but I think it was too soon. I think that if she had got used to you being around and recalling what a great guy you are we wouldn't be here like this. If it had been next week we would have been celebrating properly so I apologise for contributing to you being hurt. I could kick myself, I really could, but we have to move on and make your stay here as nice as possible, although I fear it is not going to be easy.'
'Thank you mom,' he said, 'thank you for listening to me and being my friend.'

After that, the rest of their time together was strained. The house seemed tense and the atmosphere heavy, not the best way to spend our time before Patricia goes away. It was getting to the point where we could hardly bear it. Patricia was moping the whole time and Kayvan was getting more and more confused. One evening we had some of Patricia's friends over thinking that may help. We always got on well with her friends so as it was getting late I was asked if I would take Kelly home. James and I jumped in the car and took her home; it is not far so we were only away for about ten minutes. When we got back Patricia was beside herself.

'What's up?' we said, 'It's Kayvan he has disappeared.' He just got up and left and I don't know where he is.'

'Which way did he go?' I asked.

If he turned left he would be OK, but if he turned right he could end up in trouble, as a bit down the road is not the world's best area and with his skin colour he could invite trouble without opening his mouth.

'I can't even phone him as his mobile doesn't work here.'

'Well there is not much we can do just now.'

'Let's give him ten minutes and see what happens.'

'If he is not back by then we will go looking for him. James you take your car and I will take Patricia's.'

Luckily he returned within the ten minutes much too every one's relief.

'Where did you go'? I asked him.

'I went for a walk up the road; I needed time to think and to speak to God, so I left.'

'Phew at least you went up the road and not down, it could have been disastrous.'

I explained it to him and he realised what he had done was impulsive and silly but at the same time it needed to be done. We spent the next two hours on the stairs chatting; he didn't want to join Patricia and her friends. He needed to unload and I was his shoulder to cry on and his ear for listening. What else could I do? The lad was alone and confused. I told him some home truths about Patricia, things he may not have noticed while they were on board. How she is strong willed, independent, how she thinks, the things that make her tick. Her listened intently to my every word and nodded often as if to say *'yes I know that'*, but also raised his eyebrows on occasion. What a nightmare this is turning out to be I thought.

We still stuck to the plan of seeing the sights of Scotland. The way we saw it was, well we have paid for him to come here on holiday and a holiday is what he is going to get. Who knows if he was ever to return? So we went to Edinburgh, Stirling, Loch Tay, Loch Lomond, Aberfeldy and places of historic interest. Kayvan enjoyed his time with James as he would share the history of Scotland with him. He really enjoyed the trip to Wallace Monument; he had seen the film *Braveheart* and was impressed to learn about the real William Wallace. The trip to Edinburgh castle was memorable for James too as he was impressed that Kayvan was so interested, and got quite emotional when reading the literature about the history. There was however a strange event when they were there, Kayvan had overheard a conversation and realized that he was listening to a group of fellow Indonesians. How bizarre that all these people from so far away met and chatted in Scotland's capital. He engaged in conversation and found that they were on a touring holiday. He told them that he was here visiting his girlfriend, well that was true, but by now she was meant to be his fiancé.

We took lots of photographs throughout his visit and the best one is of Kayvan and James sitting by Loch Tay just having a 'moment'. The peace and tranquillity is so obvious. I look at that now and wonder what each of them was thinking about. There is another of Kayvan, alone by Loch Lomond and I get the same feeling, that of loneliness, contemplation and yet tranquillity.

As the time went on and the date for their departure

grew closer I was beginning to feel so down. I knew that Patricia was leaving soon and under the worst circumstances ever. Every now and then the pair of them would slope away and chat in the privacy of the bedroom. I was hoping that they were resolving their differences and putting things right. Then the inevitable, Kayvan came down and told me that Patricia was crying and that he could not console her. That was it!! I had had enough. I went upstairs and asked what on earth was going on.
'I was talking to Kayvan and I realized that I don't think we could ever have what you and Dad have she said.'
'What on earth are you talking about?' I asked her abruptly.
'Well, you and Dad have the perfect relationship,' she said. 'I will never have that.'
'Perfect relationship, what makes you think that!?'
'Well you never argue, you are always together and you are always happy.'
I laughed out loud. 'You think this is perfection, well let me tell you this, it is not perfect. It is close I must admit but we have problems and disagreements just like everyone else. However we do not get heated when you and Josh were around. We have our troubles but as children you did not need to know them, these things are on a need to know basis and frankly you did not need to know.'
She looked at me in disbelief, 'Oh yeah,' she said almost glibly, 'like what.'
By this time I was so angry that I started to cry.
'I don't have to explain myself to you or defend myself but if you want to know then pin back your ears young lady because here it comes.'
I let rip, telling her all our secret problems the things that were private between her father and myself. Like having to sell the car to keep the wolves from the door, the fact that I had ran up a credit card bill that I could not control.

Then I let her have it right between the eyes, I told her about the problems I had had with James when he hurt his back when she went away and the fact that I thought that I was going to lose him. The fact that we protected her from the truth so she would not worry. She dissolved into tears hearing that her Dad had been so sick and not been told.

'You see Patricia you see us through rose tinted glasses but really we are just like everyone else, we are nothing special. Marriage is a thing that is not to be taken lightly, it is hard work. The fact that you see us as a perfect couple is, in a round about way a compliment to us that we have protected you and Josh from all the hurt and the hard times we have endured.'

We cuddled each other and then she realized that what I had told her made perfect sense.

'I am angry that you did not tell me about Dad,' she said, 'the fact that family, friends even neighbours knew but I was oblivious. I have been home for so long now and never a word about it, not even an inkling'.

'Well if it had all gone wrong you would have been told obviously, but why worry you when you were so far away and nothing you could do.'

She came to see my point of view but made me swear that when she goes this time that I would tell her everything that was going on. I agreed.

'OK babe, I promise I will tell you no matter what. No more secrets from either of us, OK? From now on I will treat you as an adult, but be prepared to take the strain of all that goes with it.'

After that the air seemed to clear a bit and the house was not quite normal but the tension was less. James told me how proud he was of me, for taking the bull by the horns and telling her some home truths.

'It could not have been easy for you to say or for her to hear,' he said.

So the rest of the time we spent with them seemed

easier. In fact we noticed that they were getting closer, the odd touching of hands and kiss on the cheek. Nothing major but at least they were OK in each others company again. Not romantic but less strained even the odd laugh between them.

The day for them to leave was upon us. We all headed for the airport yet again. This time Patricia was heading to Australia and Kayvan back home to Indonesia. It was the strangest feeling. I was sad to see them both go but relieved that this catastrophe was coming to an end. We sat about in an uncomfortable silence waiting for Kayvan's flight to be called. He was heading off first, James and I could tell that he was not keen to go but Patricia was not showing any signs of wanting him to stay.
'Well, this is it,' I said to Kayvan, 'we must say goodbye, it has been a pleasure meeting you and hopefully one day we will meet again.'
I hugged him and kissed his cheek. He whispered gently in my ear, 'Thanks mom and don't worry, no matter what happens between Patricia and me I will still look after her when we are on board. Please keep sending me emails, let me know how Louise and Cameron are doing. It is a pity I did not get to meet Josh and maybe I never will. Maybe I can come on holiday again sometime.'
'You are more than welcome in our home Kayvan, I will miss you.'
He turned and shook James' hand. James put his hand on Kayvan's shoulder and pulled him towards him, gave him a man type hug and wished him well.
'Go on,' I said, 'you had better get off, give our regards to your family.'
We stood and waved while he and Patricia headed for the departure gate and security control.
'Well one down one to go eh,' said James. 'This will be

the telling point, let's see how long she takes to say goodbye. If it is long then they have a chance but if not, well.'

…. at that there was Patricia heading toward us. I looked at James and he looked at me, not a word said.

'That was quick,' I said, I couldn't let it go I just had to comment.

'Well,' she said, 'that's it I have said my goodbyes to him and we have agreed to meet on the ship again and we will see how it goes. I don't really want to go there just now I would rather spend our last couple of hours together as a family not dissecting my relationship with Kayvan.'

So that is how it was, we did the usual, trying to keep things light and airy. We had lunch and chatted and watched the clock slowly move around. Then it was her turn to say goodbye. We all went to the departure and hugged and kissed each other. The tears were as always and we waved until she was out of sight.

'That was not as bad as last time', I said to James.

'No that was weird saying goodbye to Kayvan and then her.'

We held hands and headed back to the car.

'I suppose you will be flight-watching again,' he said jokingly.

'Yes but this time I have two sets of flights to look out for.'

'This has been an experience and no mistake; I can't wait to get home and back to some sort of normality.'

'Yes,' said James, 'that will be nice, just you and I.'

I did spend the time watching the flights as they headed to their destinations, watching over both of them. When they had both arrived safely I could then relax.

Chapter 10

It was good to be home again, just James and I. The house was quiet and relaxed not to mention clean and tidy. It was like a haven of peace and tranquillity after the last couple of weeks.

The next day was James' birthday and to make matters worse it was a double whammy as it was also Fathers Day. We kept a low profile for the day and just enjoyed the peace. Patricia had left gifts for him, forever organized. The gift for father's day was a mug. She had had it made especially for him; on the mug was a picture of her with the girl from the village in Thailand with the rings around her neck. Written on the back of the mug it read, *'sorry I can't be with you today please don't ring my neck'.*

At least she had seen the funny side of things although it had been ordered before Kayvan's arrival.

James laughed when he read it, 'As if I could ring her neck,' he said.

We had decided that after all the upset a holiday was called for, just to chill out for a couple of weeks. I spent the next week or so looking for a bargain and got a great deal for two weeks in Cyprus in August. James and I were looking forward to it as we had never been to Cyprus before.

Meanwhile, Patricia had been emailing us and telling us that the ship she was on, called *The Pearl*, was OK but not as good as *The Destiny*. She had heard that Kayvan was not going to join the ship as soon as he had hoped. He had been told that he would be there at the beginning of July, but that had changed which is quite a common occurrence. So now he was not going to get on until August. That is good, I thought, that will give her time to think things through before he arrives. She had already said that she had been a fool and regretted what had happened, but had the damage been done? A million dollar question if you ask me I thought, yet again I did not have the answer. James and I had decided to stay well clear of the situation and let them get on with it, a case of 'que sera, sera'. We liked Kayvan and he would be good for Patricia but our daughter's happiness was paramount as ever. We just hoped she did not live to regret it.

As we were preparing for our holiday, Josh had said that he was thinking of getting his and Louise's flat re-valued. They were curious to see how much money they had made now that they had got it the way they wanted it. I had told them that there are a few places that would give free valuations so they should give them a call if that is what they wanted. They had only been in the flat eighteen months, but they were curious. Personally James and I did not see the point of going to all that trouble unless they were thinking of selling it but we were told that they could not afford to sell it but they were interested, that's all.

The day of our holiday arrived and for once we set off in a good mood. This time we were heading to Newcastle airport as I could not get flights from Scotland. It is a three and a half hour drive so we decided to make a day of it and head down and stop for lunch somewhere nice. We were on holiday after all. On the way down Josh phoned me to tell me that they had decided to get the flat valued and that someone was going up later in the day to do it for them.
'Fair enough,' I said; 'let me know how it goes I am quite curious myself.'
James and I had put in an upstairs bathroom as there was only a shower room downstairs which was useless for Cameron so that may have added to the value. We always referred to it as a flat but in fact it was a flat with

a conversion in the loft space which gave them up and down stairs. We continued on our journey and discussed what Josh and Louise were up to. We were going on holiday and to pot with the kids for two weeks. We always referred to them as the kids even if they were in their twenties. The plan was to relax and recharge our batteries, so we agreed to let this flat thing go and not dissect it to pieces.

We flew out to Cyprus that night, the flight was at 23.55, and it was going to be a long night as neither of us can sleep on planes. We arrived there in the early hours of the morning and as we were the only people going to the small village of Pissouri we had been given a taxi to our hotel. Well, that was an experience, the car resembled a bat mobile and the driver was a maniac. James asked me what I thought of the island as we drove to the resort.

'I don't know,' I said, 'it is going past that quickly I can hardly focus on it.'

Talk about a white knuckle ride, I was glad when he pulled up outside the hotel. The hotel was lovely, very secluded, quiet and family run, just what the doctor ordered I thought.

As the hotel was so secluded there was not much to do in the evenings, there were a couple of restaurants nearby but the food in the hotel was so good that we spent most nights there. It was nice to chat to other guests and just chat about this and that, nothing serious or heavy. We met a nice couple called Steve and Susan, we spent a lot of time with them in the evenings just having drinks and chatting.

Throughout our holiday it was brought to our attention that there had been an incident at a UK airport and that on the journey home there would be more security than when we left. No hand luggage and no liquids, 'what on earth,' we said, 'this is becoming a habit, disasters when we are on holiday.'

As there were no televisions in the hotel we had to depend on new arrivals giving us the low down.

We had told the owner of the hotel about Patricia being away from home and asked if there was an internet café nearby. He told us that there was nothing close by but the 5 star hotel down the road had a computer that they may let us use. We dressed in our finest holiday clothes and headed there, no luck unfortunately it was for their guests only. When we told the owner he was very kind and let us use his own PC so we could check our emails and let Patricia know that we were having a good time. It turns out that Kayvan was to arrive in a few days and Patricia was quite excited about it, so that sounded promising.

The rest of the holiday was good and the temperatures were so high that it made moving from the pool a chore. However it had the desired effect and we headed home nice and relaxed and golden brown.

The day after we got home Josh appeared and broke the news that he and Louise had put their flat on the market.

'What on earth possessed you to do that, what on earth are you thinking about,' we exclaimed.

'Well,' said Josh, leaving a slight pause,

I knew there was something up, welcome home I thought, more problems.

'Well what,' James and I chorused.

'Well, emm, thing is, Louise is pregnant again.'

'What!! Are you kidding us?' we said.

'No afraid not and to make matters worse the baby is due in December.'

'We were as shocked as you are; she was 21 weeks gone when she found out.'

'We did not want to tell you before you went on holiday, so that is why I came up as soon as you got back.'
'Wait until Patricia finds out,' I said.
'Well actually she knows and has done for a week or so now.'
'We agreed not to let you know until you got home so she was sworn to secrecy.'
'So we are half way there already,' I said.
'Yes,' said Josh somewhat sheepishly. 'The baby is due on the 9th of December and before you ask we don't know the sex and we are not going to find out this time, we want it to be a surprise.'
'A surprise,' I said, 'I think you have accomplished that already'.

Once we got over the shock we were quite pleased at the thought of another grandchild. So now we know why they were so cautious before we went away. It was nice of them not to add to our stress before we went and hit us with the bombshell when we got back.

Patricia phoned the next day knowing we were home. She wanted to know what we thought of the fact that we were to be grandparents again.
'It was a shock to say the least,' I said, 'but good news none the less.'
'Can't believe you may have another niece or nephew by the time you get home.'
'You are due home on the 17th December right?'
'The baby is due on the 9th.'
'It will be just my luck for it to appear on the 17th and you will leave me stranded at the airport!'
'Would we do that to you?' I said, 'Although we may be tempted'!
'So, how are things with you?' I asked.
'Good actually,' she said, 'the staff seem nice enough and the ship is OK. Kayvan is due on board in two days.'

'How do you feel about that?' I asked nervously.
'Well, I have been thinking long and hard about that. I have realized that I love him dearly and I hope and pray he brings the ring with him. This time I will say yes and mean it with my whole heart. That is if he asks me again of course. It is the typical cliché you don't know what you have got 'til it's gone. I miss him so much and realize what a bitch I was to him when he was in Scotland. I regret it but there is nothing I can do to change it. If I could turn back the clock I would and do things differently. So we will have a heart to heart when he gets here. I will email you and let you know the full story.'
'Ok,' I said, 'just remember what I said before communication is the name of the game, if you can conquer that then the rest will just fall into place.'
Then she had a chat with James, she always makes a point of talking to both of us. I heard him say practically the same as me.
'I had better go,' she said, 'I don't have much credit left.'
'I will phone again when I get the chance.'
'Ok babe, love you, bye'

'So two days, eh, I would love to be a fly on the wall then, would you?' said James.
'Oh yes, but I don't think I could take the strain.'
'I think it will be tense times for the pair of them.'
'If it is meant to be, they will sort it out; if not then there is nothing we can do.'
'They are both adults, so have to make adult decisions.'

James and I had been talking about how our lives were changing. The kids were moving onwards and upwards and we had begun to stagnate. So after a great debate we decided to sell our house. We had been in this house since Patricia was 4 years old, so thought it was time for a change. We could even move to a two bedroom house now that Josh had moved out and as he was about to be a father of two there was no way he was coming back. So we made plans and put the house on the market. I sent Patricia an email to tell her of our decision. Her reply was simple, 'if you move before I get home can you make my bedroom cream tones please.' She took it in her stride but said it would be funny to come home but not home, as in the house she had known since she was little.

So that was it, the *For Sale* sign went up and details of the house went into the local property centre. All we had to do now was wait and hope that people were interested in a three bedroom, mid terraced house.

It was heading towards her birthday again, *'two years on the trot she has not been here I thought to myself, it is becoming a habit.'* When she was home we bought her an MP3 player and that was meant to be her birthday present. She spent some time before Kayvan arrived putting all her favourite music on it. However, yet again I packed up some small gifts and posted them out to her making sure it would be there in time. You can't have a birthday with no gifts from home, nothing to open.

So here we are again another birthday, I bet it is not as exciting as last year we said. I checked my emails and here was what was waiting for me.

'Well all I've had a very busy day,

At 12 pm I was proposed to, yes Kayvan was on one knee along with a chocolate heart shaped cake with 'Patricia, marry me' on it.
We were in the bar with all the shoppies whose jaws hit the floor. It was amazing.
We got drunk, and had a good night, I wish so many of you could have been here.

I've also had a bunch of flowers sent to my work today so he is really taking care of me.

I am very happy, I can't believe it.
I'm also calm and just waiting to see what happens but we do plan to marry in Aug/Sep next year so get the hats out.

I will call u all soon as I know this is not the best way to find out but I've just not had a spare min.

miss u all
xxxxxxxxxx

'James, I screamed, come and read this.'
'What is all the noise about,' he said.
'Just come and read this.'
He leaned over my shoulder and began to read the earth shattering news.
'Well, well, well,' he said, 'it looks like they have sorted themselves out and you my dear have a wedding to arrange'.
I sent back this reply

Well, well, well, just a wee note to let you know Dad is preparing a celebratory meal for us, a birthday and an engagement. Let Kayvan know Dad says he is having one of the whiskies he gave him for his birthday. We are having wine too so we can raise our glasses to the happy couple.

Love to you both
Mum and Dad xxx

This is the reply we got back

aw, u guys r so cute.

I'm learning every day what Kayvan expects from me, and looks like I'm not the only high maintenance person in this relationship ha ha.

Lots of passengers asking to see my ring again 2day, it's odd but I'm calm this time so all is well.

Miss u guys so much and wish u were here to see us.

Get working on that speech Dad and be nice ha ha

xxxxxxxxxxxxx

I knew now that there was a wedding to arrange. Wow, a new grandchild and a wedding, and of course moving house. It is going to be a busy time.

Chapter 11

All I can say is thank goodness for the Internet. I spent hour after hour searching for wedding ideas and sending them off to Patricia. This was to be a virtual wedding, well at least the planning part so we had to keep in touch at all times and about every detail. At least we knew what her dress was like. That was a major obstacle already overcome. I spent time sending pictures of invitations, flowers and bridesmaid dresses. This kept her informed of every step. She would then confirm if she liked my ideas or not.
A few days later I received this email

Hey momie.
How's it going? Any interest on the house?

Can u please do me a favour and send a picture of my ring to Mel cos God knows when I'll see her to show her.

Me and Kayvan were talking and I think we r going to get the invites and favours from Indo when I go in April time. Don't know about cheaper but different for sure.
We r also thinking Indo fans (or something indo) for the favours. They will have our names on.
Don't know though, it would be cool. I'm going to ask his sisters to help me out there cos Kayvan is crap.

As for rings I think I'll leave that to him and his Mum again, they got it right 1st time.

Also we have decided noooo cars. Even he looked at me like I was nuts when I suggested cars to the venue.
He says it's a waste of money. So I reckon we head to the hotel in the morning, that way no1 need see us arrive, I'll just come from upstairs.
And Dad's car is well nice enough to take Kayvan and

who ever in. We can put red and white ribbon on the front.

*Anyway I'm going to the gym cos I've a dress to fit into.
Miss u lots
xxxxxxxxxxxxxxxxx*

This was my reply.
*Well kid I am all over the place just now and loving every minute I may add.
Just dropped Mel an email cos she replied to the one I sent her this morning with pic of your ring.... she loves it and wonders if Ibu would make us one hee hee*

*We are trying to arrange a date so we can go dress hunting; we are also discussing Hen night....................
Oh boy........ BEWARE!!!!
Still not posted that stuff yet cos some of it is now irrelevant if you are getting Indo invites etc (stonkin' idea)
What a carry on Dad and I had this evening. We needed to find the certificate of completion for the upstairs loo as the solicitor needs it for when we sell the house to give to new owners (if we sell that is) Well we turned this bloody place upside down, we were in the loft, cupboard in kitchen, living room, under the stairs etc only to find it in the bedroom. Dad was convinced I had chucked it out when I was going mad cleaning out the cupboards the other day. Cheeky bugger. Then I needed details from the building society and would you believe he had just chucked them out himself while looking for the other thing, I thought I was going to wet my knickers. The daft sod. Would you believe it was 10 years ago we put that loo in, I nearly fell away, where has the time gone????
Well monkey, I am off to do a bit more searching
Love you, you are so special to me
Mum xxx*

It had been decided who she wanted for her bridesmaids, Louise, Mel and Kelly, so I arranged to meet them in town and go dress shopping. Poor Louise could not try any on as she was very pregnant by this time but at least she could have a say in the matter. The shop we went to was very good; we explained the situation that Patricia was in Australia so they let me take photos of the dresses that Mel tried on so I could send them to her for approval. The dresses were gorgeous, a bit pricey but gorgeous. Fortunately I know what Patricia likes and knew it would have to be something different. Mel tried on various styles and colours so we had a wide range for Patricia and Kayvan to look at. Kayvan had said that he wanted to wear traditional Scottish dress and therefore wanted to wear a kilt. *'Well, that's different,'* I thought, *'an Indonesian in a kilt,'* but you know I wasn't surprised. This was going to be a great and quirky wedding that's for sure. It was to be a Scottish/Indonesian feel, with the red and white theme and the groom, father of the bride and best man all in kilts. What tartan I wondered, so I went and had a look in the shops and I knew that it would be best if it was a red tartan.

Things were getting complicated as I received this email the following day.

Hey Mum, sounds good.
I've also been thinking and we may have a slight hick up.
Ok 1st of all Kayvan has told his Mum and to know if/when I'll become Muslim.
I've said no way and I'm about to mail the family and put them straight. It's stressin me and Kayvan out.

Also was thinking even if we do get married there is no guarantee that he gets to stay in Scotland so I want to

scale the day down.
I would really appreciate it if u could look into the hotel with the beautiful 30 person room. How much, what's included. etc then we can have big party.
I know I love the other hotel but that wee one just still sticks in my mind so I really want to check it out.
I reckon we will save a lot.
Maybe worth a second visit. More and further details.
i.e. how much is small room and big room for party.
Do they do package...food, drinks, cake knife etc etc.
Of course we will go with the best deal.

And as for not spending on irrelevant stuff, bugger, cos who knows, I may not be welcome in Indo in April.
xxxxxxxxxxxxxxxxxxxx

She also sent me a copy of the email she sent to Kayvans family.

Hello guys,
How are you?

It's Patricia here.

I hear that Ibu is asking if I will become Muslim when I marry Kayvan.
Well guys we decided that he will remain Muslim and me Christian.
I will not change religion and I do not want Kayvan to either.
To us religion is important to us but in our own way.

I will be a good wife, mother and I will look after Kayvan even though I am not Muslim.
I believe God loves us and so does he, I'm sure that is all that matters.
I fully support Kayvan, his way of life, prayer times, his

views and I don't believe I have to be Muslim to be the best person, and wife I can be.
You guys can believe me when I say I love him but I will not become Muslim.
Not today, tomorrow or in the future.

I would love to know how you guys feel and what you think about this.
We need your support.

I miss you all and hope you are all well

Patricia
xxxx

'Could this be trouble I wondered?' Ibu had met Patricia and seemed to welcome her with open arms when she was in Indonesia, so why is she being like this. I thought it through and decided that like all mothers she wanted what she thought was best for her son. She is entitled to voice her opinions and ask questions just as I did.

A few days later I got another email to tell me that things were OK again. Kayvan's family gave them their full support and had spent time explaining things to Ibu. She was coming round to the idea. Patricia also mentioned that she and Kayvan were doing well. She said that when I am not with him I miss him; she was even waiting until he had finished his shift before she ate so they could eat together and that she could not sleep if he was not there even if she was exhausted. She had said that more passengers were giving them cards and gifts and was overawed by it all. Then a poignant few words, 'I love him more than words can say, just remind me when I get home if I ever doubt myself again'.

Nothing daunted I proceeded to send the details I had of

invitations, tartan swatches and even details of how to measure Kayvan so that we could order the kilt in the right size. As we were going to hire them we have to order them well in advance to ensure we get what we want.

I made enquiries at the smaller hotel about prices, sizes of rooms etc as Patricia had asked. The hotel was nice but not as nice the one we had set our hearts on. So I sent her the details but advised her that both James and I wanted the best for her and Kayvan, so they should go with that one. I explained that we knew that it is her and Kayvan's day and that we will do everything possible to make it perfect for them. 'We can always make economies elsewhere,' I explained, 'we had already saved money by not having wedding cars.'

Meanwhile in amongst all the wedding preparations we were still selling our house, but it seemed that every time we went for a house we failed to get it. It seemed to me that the house was telling us to stay put. James thought I was losing the plot.
'How can a house tell you to stay put,' he said.
'I don't know, but we keep hitting problems, it is like something is telling us to stay.'
The next day I got up as usual and went into the kitchen to make coffee. I noticed a strange smell there. What on earth could it be? It turned out that there was a leak into the foundations of the house. There was a huge puddle down there and the smell was that of stagnant water.
'See what I mean,' I said to James, 'the house wants us to stay.'
We had to withdraw the house from the market temporarily until we got the problem rectified.
Josh and Louise were having trouble selling their flat too. So as time was marching on they decided to fix the price of the property. That way there was no haggling

over the price it was a case of this is the amount we want so meet the price and it is yours. They had to make sure that they had sold their flat and got another house before the baby arrived. They wanted in and settled before then.

Between our emails Patricia had decided that she wanted silk flowers for her bouquet not real ones. So back to my faithful PC and I sourced a great site for them. I contacted them and asked if it was possible for them to do the flowers. The reply came back yes that would not be a problem, all we had to do was chose one of their designs or send a picture of what Patricia wanted and they would copy it for her. They told me they also do hair flowers and table flowers so nothing seemed to be any trouble. This was strange doing this by internet, but they seemed very capable and professional.

The emails were fast and furious, sometimes two or three a day, it was manic. I sent pictures of bridesmaid dresses, and flowers so they could have an idea of what I was looking at for them. Patricia did not like any of the dresses Mel had tried on so we decided that it would be best if we waited until she came home. We would have enough time she said as I will be home about Christmas again and we are hoping for a July wedding.

That created a debate and a half; James and I thought that July would be cutting it fine. After all Kayvan was on the ship until March/April and then he had to apply for another Visa. This could take months. It is a fiancé Visa this time, a bit more complicated. 'Imagine if we go ahead and book everything for July and he is not in the country, we could lose a lot of money.'

She agreed with us but at the same time she wanted a summer wedding. 'I know this sounds a bit strange,' she said, 'after the carry on I had in the summer but I want to marry him as soon as possible.'

So after all the emails going to and fro they agreed on a date, the 29th of September 2007 was to be the big day.

So we have a date to work on now. I can go ahead and make all the arrangements as far as I dare. I want Patricia to be more involved but at least I can book the things she liked and we can finalise them all when she gets home.

The house problem was sorted, so again we were open to viewers. We had a great response. There seemed to be lots of interest which was great. One couple seemed especially interested. They came up to see the house on the Saturday and on the Monday put in a good offer which we accepted.
'See it is all coming together now, all we have to do is find a place for us,' said James.
'Yeah, I guess the house has decided to let us go after all,' I laughed.

As it turned out we ended up having to withdraw our acceptance for the house, because to fix the problem in the foundations properly would mean that the water people had to dig up the entire garden at the back of the house and the path at the front of the house. This could mean that it may be an expensive repair so we had no choice but to back out of the agreement.
'It seems the house has changed its mind,' I said. James just looked at me, 'so it would seem,' he said. 'I don't understand how things could have gone so wrong.'

So that was it, no new house for us. 'Everything has a reason, there must be something stopping us for whatever reason,' I said. 'I don't know what it is but it will become clear in the future.'
'You are a strange one, you have some weird ideas,' said James

Meanwhile Patricia phoned to tell us this lovely tale. On cruise ships there are often formal nights where everyone gets their best dress on, lovely evening dresses for the ladies and dinner suits for the men. So Patricia's boss had argued that her staff should be able to attend. *'They always dress up for theme nights,'* she said, *'so why can't they dress up for a formal night once in a while?'* She won the argument so Patricia took out her beautiful long black evening dress and black sandals; she was going to look stunning she thought. She had her friend do her make up and her hair, she wanted to look stunning for Kayvan. So she went to meet him when he finished work.
'You look gorgeous,' he said. He took her hand and placed it on his chest, his heart was racing. 'I have never seen you look so beautiful, feel the effect you have on me. I am so lucky.'

We took this opportunity to tell her about the house saga.
'Well I am disappointed for you because I know how excited you were about it but at least now I will be coming home,' she said. 'You can still paint my room cream if you want,' she said trying to keep things light.

We chatted for ages about wedding plans. She said it would be a good idea if we could get a sample of the flowers that would be used as she was a bit apprehensive in case they looked artificial. She had decided on lilies, jasmine and thistles in her bouquet with coordinating buttonholes for the men. We could have spent hours talking but as ever her credit was running low and she wanted to phone Josh to see how he and Louise were doing, so we agreed to keep up with the emails.

Back to work for me, back to tracking down the best

value for entertainment, invitations, photographer and all the rest that goes with weddings. James and I wanted Patricia and Kayvan to have the best wedding ever, but being Scottish we were wanting the best value for money, so we kept looking and checking and comparing.

Chapter 12

The e mails bantered back and forth, three, sometimes four a day. The details were becoming more detailed and more defined. So far they had decided that the colour scheme was to be red, white and silver. The invitations were chosen, white with embossed white and silver hearts on them. I had received samples of flowers and taken photos of them and sent them on. They looked real to me and Patricia was chuffed. I also received small Jasmine flowers on a sprig these were for the bridesmaid's hair. So I tied up my hair and placed the sprigs accordingly, took a picture and sent that on to. The problem was that I had put on a strapless top to have my picture taken and it made me look like I was naked!

James and I went to the hotel and met the manager to discuss times, meals etc. She was so good, coming up with lots of ideas and gave us samples of menus there were five different menus with varying prices. We were there for almost three hours discussing and debating everything. I had to take notes as I had to pass all these details on in an email which was not going to be easy. She let us see around some of the bedrooms, the bridal suite being the most beautiful room I had ever seen, dominated by a beautiful big, silver four poster bed. She was kind enough to let us take photographs so we could send them too.

I sent all the information off to Patricia and Kayvan for them to digest. They had to tell us what they wanted as I had to make bookings on their behalf. I also told them that the hotel had a resident DJ if they were interested. Patricia asked me if it was possible to hear him to see if he was any good. I contacted the hotel only to find that the manager had left and there was now a chap from

New Zealand running the hotel but he told us that all was under control and that the DJ was playing at a wedding the following weekend and that we could pop in and hear him and maybe have a word with him. So off we went again to hear what he was like. We felt a bit cheeky as we were in fact gate crashing a couples wedding! We did make an effort to dress nicely so we would blend in and not look like a pair of nosey parkers although that is what we were!

As it turns out the DJ was a man not in his prime shall I say, but he was very nice and polite and the music he played was very modern and he seemed to know what he was doing. He told us that if Patricia and Kayvan gave him a list of songs they wanted he would arrange to have that for them. James and I were more than pleased and his price was very reasonable compared to some of the quotes I had received. I told him that we would pass the information on to them and get back to him in due course. He gave me his phone number so I could contact him if necessary.

Back to my faithful PC I passed all the details on, including the fact that we were dealing with a new manager, although he seemed very nice and well informed. I did not tell them I was somewhat apprehensive about the change. I felt that it may be a disaster moving from one person to another but James said that these people do this all the time and as long as they had all the details it would run smoothly.

Patricia had emailed me telling me that she and Kayvan had had an argument, about nothing in particular but enough for them to be in the huff with each other. I had said to him when he was here that he should be stronger with her and not let her get away with everything. He had to stand firm and take no nonsense, not exactly bully her but make his point and I think he went too far. It was short lived and he ended up going to her cabin later as he could not sleep without her. At least he tried but did not last long. *'Oh the path of true love never runs smooth does it?' I thought.*

They had also chosen the menu from the information I had sent them. The starter was to be either Tomato with basil soup, or king prawns with garlic. The main course was to be a Scottish fillet of beef with peppercorn sauce or chicken with mushroom and tarragon sauce. Dessert was to be either sticky toffee pudding with ice cream or cheese and biscuits. As the choices were from several of the menus I had sent, we would have to have the prices changed.

Due to the complexity of having to get Kayvan a Visa, it may prove difficult for him to get work for a while so James and I had thought that it would be best for them to live with us after the wedding, even if only for a while maybe a year or so. That way they could get on their feet financially before moving out. We put this to them and they agreed that this would be a good idea. With this in mind James and I thought that maybe a bigger house would be a good idea. Our thought was if we had two bedrooms, and a third room that could double up as a second lounge for Patricia and Kayvan then they could have privacy as a married couple. So, it was back to the house hunting scene. We looked at all the properties that met our needs but it turned out that they were all out of our price range. So the next best thing was to transform what used to be Josh's bedroom into a lounge for them. We bought a settee that could convert into a bed if needs be and thought that with a coffee table and TV would be a nice space for them to spend their time. That way we could all have privacy. Everything was coming together and it was easier than I thought to do all the arranging by email.

One day when we got home from work there was a card through the door advising that there had been a parcel delivered but as we were not at home we would have to collect it the following day at the post office. *'Strange,'* I thought I have not ordered anything and I am not expecting anything either. However the next day I hurried to the post office to find it was a parcel from Australia. It can only be from Patricia but why is she sending us a parcel, it is normally the other way about. When we got home from work we eagerly opened the parcel to find two somewhat funny hats and a load of chocolate. James' hat was a stereo typical Australian hat with corks dangling from it and mine was a Stetson style with the word *'Australia'* blazed across the front. The chocolate were types that we can't get here in the UK which were delicious. The letter inside read *we saw these and thought of you. 'This is a little thank you for all the hard work you are doing for us,'* lots of love Patricia and Kayvan. Another photo opportunity, so we donned the hats and took lots of silly pictures then sent them to the pair of them. The reply was merely *'ha ha ha ha ha ha ha ha ha ha ha ha ha.'*

Out of the blue Patricia emailed me to tell me that she was planning a trip round Australia when she finished her contract.
'I know it means I may not be home for Christmas, but I may never be here again so thought it may be a good idea to see some of the country before I head home,' she said. 'I know we have a wedding to plan and bills to pay, but it is a once in a lifetime chance.'
She was thinking of going to Alice Springs and she wanted to see Ayres Rock. She had been checking it out on the internet and said she could do it quite cheap. James and I were a bit apprehensive at the thought of

149

her touring around on her own but I know her, and nothing will stop her once she has made her mind up. I will tell her our concerns when I reply. Hopefully she will see sense.

Literally the next day the phone rang, it was Patricia and she was somewhat upset. My thoughts immediately turned to her and Kayvan, had they had another argument? Not that simple as it turned out. It transpires that the cruise company was going to cut her contract by two months. She was to return home towards the end of October. She was so upset, and so angry she could hardly speak. James and I had to calm her down and get her to settle so she could tell us the full story. Apparently another member of the crew was leaving and being replaced by a young guy. However his fiancé wanted to join the ship with him so to make room on the ship for her they had to send someone home and it was to be Patricia. I found this unbelievable and so unfair. Patricia and Kayvan had been through so much recently and now they were together again and so happy. *'How could they do this to them?'*

Patricia told us that her boss was trying to fight her case for her as she knew that Patricia wanted to be with Kayvan and vice versa. She was going to approach head office and try to find out if there was anyone else that could be sent home, maybe someone whose contract was nearing its end. She knew that Patricia was a good worker and that the girl that was going to replace her was not as conscientious; she had worked with the girl before and was not pleased that she was going to lose a good team member. So it was in the hands of the Gods, will they send her home, we would have to wait and see.

Meanwhile I emailed the company and expressed my

disapproval and told them how angry I was. Angry! I was livid and so upset! They really did not need this. They needed the next two months together. How dare they do this? I felt useless so I sent the email in a torrent of anger, hoping to get a reply telling me that they had changed their minds and that Patricia could stay. I had hoped that if her boss and I bombarded them then they would cave in. I had to be careful how I worded the email as I knew that they did not condone inter-staff relations so I based it on the fact that they had cut her contract and therefore her income and how unfair it was to replace her just so someone could be with their fiancé. Pot calling the kettle black I know but it was the only thing I could do. We all just hoped and prayed that her boss would come through. I phoned Josh to tell him what was going on, he was as distraught as us and Louise was furious.

I got this email a day or so later

Well we are calling the office 2mr morning so hopefully we will know more but if my boss goes out 2nt and gets trashed I don't see it happenin but let's see. , Kayvan won't let me go at night and when he thinks I am sleeping he is whispering in my ear he will miss me and loves me. He said he will never survive another 4 months on here without me.

He's amazing. I have to say if I'm comin home I will be happy but gutted too. So in preparation for comin home I went out in the sun and FRIED....just in case. I can't come home white!!!.

Anyway.....

The room thing sounds logical but we can put all this on hold till I find out what I'm doing here 1st cos I don't want to be living in the tiny room from Oct this yr when there is no need .

xxxxxxxxxxxxxxxxxxxxxxxxxxx

So no news yet then, we were all hoping for the no news is good news scenario. That included a reply to my email so we were all pinning our hopes on the fact that maybe they were communicating with each other and working something out. If only they knew, I thought. If they knew the full story and maybe if they had a heart they would let her stay.

A few days later James got a text from Patricia confirming the worst. They were sending her home she was going to email to tell us the full story. This is what I received

I'm guessing u got my text by now on Dad's phone ....I'll be seeing u in 2 wks. Can u believe it?
Fuckers.
They said that we should let them know the name of my boyfriend in order for us to be together next contract......DON'T THINK SO FUCKERS.

Kayvan is gutted but only cos he is worried. He is worried I'll freak again, start stressing etc just like last time. He is sooo scared poor wee thing.
I've told him I won't but we really needed the next 2 months for me to store confidence in me in him.
Well tough shit ah.
I am really lookin forward to getting home though cos I'm not happy here, I mean I've had laughs but it's been pretty shit.
So bring on 25th ....what else can I do?
At least this time when I get home I won't be fucked.
I've not been drinking so my body is ok, I'll just be knackered.
Don't even know flights or anything and prob won't til late next week......

Can u please get in touch with Susan and see what the crack is. I'll drop her an e mail now. I'll tell Mel too, I reckon she will be glad to get me back.
Maybe I can stop her going and get her to work with me.....just like the gold old days.

Anyway I plan on calling u this morning so I'll go for now xxxxxxxxxxxxxxxxxxxxxxxxxxx

The tone of the email said it all. The poor souls, what have they to do to find the happiness they deserve? I phoned Mel and told her what was going on. She had just been told that she had been accepted to join the same company as Patricia.
'I didn't think they could do that,' she said.
'Well neither did I but there you are, so be prepared. It seems to be if your face fits!'
Meanwhile we continued our emails and I sent as much information as I could to her so she and Kayvan had exciting things to speak about and things to arrange before they separated again. At least I had already sent them the forms to complete for Kayvan to apply for his fiancé visa so they could get that all sorted too.

Then this came in
Hey mommy,
Been lookin for jobs and cant see anything ....oh oh
Can u please send my CV to some travel agents....I trust u to write me a good strong appropriate cover letter. I really don't want to back to selling clothes....
Thanks for the supermarket manager thing, that was 1st on my list but don't need to look now though.
Got myself all upset last night, sobbed just like when I left u guys the 1st time. I was in total shock. My boss said she will call head office today again but I don't think she got up this morning. I couldn't stop crying and my

153

eyes still sting today and the head ache still lingers but I'm over it now.
I'm ready to head home, I just need to remember how I feel when I'm with Kayvan and that is amazing.
He loves me so much and I must not forget. He is shitting himself about me changing my mind but I must be strong.
He had a go about it to me last night again and I can see he isn't soft, he is just soft with me and if I don't watch myself I'll have barriers up b4 I know it .
We really needed the next 2 months to sort things out and just be happy but now I realize that will never happen till we settle down cos I'm not happy here anyway.
So maybe I'll marry some1 I don't know that well, but I know he loves me and I'm gutted to be leaving him so we will just have to get to know each other later.
Water and fire always go well together. I have to just be careful not to set him alight too. haha .

Anyway I'm getting away from this bloody place can't find jobs here so I'll just have to rely on you sending some CVs out for me.

Ok bye for now
xxxxxxxxxxxxxxxxxxxxxxxxx
Right behind came this email

Well u got my txt this morning, so I am coming home for sure. My boss mailed the office again 2day cos she could see how upset I was and they still say no!!. She even said I will not be coming back if this is the case due to having a wedding to plan.
Good escape route really haha .

They sure organized it quick enough any way.

I am looking forward to coming home, and I will go to Indo in Feb now instead of April so it is still the same amount of time apart.
I feel heart broken once again but the good thing about being heart broken is I know I love him and that one day it will all come together.
I keep crying but I'm actually ok....as long as I don't talk about leaving him.

So prepare for big hugs for me but don't tell me it will all be alright. Cos I swear it will make me cry.
If it wasn't for him I'd have left here a long time ago so I am very excited to come home. I miss u guys more this time, and I can't wait to see the wee man and get all my wedding pieces into place.

Mum ...can u txt Mel and see if she knows when she is free after I'm home cos I want to go see that dress on her cos I have funny feeling she will leave in November ...but not said that to her cos might get her hopes up.

Talk soon guys
xxxxxxxxxxxxxxxxxxxxx

I cried buckets when it was confirmed that she was coming home. Normally I would have been delighted to have her back again but with all the upset that they had been through I was sad to hear she was leaving Kayvan again. Two months more together would have been ideal, but it is as if they are being tested. *'Is someone up there testing this relationship, putting barriers in their way? Seeing if they are strong enough? Keeping them apart seemed to be the order of the day,'* I thought. These thoughts ran through my mind and there seemed to be nothing I could do to stop them. *'However they are a strong couple, they can come through this,'* I thought.

Things have to move on and we had to stay focused so I sent her CV out to various companies and also uploaded it on a web site so with a bit of luck they will contact her. Then I sent a text to Mel as instructed. If Patricia asked me to jump in the river just now I would, I will do everything I can to keep her and Kayvan happy they did not need any more pressure.

Heavens above, another email and I really could not believe my eyes when I read it. It appears that the girl that was replacing Patricia did not have a Visa therefore she could not join the ship. Was this the stroke of luck we had all been praying for.? Patricia had said that she may be asked to extend her contract now and not go early but that would mean she would be away for Christmas and miss the birth of her new niece or nephew but that was ok. *Were Patricia and Kayvan being allowed to stay together after all?* Emotions were running thick and fast through the Gilmour house. At last a ray of hope amongst all the chaos. It seemed the cruise company could not make their minds up, but we were not complaining if it meant they could stay together.

Then it changed to could you do one more cruise for us until this girl arrives. Patricia was not best pleased at being used like that but it meant that she could be with Kayvan for another two weeks so she agreed to stay.

As I said before the company are somewhat disorganized so the next thing we knew she was being sent home for sure on the 25th October. That was it! Patricia was so mad that she could not wait to get off the ship. She knew she would be leaving Kayvan behind but she had had enough of it all. She even discarded the idea of travelling around Australia. 'I just want to come home,' she said. 'I will focus all my energy into the wedding, get a job and organize a trip to Indonesia when Kayvan is due home.'

Chapter 13

So it is final. Patricia is coming home for sure so things will change with regards to wedding preparations. It will be good to have her here for that, I thought. We can spend time doing things together, making plans and doing the mother/daughter thing. We always have fun when we are together and I was determined to make this fun too. I sent her an email to tell her that I intended keeping her busy, that way time will pass quickly and before she knew it Kayvan would be here permanently.

I continued to send all the emails I could, giving them the information I had. I told them I had prepared a wedding box full of all the information, flower samples, invitations etc.

Meanwhile I was searching for a job for her. I knew she had no intentions of going back to the ships; she had had enough of that so I had to find her a job and one that paid well as she was to be a married lady in less than twelve months.

She continued to send me details daily. Having put her CV on that web site there was lots of interest in her. She would then send me details and ask me to send prospective employers the details they required. They knew she was out of the country at the time and were more than willing for me to act on her behalf. They even phoned me on a few occasions for information.
This was good; it kept her concentrating on other things, making her think about things other than her obvious approaching departure. I also checked our local paper and copied details and pasted them into my emails to her. I sent lots of information, enough to keep them going for a while.

Things were going well on the job front, applications were going in and replies being received. I spent my time reading letters and sending information, keeping Patricia up to date with what was going on. It was strange that the prospective employers were willing to wait for her return home; her CV must have been stronger than either of us realised.

In the midst of all this I noticed that Josh was constantly complaining of stomach upset and stomach pains. I told him that if this kept going that he should go and see the doctor. He just looked at me as if I were possessed.
'I will be keeping an eye on you,' I said, 'this has been going on for too long now. Maybe you should lay off the beer for a while,' I suggested.
Well, you would have thought I had asked him to cut off an arm or a leg.
'Don't worry about me,' he would say, 'I have just got a virus or something.'

The time was getting close to Patricia coming home. Her emails were getting less and less frequent. I knew in my heart that she was hurting and that the only way she could cope was to stay silent. Putting her feelings into words would make it more difficult, so if she stayed quiet it would hurt less. I could hardly keep my composure when I thought of the pair of them, what they were going through, the pain, the upset, the torment. We all knew we were planning a wedding but it seemed that we were preparing for a departure first. It was a bitter sweet feeling, knowing that they had to say goodbye yet knowing they would meet again.
James would check on me daily, knowing I was going through the pain with them, step by step, even through the silence. I knew he was too but he was stronger than me and hiding his feelings well. He knew his little girl

was going through hell and he hated it because he had no control over the situation.

Josh knew what we were going through so he kept popping in with Cameron; he always took my mind off my troubles. He always wants me to play with him and do all the silly things. He drags me everywhere and we do all sorts of things together. This is a blessing to Louise as she is showing a proud bump now so she can't do all the silly things he likes, so she is quite happy to let me do them. Josh is still not feeling great but still won't go to the doctor. This is really starting to worry me. 'Maybe he is stressed about the baby,' I thought to myself so I put it down to that. 'Maybe once the baby is here it will settle down.' I remember when I was pregnant with him and was worried about finances and how I would cope with two young children. So maybe he is doing the same.

Then it arrived, the email telling me her flight details. There was not much else in the email just the details we needed to know. Between the lines I could read how tense she was, how angry and upset she was feeling. I jotted down the information so I could check out her flights again! I replied to her just so she knew that we were thinking of her and Kayvan and that we would be there waiting for her with open arms. I know the path of true love never runs smooth but this was the bumpiest road I had heard of.

So again back to my trusty PC, flight watching. Watching each stage as it unfolded, knowing our lovely daughter was going through such torment, such heart ache and all alone. Just before I went to bed I did my final check, I am glad I did as there was an email there for me from her, she said that she was doing OK and fortunately another guy was leaving the ship and they were travelling together. I was glad she was not alone. She said I had not to worry, she had cried but Alan, the guy she was travelling with was keeping her laughing. That was all the information she gave me, nothing about the final farewell which was just as well or I would have cried the night away and I had to be strong for her arrival tomorrow.

The next morning I checked again and her flight was running half an hour late. Yet another email, now Alan had left her as he was heading south so they had parted company. She just said that she was now desperate to get home and get on with the wedding. Great I thought she seems to be holding it together. James was pleased to hear that she was not all soppy. He finds it hard to deal with soppiness. He is a tower of strength most of the time but in these cases he buckles and doesn't like that.

We began our familiar journey to the airport.

When we got there we did not have long to wait before we saw this weary traveller walking through the doors. She was looking a bit worse for wear, but a big smile on her face. That came as a surprise to us all. I ran down and hugged her as always and she gently whispered, 'Thanks Mum, it was worth the journey just for that' and gave a small sigh.

'How was the flight then?' asked James.

'It was OK, I am sick of doing it now though. I have had enough and if the cruise company phone me to go back again I am going to tell them in no uncertain terms what they can do with their job,' she said. 'I have better things to do with my time now, don't I Mum?'

'Oh yes pet,' I said, 'we have lots of work to do and things to plan. Your head will be spinning by the time I am finished with you. Firstly you have to find a job, and then we will get cracking on the wedding plans. I may let you have a week off before we start, get you back on UK time so your mind is clear.'

We headed off in the car, keeping the conversation plain and simple, nothing of any great importance and only mentioning Kayvan when she did. I knew if she talked about him it was OK but we didn't want to push it in case it caused tears, I don't think James could have coped with that while he was driving.
We got home and began what was becoming a ritual of settling Patricia back home again. Her body clock was all over the place, feeling sleepy when she should be alert and vice versa. It took a few days before she was back to normal. I had deliberately not mentioned the wedding or the plans ahead, no point as I doubt if she would have taken it in. I would wait for her to start then I would know she was ready.

Her priority was to get herself a job; she knew she had to get that established before anything else. So once she was back on track she began her plan. Phone calls were made and letters written. She began following up the emails she had been sent about possible positions. This took her a few days and things were moving along nicely. She had a few interviews and was amazed that people were willing to pay her what she was asking without any questions. Her experience on the ships and previous jobs seemed to impress the people interviewing her. The jobs were OK but not exactly what she was looking for.
Then she said, 'You know Mum maybe we should take the opportunity of getting wedding plans underway while I am not working, so how about a trip to Edinburgh next week and we will go and see about my dress and an outfit for you. They say it takes a while to get my dress ordered and fitted so maybe we should get a move on.'

'Hurrah,' I thought to myself, 'this is it, all the ideas I have in my head will be coming together soon.'

I arranged to have the Wednesday off next week and we booked seats on the bus to take us to Edinburgh. We thought that her friend Mel should come along too as she was to be a bridesmaid and she could help us choose dresses for them.

Chapter 14

Wednesday came along and the three of us piled on the bus in a rush of excitement. It only took us an hour and a half to get there and we knew where we were heading this time so that made things easier. First port of call was for my dress. I tried on several, various styles and colours. Some of them made me look like a typical mother of the bride, something neither Patricia nor I wanted so we headed for something a bit out of the ordinary. I was in and out the dressing room like something possessed. I tried on one that was shocking pink. Not quite my colour but the style was ideal. It was plain and simple. It was actually a two piece, a rouched, strapless top with long ties at the back that once tied flowed all the way to the floor. The skirt was plain and ankle length. All we had to do was to choose a colour. We poured over the swatches trying to envisage what it would be like in various colours. We knew that the bridesmaids would be in red and Patricia in white, the tartan for the guys was an assortment of red, blue, and green, not wanting to stand out like a sore thumb we decided on a lovely shade of green, almost bottle green that way I would blend with the tartan. Accessories, shoes bag etc to be gold. Nice autumnal colours for a September wedding.

Next was the big one, the wedding dress. We headed off to the shop and were greeted with a big smile from the lady behind the counter. She showed us down to the area where the brides tried on their dresses. It was lovely, lots of ornate furniture and mirrors. Dresses galore hung proudly on the hangers and tiaras sparkled in glass display units. Patricia went through all the dresses looking for the one she had seen before. There it was, just as we remembered stunning, and beautiful. She handed the dress to the girl who held it above her head so that it didn't trail across the floor and escorted Patricia to the dressing room. Well out she came, wearing the dress she had been dreaming of and Mel and I burst not into tears but into laughter, the dress was about six sizes too big, I could have got in it with her. We took handfuls of material and gathered it and pinned it until it fitted. She looked radiant even if most of the dress was pinned in. 'This is certainly the one,' we all said. So that was it. We ordered the dress in her size and paid the deposit. We were told that they would phone us when it came in as it had to be ordered from America, it should be here about April. That still left plenty time for any alterations to be made.

Then we looked at dresses for the bridesmaids. There were a few that were quite nice, but so expensive. Patricia decided to look elsewhere for them. So off we went for lunch and then to main high street stores to look at dresses. With it now being November and coming up for Christmas parties there was an abundance of red dresses. Mel tried on a few but they were not quite what we were looking for. Then to our amazement we found a lovely red dress with a black taffeta underskirt and black ribbon around the waist. It was just below the knee and with a few alterations could be ideal. So we bought three of them there and then. Patricia had decided that she wanted all the black removed to be left with a plain red dress.
'I am sure I know someone who can do that for you,' I said. 'If not I will find a dressmaker and have it done.' Once all that was removed no one would be any the wiser that it was party not a bridesmaid's dress. What a great day, all three dresses organized in one swoop.

As we passed a shoe shop Patricia noticed that there was an advertisement in their window saying that they were opening a shop in Dundee and were recruiting for staff. Nothing daunted, she and Mel walked in and asked for details. The girl there said that they were opening a branch in Dundee in December and gave them the address to write to. The pair of them came out grinning from ear to ear. Chatting like a pair of school girls and already discussing what it would be like to work together again if they both got jobs there. Patricia said that they are looking for all staff from sales to manager so she was going to write to them and so was Mel.

'I can't believe it,' I laughed.

'We came here for dresses and may have landed you a job too, Patricia.'

Shoes, every woman's desire and Patricia was no exception. She had already asked about discounts!

As we headed back home I listened to the pair of them chatting and planning and discussing what to put in their letters. I was glad to be sitting on the bus as my feet were aching; I had not walked that much in ages. It was good to have my shopping buddy back again.

James met us at the bus station and took Mel home. She lived in Carnoustie, and on the way there we passed a gym. Patricia announced that she wanted to tone up for the wedding so asked if we could pull in so she could make enquiries. We headed in and had a whistle stop tour of the place. It looked good, lots of machines and weights not to mention a pool and sauna.

'Well how about it,' she said? 'Me and you Mum, we could work out together. Then we will both look even more gorgeous'

'Emmmmmmmmm, not what I planned,' I thought, 'but what the heck, I had lost lots of weight so maybe it would be a good idea to tone up.'

So that was it, we signed on the dotted line and became members. James laughed when we got back in the car and I told him what we had done.
'Good for you, that's what I like to see, total commitment,' he said
We got home later than expected and ended up buying Chinese food as none of us could be bothered cooking. Just as we sat down the phone rang, yes, Kayvan was on so bang went the food as far as Patricia was concerned. She spent the time telling him of her day in Edinburgh, although no details of her dress were given. Only her Mel and I knew, and we were all sworn to secrecy. When she put the phone down she was as high as a kite, James' head was buzzing listening to all the details and she took advantage by teasing him about her dress.
'Oh lovely,' he kept saying over and over.
She burst into the room with one of the bridesmaid dresses.
'What you think of this Dad,' she asked.
'I can't tell really without seeing it on,' he muttered.
So I ended up having to model it, and I am pleased to say that it was too big for me! I had not realized just how much weight I had lost until then.
'Very nice,' he said, 'I like the petty coat thing.'
'That's too bad,' she said, 'as that and the belt is coming off,' she looked at me and giggled.
'Oh, what was the point of buying them if you are going to change them?' he asked.
'About £100 a dress,' I said.
'Good point,' he laughed.
'I told you I could do this on a budget and I will.'

'There is not much point in spending a small fortune on so called bridesmaid dresses when these will look as good when they are altered and a small fortune saved that can be spent elsewhere,' announced Patricia.

A girl after my own heart I thought. As I said before, weddings are expensive but things can be done at reasonable prices and no one would know the difference if done properly.

'You are a shrewd woman,' James said.

'I will make this a wedding to remember,' I said.

'This is a once in a lifetime experience for me and I intend to make this perfect.' Patricia looked at me and agreed that between us we were going to make this a day to remember.

We both had ideas that when put together would be fantastic. Now we had the dresses organised it was time to concentrate on all the other things that were needed. The theme was to be red and white and Scottish/Indonesian. So we got our heads together and planned all sorts of quirky things that we could do to make this work.

Chapter 15

Patricia and Mel sent off their letters for the jobs in the shoe shop. So now all they had to do was wait. Patricia had another couple of interviews and some looked promising but she held off until she had heard from the shoe company.
'I just have a feeling about this one,' she said.
A week or so later she got a call inviting her for an interview and so did Mel. So the pair of them went off. Mel was hoping for sales assistant but Patricia was looking for the assistant manager's job.
'I need more than sales wages,' she said, 'and assistant manager would be great because although I would have some responsibility it is less hassle than the manager's job.'
Their interviews were held in a hotel and Patricia went full of confidence and dressed in funky clothes.
'Well it is a funky shop,' she said. 'I am sure they are not looking for someone plain and simple.'
'Good for you,' I said,' I wish you luck. Let me know how you get on'.
The hotel is not far from the office where I work so later in the day she phoned me and asked if I could meet her.
'Of course no problem just let me know when and where.'
I arranged to meet her at the hotel at 4 pm. I headed up at five minutes to four. I knew she had had a good interview as she was beaming from ear to ear.
'Well?' I asked.
'Well?' she said, 'I got the job, assistant manager and again the salary I asked for. They were impressed with my knowledge of retail and seemed to think that I was what they are looking for. In fact they were so impressed that they asked me if I would sit with them on the rest of the interviews to help pick a team.'
'Is that not for the manager to do?' I said.

'Apparently he is working in Aberdeen at the moment so can't be here to do it and because I am not working and have time to spare it seemed the logical answer. So I have to meet them tomorrow and do interviews.'
Then along came the next dilemma.
'What do I wear?'
So it was a mad dash around shops in the town centre to get more clothes. After all she couldn't be seen with the same clothes on more than once could she?
So that was it. Everything was falling into place for her. A good job and a good wage, Kayvan would be pleased. The problem was that when Kayvan arrives in the UK he would not be allowed to work until after they get married and he gets his next visa, so money was important she had to earn as much a possible to be able to support him until he could work.
The next day off she went to do the interviews. She was quite funky yet professional looking. She sat in with them during the interviews and asked relevant questions about experience and retail in general. Her input was received well and she chose the people who she thought were right for the job and gave valid reasons why she thought that. Now, they needed a supervisor too so obviously she suggested Mel. Patricia had obviously impressed so much so that Mel got a call and was offered the supervisors post. So they had been right, they were to work together again, just like before.

They were sent off to Aberdeen for training a week later. This was the nearest of their shops and the manager there was to train them. The shop in Dundee was almost completed and the date set for the opening.
However, there was a problem with the person that had been chosen for manager. He had accepted the job but when it came to it, he never showed up. So the grand opening of the shop was left to Patricia and Mel after only a week's training. This situation was to carry on for

a few weeks until they found a manager. After a few weeks had past and no sign of a manager Patricia stood up and said, 'Look I have been doing this for weeks now and I think you should give me the manager's job.'

They took this onboard and told her that if she made it to January without making a mess of things then the job was hers. The gauntlet had been thrown down!

In the meantime Christmas was approaching and along with it the impending arrival of our next grandchild. Louise was keeping well, a very pregnant bump was now developing but Josh was still complaining about feeling unwell. This was annoying me as he refused to go to the doctor. 'One of these days,' I thought, 'he will pay for this, and he will be sorry. Maybe once the baby arrived safe and well he will calm down and feel better, we will wait and see.'

I spent time preparing for Christmas and the odd wedding plan here and there. Some of it was emails to family, keeping them updated, but most to the lady I had contacted regarding the silk flowers. First it was to be a bridal bouquet and three bridesmaid posies, buttonholes for the men and a cake top, but it kept changing hence all the emails. It was quite surreal doing all the arrangements without seeing the actual flowers and not meeting the person, I was totally dependant on her understanding my requests and sending pictures for her to get an idea of what Patricia wanted. Quietly confident we kept in touch more or less on a day to day basis and things were coming together nicely.

The telephone rang about lunch time, it was Josh, Louise had gone into labour and he had taken Cameron to his grannies house to be looked after so he could be with Louise. So back to waiting and pacing while we waited for the news of our new grandchild. We all kept busy doing various tasks, it was better to be busy then sitting by the phone. James washed the car and I spent the afternoon cleaning and scrubbing the house. Patricia was at work so she was busy enough.

The shop had taken off really well and she was learning all the duties of a manager, so she was oblivious to what was going on at home and the hospital. It is now 9th December so everyone had gone shopping mad with Christmas just around the corner.. Patricia was pleased, as the more money the shop took, the better it was for her and the possibility of her getting the manager's position increased. I did call her to let her know of the situation and the likelihood was she was going to become an auntie again soon.
She said, 'keep me up to date with what is going on then, but I must go as this place is going like a fair.'

We didn't have to wait long for the news, second babies are usually quicker and Louise was no exception. Josh phoned and announced he was the proud father of another baby boy, his name is Jack and he weighed in at a healthy 8 lbs 1 oz. Mother and baby are both well and it was clear he was as pleased as punch.
'When can we see him,' I asked, 'today?'
'Not sure Mum,' he said, 'by the time they get things organised here and get them up to the ward it will be after visiting hours, so maybe tomorrow. I have taken a sneaky photo with my phone so I will pop in on the way home and let you see it.'
'OK, we have waited all this time so another day won't hurt. Congratulations to you both. Tell Louise I said well done and will see you all tomorrow.'
I hung up the phone told James the news and began calling the family to let them know and I sent emails to the ones I couldn't get. James asked if we could go to the hospital but I said, 'No, not likely.' although I wanted to take flowers up.

'Well surely you can take them up and leave them with the nurse to give to them,' he said.
'Good idea, grab your coat,' I said.
We went and bought a lovely bouquet of flowers and headed for the hospital. We went straight to the labour suite and asked the nurse there if she could give the flowers to Louise.
'Hold on one moment,' she said in a snipey voice, 'I will see if the Sister will allow her to get flowers.'
'Thanks,' I said, trying to stay composed although she had annoyed me with her attitude.
She was away a few minutes and when she came back she walked over to me and whispered, 'If you want you can take them in yourself!'
I was flabbergasted, 'Me, take them in?' I said with bated breath.
'Yes I have cleared it with Sister and with Josh and Louise and they are more than pleased for you to go in.'
I looked at James, 'Go on,' he said, 'you know you are dying to, I will wait here, I don't want to crowd them.'
I took the flowers and followed the nurse; she leaned on a heavy door and signalled for me to go in. I popped my head around the door and there was Josh with a grin from ear to ear and Louise was beaming as she cradled little Jack.
'Come on in,' they said, 'come and meet the newest member of the family.'
I walked in as if walking on eggshells not wanting to make a noise and disturb such a perfect picture. I placed the flowers on the table at the side of the bed and looked down to see my new grandson. He was perfect as I stroked his little cheek and felt the softness of his baby skin I felt a lump in my throat.
'He is beautiful guys, just beautiful, and Josh he is your double.'
'Do you want to hold him?' asked Louise.

'I won't just now,' I said, 'he is quite content and I never disturb a contented baby, I am pleased to look and share this moment with you all. I am only staying a minute as I don't want to get you into trouble with the nurses as I am sure they want to get you to the ward and settled in there. Dad is waiting outside and I don't want to keep him waiting, I will go and tell him what a lovely grandson he has.'

So I walked out on a little cloud and told James about little Jack, and Mum and Dad of course.

We all went to the hospital the next day and admired the new arrival. There was an entourage of people from both sides of the family and we all agreed that we were delighted and relieved that all went well and that Mum and baby were OK.

Before we knew it Christmas was upon us, we spent the day somewhat quietly and just enjoyed the day. Exchanging gifts and eating seemed to be the thing to do. Josh and his new family came up for a little while but with a new baby they did not want to be out and about all day. Cameron was coming to terms with the new baby and I made a fuss of him because as is often the case with new babies they get all the attention and the older one gets ignored. He and I spent time running around; him on his hobby horse and me on mine, which was the broom from the kitchen. He did not seem to mind that his hose had a head and made galloping noises and mine swept the floor as we went. Needless to say it was a great photo opportunity for the rest of the family.

Kayvan called later in the day to wish us all a Merry Christmas. He said that the passengers on the ship were very nice and appreciated the fact that the crew were away from home making sure that they enjoyed the Christmas Cruise. He chatted with Patricia for a few minutes but as the rest of the staff wanted to call home he did not want to spend too long tying up the line. He is such a considerate lad, he thinks of everyone.

Christmas and New Year over it was time to get down to serious wedding plans. We had lots to do and if we wanted this to be a perfect day we had lots to organise. The biggest thing was to get Kayvan's Visa application sorted out. After all no groom ..... no wedding. He was due to leave the ship in February and he was going to put in his application as soon as he got off. He was going to the Embassy in Jakarta before heading for home in Sukabumi, that way he did not have to travel back and forth. So we had to make sure he had all the documents he needed from us before he left the ship. This was not a problem as we had done it all before. James and I just needed up to date letters from our employers which were easy enough to sort out.

Chapter 16

Patricia had been looking at the price of property and realised that if she did not strike now, then she doubted if her and Kayvan could afford to buy a place of their own once they got married, as the market was going crazy. So she began to look at possible properties. She knew a house would be out of the question but a flat was more likely.

'I am not saying for certain that this is what I am going to do, it is just an idea,' she said, 'but there is no harm in looking is there?'

'Well, no, but you may want to see how much of a mortgage you would get before you start thinking along those lines. It is not as easy as you think, remember you also have to think about utility bills, insurances etc not just paying for the house.'

'I understand,' she said, 'maybe I will just look for the moment and see what is out there.'

Well, it is as if someone up there was listening to her, because when she came home that night she told us that she had got the manager's job and her wages had increased dramatically. So that was it, she started to look seriously at flats, and made an appointment with the bank to see what kind of mortgage she could have, based on her new salary.

So now we were looking at possible flats, arranging a wedding, a visa application and a new grandson! Wow, things were going crazy.

'Never a dull moment these days is there, James,' I said, 'what did I do with my time before all this?'

The next time Kayvan phoned Patricia told him of her idea, the fact that they would not be living with James and I but have a place of their own. He seemed quite concerned about it as he was looking forward to living with us but once she explained the reasoning behind it he was quite pleased with the idea.

Meanwhile, I had convinced Josh to go to the doctor as he was still feeling off colour.

'Go on,' I said, 'even if it is only to put my mind at rest, go and see what is wrong. You are maybe just a bit run down.'

So off he went anything to keep me happy.

'The doctor has taken blood samples,' he said. 'He is not sure what is wrong with me so this way it may show something.'

The blood results came back quite quickly and showed that there was a problem; he was showing signs that there was inflammation somewhere, but where? So more tests followed to try and find out what was causing the elevations in his blood.

It is now February and Kayvan has left the ship and sent in his Visa application before heading for home.

'So another waiting game, we are all getting good at this,' said James.

We were quietly confident about this too but things can go wrong so the sooner he has confirmation about this the better. Patricia had arranged to go on holiday to Indonesia in March so she could be there for Kayvan's birthday; she also thought it would be a good idea to go so that if there were any questions needing answering then she would be there to help him.

So now we had another thing to organize. 'At least Patricia can do that herself,' I thought, 'she has arranged travel details before so she knows what she is doing.'

She arranged her flights and time off work so was heading away to Indonesia on the 5th March. She had also arranged to stay in one of the best hotels in the area as a surprise for Kayvan's birthday.

'Well,' she said, 'I thought this could be an Indonesian honeymoon and one in Scotland for the real honeymoon. I am not greedy but two honeymoons sounds good to me,' she laughed.

Now a bombshell.

Josh has been told that he has to go for a colonoscopy as the doctor things he may have Crohn's Disease or IBS. Back to my trusty PC; I look up the disease and he has been showing all the classic symptoms of Crohn's. My heart sinks; 'I knew nothing good was going to come of this,' I said. 'It may not be Crohn's it is only a maybe just now, but my gut reaction tells me otherwise.'

Patricia headed off to Indonesia to spend two weeks with Kayvan and his family. She went taking gifts for his birthday and also gifts for his family. She had found out that his sister was expecting her first baby so she bought some nice baby clothes to give to his sister and her husband for their new arrival. Flight tracker back in play once more! As ever she called when she got there to let us know she was safe.

This time there were no travels to see the rest of the country; this holiday was to spend quality time with Kayvan. They spent time in the hotel that she had booked, however Kayvan was uneasy as he is so used to waiting on people he felt uncomfortable being waited on himself. The hotel was lovely though and it was nice just for the pair of them to be together without family being present.

Ibu and family had arranged a party for them both. Not an engagement party as such but a party none the less. It was another chance for family and friends to meet Patricia, this time they knew that he would be leaving for Scotland and that Patricia was to be his wife. Patricia was dressed in traditional clothing and spent the day socialising and having Kayvan translating for her. Neighbours came and entertained them throughout the day. Such a close knit community and they shared the food with them.

They spent their time together not wasting any precious moments; being a couple and planning their life together. I would get the odd text message from her and I could sense that she was having a great time and enjoying her time with Kayvan. She had told me that they had bought favours for the wedding. They had bought traditional fans and down the spine of the fan were their names along with the date of the wedding and they were in red sheaths so those on white linen table cloths would be part of the red and white theme. She had also bought an Indonesian wedding magazine so was looking for inspiration and ideas to help make it an Indonesian/Scottish wedding. The main and most important piece of information was that Ibu had made their wedding rings. Very Indonesian, white gold and diamonds, I was told not to say anything to anyone but she would show me a picture when she got home. I could not see the real thing because Kayvan was bringing them with him when he came over. At last, things were as normal as they can be when having a long distance relationship. As always all good things must come to an end and once again they were to be apart. Was this to be their last separation? The next time they met would be when we pick him up at the airport to start his new life in Scotland.

While she was away it was confirmed that Josh did have Crohn's disease and that he had to be seen by a specialist. There is nothing Patricia could do so I did not tell her until she returned home.

Chapter 17

Patricia arrived home safely and full of stories of her trip and I saw the picture of the ring. It is so beautiful and unusual.
'Typical of you,' I said, 'no one else in the world has a ring like that it is unique, just like you. Now we have to get this wedding on the move. I have the invitations, the flowers are coming along nicely, the hotel is booked and the deposit paid. I have sourced a dressmaker to alter the bridesmaid's dresses so now we have to see about a photographer and cake. I have been chatting to one of the girls at work who got married last year and she recommends the guy that done the photos for her wedding. His name is in the phone book, how about we make an appointment to go and see him?'
'Sure,' she said, 'I am off work on Sunday so see if he can fit us in then.'

I called the photographer and arranged an appointment for Sunday at 2 pm. So we all went to see him including Cameron, we had him for the day to give Josh and Louise a break. We all fitted into his little office and he seemed to think that Cameron was Patricia's baby!
'Heaven forbid,' we said, 'it is one thing that she is not interested in, well not at the moment!'
She shot me a sideways glance when I said that! The photographer let us see samples of his work and gave us a price, at which to be honest I was surprised, as I thought it would be much more expensive. We told him where the hotel was and he said that he would drive up and have a look as he had never been there before. He would look for nice places for photographs and asked if there was anything special that she wanted.
'I am willing to leave that to you as the professional,' she said.

'Now, have you thought about your wedding cake?' he asked. I know a lady that does them and I highly recommend her. I know her prices are very reasonable. Here is her number, give her a call and see what she has to offer. Obviously you are not obligated but I know weddings are expensive so if you can save a pound here and there then all the better, right Dad?' he said with a devilish grin.

James grinned back at him, 'You bet, if I can save a pound here and there it means an extra drink for me on the day, and I think I may need it.'

'Well that's it then, I have it in my book, I will have a drive up and look around to get a feel for the place and all you need to do now is come and see me a week before the wedding and finalise everything.'

'Great, that's another thing in place; let's give the lady a call about the cake.'

Patricia pulled out her mobile and called the lady, she arranged to go and see her on Tuesday evening.

Tuesday came and I met Patricia and we headed off to the gym. I had spoken to one of the instructors and had a plan all mapped out for me to tone all the wobbly bits as I called them. Once we had been there and freshened up we drove up to the ladies house to discuss the wedding cake. Patricia had a picture that she had cut out of a magazine and when we met Mrs Green, she handed the picture over and asked if she could possibly do something similar. Mrs Green took one look at the picture and said. 'Well if you want inferior then no, I can't do it. I mean look at the icing, there are gaps everywhere, and my cake wouldn't look like that. Look at the shape, it is not even!'

I had been impressed by the cake, it looked lovely to me but I suppose to a trained eye it did have flaws.

'So I propose I do this …..and that,' she explained in great detail.

Patricia and I looked at each other, not saying a word but we thought the same. 'Wow she is good!'

Patricia explained that she wanted a two tier cake one sponge and one fruit. But she wanted the sponge to be the bigger of the two. We thought that this may be a problem because the fruit being heavier it may fall through the sponge one.

'Not a problem,' she said 'I have a gadget that would prevent one falling through the other. It is a Perspex sphere that distributes the weight on the bottom tier so no worries there. Now the top of the cake what do you want for that?'

Puzzled looks again from the both of us.

'Well,' she said, 'what flowers are in your bouquet?'

'Lilies and Jasmine,' we piped up in harmony.

'OK, how about I make icing lilies for the top and fill the sphere with Jasmine?'

'That sounds great.'

'The cake you see on the sideboard behind you is for a wedding tomorrow, as you can see there are lilies on the top of that one. What do you think?'

I stared in amazement, the lilies were perfect.

'Oh yes,' said Patricia, 'we'll go with that for sure.'

'So we are having two tiers, one sponge, and one fruit and lilies right? Ribbon? Do you want ribbon?'

'Well actually,' said Patricia, 'what I want is the words *I love you, in English and Indonesian all around both tiers*.'

She produced a piece of paper with the Indonesian spelling for her.

'I want it in white icing so that when people see it they think it is a design but in fact it is writing.'

Mrs Green seemed to like this idea. 'OK then, but I still think that ribbon around the base would be a good idea, that way it is not all white.'

'Well the theme is red and white so how about a red ribbon,' I said.

181

Mrs Green leapt up from the table and came back with various shades of red ribbon.

'You chose the one you want and I will do that for you.'

'So you will make the cake, put on writing, ribbon, lilies and jasmine in the sphere is that right.'

'Yes,' said Mrs Green. She reached over and brought out a big book full of orders and marked it up with what looked like hieroglyphics, a few figures thrown in for good luck and said, 'the cost will be £90.'

I couldn't believe my ears, a bargain!

'The only other cost is a deposit for the sphere but you get it back when you return the sphere to me.'

So that was that, all we had to do was pick it up the day before the wedding and that was it. Easy! Patricia and I left Mrs Green's house and on the way to the car we discussed the price. We were both gob smacked and we giggled about her tearing the picture apart and finding faults with it.

'Your Dad will be pleased when we tell him the cost, not that *we* are bothered about it, but every penny counts.'

James and I decided that maybe a holiday was called for. We knew that the wedding would start to take up most of our time in preparations and if we didn't take this opportunity we would not get a break until mid October. That was a long time to wait so we booked a week's break in Spain.

The hotel was lovely and the resort was very peaceful as it was out of the main holiday season. A great time to spend charging our batteries knowing what was to come. We spent time reading and walking and with the odd jug of Sangria made for a very relaxing time. Of course we would look around the shops too and we stumbled across beautiful wooden boxes full of everything a wine buff would like. There was a bottle stopper, a thermometer, cork screw and wine pourer, what a nice gift that would be for someone we thought. *Then a brain wave, I wondered if Patricia would like to use them as gifts for her ushers*? I texted her to let her know about the boxes as we had not seen anything like it in Britain and we know she likes unusual things.

'Great idea,' came back the reply. So we bought two of them.

'Funny,' said James, 'even on holiday you can't take your mind off the wedding.'

'Well,' I said, 'strike while the iron is hot and I thought she would like the idea as she was asking just the other day what to buy for Sean and Phil as gifts, so the problem is now solved, right?'

'I wouldn't mind one of those myself,' he said, 'but I suppose that is out of the question seeing as they are being given to the ushers.'

'You have hit the nail on the head there,' I said, 'if you had one then the gifts would not be unique. Sorry!'

I gave him a broad smile and hoped I had convinced him.

He smiled back at me and replied 'I don't mind really three would take up too much space in the luggage anyway.'

I had got away with it - that was a close call. Then we found nice pearl earrings, just small studs but they would look great with the necklace I had bought in an antiques shop when we had been visiting friends in Harrogate. The necklace was actually dated the same year as I was born........ Not quite an antique but it was exactly what I had been looking for. It consisted of a heavy old gold chain and the front had been set in small flowers with green stones and between the flowers were small pearls so the earrings would be ideal. Another purchase made and James said. 'Funny that you manage to get something you want but I can't have what I wanted.'

I thought he was being serious and almost backed down and told him to buy another wine set until I caught the glint of mischief in his eye. Cheeky monkey! I did feel somewhat guilty so when James went to order lunch I made my excuses and went back to the wine shop. I didn't buy him the full set but did get the funkiest bottle opener I had ever seen. I had seen him admire it when we were there together so I knew he would like it. I presented it to him after lunch and he was delighted.

'I couldn't have you doing without,' I said and we both burst out laughing.

The week away continued to flow at a nice easy pace and the weather was nice and warm not burning sun like in the height of the summer.

One day we decided to go for a walk along the beach to the next resort which was apparently very nice too. On the way home I thought we would walk back along the beach again but this time when we got to the rugged rocks we didn't walk around them. I decided to stay in the water and walk across them that way. James went up on the path to take a photo. This was unusual for me as I never go in the sea.

As I was climbing over the rocks my foot slipped just as a massive wave was heading towards me. The next thing I knew I was being dashed across the rocks and could feel my knees being cut. Then I fell onto my bum with a crash. I thought to myself *'it is OK, even if you get pushed out away from the rocks, you can swim, so you'll be OK'.*'

But it was not as easy as I had thought and I struggled to get to the shore. James couldn't do anything to help as he was too far away. He looked on helplessly as he scrambled down the rocks towards me.

I finally managed to get back onto the beach and looked at the damage, my knees were grazed and bleeding and my bum felt badly bruised. I would check that when I got back to the hotel I couldn't do that on the beach! I also

looked like a drowned rat, soaked to the skin and my wet hair slapped to my head. What a pretty picture!
'I won't do that again,' I said to James who had made it down to the beach by this time in a desperate effort to rescue me.

Back in the hotel I looked in the mirror at the damage, I was right my bottom was bruised, as were my knees. I had a shower and washed my hair and put on a pair of nice trousers and top at least that way my injuries were covered. At least we were heading for home the day after so I didn't have to try and cover up the bruises for long fortunately.

As always, when it was time to go home, we felt as though the end of the holiday had come around too fast but at least we had enjoyed the time away despite my obvious bruises! I wasn't looking forward to sitting for a couple of hours on a plane with a bruised bottom but it had to be done

So now the flat hunt was on seriously. We all knew that she would have to move swiftly as the chances are that any property bought would need refurbishing and with everything else going on it may be difficult to do everything at once.
James and Patricia spent time looking through the property papers and on the websites of local estate agents and making appointments to go and view them. This is where James came in, this was his forte, he saw to the flat side of things. He looked at the properties with a critical eye and objectively whereas Patricia and eye would have just admired the surface. James checked out the more structural side and was aware of any repairs that may be needed. He would point them out to Patricia and advise her of what it may cost to put right. So I looked after the wedding arrangements and Patricia

was trying to balance her time between both of them. Our lives were starting to look and feel like a three ringed circus, all of us doing various things at various times, we had to stay focused and in control. *The word mayhem springs to mind!*

Flats were now the focal point, James and I spent time viewing properties with Patricia, we did not want her to buy the first thing that came along, it had to be right and in the right area. She realised that to get this she would have to pay for it, but better that than getting somewhere cheaper only to find that it needed too much work done or that the area was not suitable. Scottish law is somewhat fickle when it comes to buying property; it is advertised at 'offers over' so if it was advertised at offers over £70,000 realistically you would have to offer something in the region of £90,000 to get it. So keeping this in mind she looked at price ranges that she knew she could afford without breaking the bank. She had seen a few that she liked and put in offers but every time she was out bid! This was really starting to annoy her but as I said before. 'Patience is a virtue, there is something out there waiting for you, it is a case of finding it that's all.'

We went to see one flat that was out of this world and even though the offers were within her price range it was obvious that it would go for well above what she could afford. Another was not far from where we lived but next to a pub which would be a bit noisy. Then there was another which was nice but weird, there was no door on the bathroom! The girl selling the property said that the previous owner had put in a new bath and as the bath was too big for such a small room, his solution had been to take the door off! Not great if you want a bit of privacy, we both thought. We didn't need James to keep us right on this one, it was definitely not one to be considered. The worst one of all was one that we went to look at, just to see the area. James drove up and found that he could not turn the car round, so he went up a side street only to find it swarming with policemen! At the side of the road was a car with a big dent in the roof. 'Not looking good here,' he said, 'I am not getting out and I suggest you guys don't either.'

So we left in a hurry not knowing what had happened but the next day in the local paper it read *'man jumps out of window and damages car.'*

'Don't think we will pursue that one Dad,' she said. 'I don't want people jumping out of windows onto my car!'

Then one Monday evening, off we all went to look at yet another flat. This one had lots of potential, two bedrooms, with a lounge, bathroom and galley kitchen. It was owned by an elderly couple who had decided that they could not manage the stairs to the first floor and were moving to a ground floor flat in another part of the city. The lady showed us around whilst her daughter and grand daughter waited in the lounge. Once we had finished the grand tour we got chatting to the family and found out that the grand daughter was married to a man from Sri Lanka, so immediately there was a bond, as we told them that Patricia was about to marry Kayvan who came from Indonesia. This seems to strike a chord with them. The grand daughter was speaking about the crazy system in Scotland and the 'offers over' scheme, She found this most annoying as she had moved here from England a year or so before. She said that she got so frustrated when looking for a house that she ended up sitting in the lounge of the sellers and saying. *'Look! What do you want for it and if I can afford it then I will give you what you want.* It seemed to work,' she said and she had got the house she wanted at a price she could afford. James, Patricia and I looked at each other and some sort of intuition seized us all, at the same moment and it did the same to them. They told us that if

Patricia put in a decent offer they would consider it, as they appreciated what it was like to buy your first property. We shook hands and left with a bit of a spring in our step.

'I think you may have scored brownie points there hun,' said James. 'Get your solicitor to put an offer in tomorrow morning, strike while the iron is hot.'

Next morning she had her solicitor put in what she thought was a good offer, only to find that someone else who had seen the flat earlier had also put in an offer.

'Oh, maybe not as easy as we had hoped,' we said. Patricia increased her offer and low and behold it was accepted. Hurrah!

'There you go babe, your first place of your own, and a nice little starting point on the property ladder.'

We were all tickled pink,

'It doesn't even need much doing to it,' said James, 'just a lick of paint here and there. You will be in it before Kayvan gets here, what a bonus.'

The weeks past and things seemed to be falling into place nicely. The wedding plans were all in place and Patricia had signed for her flat. Everything was in her name as Kayvan was still not in the country. She felt a bit uneasy about that but he understood the politics of it all. He understood that when he got to the UK he could not work as his Visa did not allow it until he was married and then he would have to apply for another Visa which would allow him to seek employment. Until then he could not begin to settle into his new life in Scotland properly.

Patricia took over the house in June 2007, three months before the wedding. That was plenty of time to get things organised and any alterations done.

'It will only take a few weeks to put that place in order,' said James, 'but it means all hands on deck as it were.'

We were all up for that, it would mean spending every spare hour there but it would be fun.

The day she got the keys she went up and had a look around, full of excitement knowing this was going to be the place where she and Kayvan were to start their life together. She looked around and soaked in every nook and cranny of the place. She was delighted. The same day she heard from Kayvan that his Visa had come through and that he would arrive in the UK on 17th July. The look on her face was one to treasure, she beamed from ear to ear mixed with a hint of relief. Brilliant, the flat would be ready in time for his arrival and they could move in together and get settled in before the wedding. That would take the pressure off everyone and give them both time to become accustomed to being together as a couple for the very first time. Things were moving along and all was calm in the family.

That evening James and I went up to look around the flat. It looked different with no furniture in it. James looked carefully and hummed to himself. He now had his working head on so to speak and went over everything with a fine tooth comb.

'This may take a bit longer than I thought,' he said. 'Now I can see it for what it is and there is a lot of work to be done here. Just looking at the kitchen, the cupboards are old and tired and the décor is bad. Then the bathroom - it needs a new toilet and wash hand basin. There is also a shortage of sockets for appliances.'

'Stop!' shouted Patricia. 'So now how long do you think it will take to get it looking nice?'

James hummed again. 'Well put it this way, I don't think you will be moving in when Kayvan gets here.'

'Oh!' Said Patricia, 'you said all it needed was a lick of paint.'

'Well, yes, but that was before I had a proper look. Don't worry we will all pull together and get it done as quickly as possible. We do have deadline you know. Not that I

am in any hurry to see you go, but Auntie Carol and uncle Mick are coming from Canada on the 22nd September.'
'You are kidding me aren't you; it will be done long before that surely.'
'Yes but what I really mean is that we will all have to pull our socks up and dedicate time to this project.'

And so the fun began! James and I spent every spare moment in the flat. We would go to work at 8 am and be at the flat by 5 pm stay there until 9. Patricia would appear about 7 pm and help out. First we started stripping the wallpaper off. That was the easy bit. It looked like we were making good headway but then we noticed other things, like cracked walls and poor lighting. Nothing daunted we kept working away spending all our weekends there too. Patricia wanted to replace the doors in the flat as they were old fashioned and ugly. Then James noticed that they were actually old doors with boards over them to make them look more modern! So we pulled the boards off to reveal lovely panelled doors, made of solid wood.
'You can't buy doors like that now; well not without costing the earth,' said James. 'Can we do anything with them?' asked Patricia
'Maybe …your Mum used to be good at restoring things so perhaps she has an answer.'
I had a look at them and said, 'well if we can get the paint off and bring them back to wood, then yes, they would be nice.'
'Ok,' said James, 'that is your task.'
'There are six doors in total,' I said. 'It will take a lot of time but I will have a go.'
From there on I was assigned 'door restoring duties'. That was all I did. I tried using chemicals to remove the paint but that didn't work. So we got a hot air paint stripper which worked a treat but it was still time

consuming. I had been given a challenge and would not give up until I was satisfied.

Meanwhile James and Patricia were decorating the lounge. But this meant removing an old fireplace and blocking up the chimney, then replacing the wall. Then they had to concentrate on the electrical side of things, adding more sockets and putting in small down lights in the ceiling. Josh helped in that department but with him not being 100% fit I was reluctant to let him do too much. Patricia and I chose colours for the walls and curtains for the windows. She went for lovely brown shades, nice and mellow. At last we could see one room taking shape. I continued with the doors and I was developing muscles as a result of stripping paint and sanding them down to reveal their natural beauty. We would go home at night and fall into a heap. It was hard work, 13 hours work a day and no days off.

Kayvan called often and at one point he said. 'Don't do everything; leave something for me to do when I get there. I can't work after all so it will keep me busy.'

'I have a feeling he will be busy,' said James, 'there is no way this is going to be done any time soon.'

Days rolled into weeks and it was time to pick up Kayvan. We were not nearly finished.

So we went to the airport (a familiar scene now) and waited patiently for his arrival. Patricia asked if she could meet him on her own this time. So James and I headed off for a coffee and left her to wait for her husband to be. Fortunately it was a nice sunny day so James and I sat outside the airport and watched the people coming and going. There must have been a concert or something on as there were lots of people from Australia roaming around and all pushing instruments around.

'He is taking his time getting through customs,' I said to James, 'I hope it is ok'
'I suppose there will be lots of questions to answer and checks to be made,' said James, 'remember he is not here on holiday this time.'
'True enough, I am just worried in case there is a problem.' *Imagine going through all this and him being refused entry.* It didn't bear thinking about.
I meandered over to the door and peeked in; Patricia was standing there waiting patiently. I wandered over to where James was sitting enjoying the sun shine.
'She is still standing where we left her,' I said.
'Stop worrying,' said James, 'they will be out soon.'
I sat down again and checked my watch, 'his plane landed over an hour ago,' I said.
Then all of a sudden I heard, 'Hi Mom!'
There they were both grinning like Cheshire cats arms around each other. I heard a sigh of relief and realised it wasn't from me but James. 'OK, OK,' he said, 'I was getting a bit apprehensive too.'
We laughed out loud and went to greet our new son-in-law to be. We chatted all the way home asking how he felt to be here and how his family felt about things. He admitted he was nervous and his family were upset to see him go, especially his Mum.
I don't think I could let my kids go so far away from home but I suppose there is not much you can do if they have made their minds up is there? We did not go to the flat that day. We would leave that for Patricia to do.

We all spent a couple of days recharging our batteries knowing what lay ahead. Patricia took Kayvan to see the flat and when we asked him what he thought he said. 'It is very nice.'
Well that is not the term that springs to mind but we knew what he meant. However, we later found out that he had no experience of DIY so that could be fun.

James had a new pupil. James is a very patient guy and a great teacher but Kayvan will have to learn quickly!

As the days went by we noticed that things were not exactly as we had hoped between the future bride and groom. Things were tense, to say the least. I had this dreaded fear that maybe there would be no wedding. I watched their every move. There was no body contact and Patricia kept complaining that Kayvan snored. I was on heckle pins and James was no better. The feeling of de ja vu was immense. I had to take Patricia to one side and ask if everything was alright.

'Sure,' she said, 'but the snoring thing is driving me crazy.'

The one thing Patricia excelled at was sleeping and to disturb it was a sacrilege.

'It takes a while to settle down that's all. Don't worry it will be ok.' Easy for her to say! Not so easy for us to do especially having been through the upset the year before when Patricia had called off the engagement. I headed for the local chemist and asked for a snore remedy, maybe if I could help resolve this things would be easier. So the girl gave me a throat spray and said it was very effective. I hurried home that night and presented it to the pair of them.

'I know you are not one for taking medication,' I said to Kayvan, 'but if you don't do something about the snoring I think Patricia may kill you!'

He laughed and said. 'OK Mom, I will try anything if it makes her life easier.'

So James and I decided to let them get on with it and if it all went wrong then so be it. I must admit that James and I were both worried that all our money could go to waste; but in the same token agreed that if it was not to be then best find out before the wedding and not after!

This feeling of unease continued. We would work at the flat during the day and return home to a feeling of unrest and dreaded fear. Patricia and Kayvan would sit there watching TV not even together but him on one couch and her on another. I could have cut the atmosphere with a knife, James and I would shoot looks at each other across the room and just look skywards, raise our eyebrows or just shrug our shoulders hoping we would go unnoticed. When James and I went to bed we would discuss the situation willing the should be happy couple, to be happy.

I went into the shop one lunchtime and spoke to Mel about it. I was looking for some sort of feedback hoping that maybe Patricia had spoken to her about what was going on. Mel said that as far as things were concerned everything was OK. Patricia had not given any indication that there was a problem. I had seen a pair of shoes that would be lovely with the dress I had bought for the wedding but was reluctant to buy them until I knew there was to be a wedding! Mel laughed when I told her what I was thinking.
'Maybe I am reading it all wrong,' I said to her, 'but I just have a horrible feeling about the whole thing.'

The days continued to pass, keeping busy and working in the flat every hour God sent. Kayvan and I would chat away as we had done before when things went wrong. This time he was more reluctant to give much away in the way of emotion.
'You know Mom,' he said, 'we are always like this when we get together, strained and uncomfortable with each other.'
That was some consolation coming from him at least they were both saying the same thing.
One night we headed off home again, Patricia had gone straight home from work and was waiting for us to return home as she had prepared our evening meal. It was bizarre, it was like someone had waved a magic wand

and everything was relaxed and for the first time since Kayvan arrived they were as they should be together. James and I just looked at each other yet again and smiled, could this be the turning point?

Yes it was the turning point for them, they seemed so happy and in love. I could hardly believe the difference. They sat together, holding hands, cuddles galore and the odd sneaky kiss. Phew, what a relief. We don't know what had happened between them but we are glad it did. It seems that it was as they had said they were comfortable with each other again. Now I could relax and enjoy the run up to the wedding.

Chapter 18

It is two months to the wedding now and everything is calm. We were making headway in the flat although there was a still a lot to do mostly decorating but it was all taking time. I continue to work on the doors. I still have two left to do, but the ones that are finished look amazing.

The Hen and Stag parties are all arranged. Patricia has decided to have a two day event. The first is made up of close female friends and relatives having a Spa Day. This consisted of all the facilities at the spa, swimming, sauna, steam room, gym followed by lunch. Then a massage and hand pamper including French polish. The next night was a party at the house with all her friends. The stag day consisted of the guys going to play paint ball during the day then a BBQ and booze late afternoon until………………whenever!

The work continued painting, wallpapering, new kitchen, new toilet and wash hand basin, doors, sanding wood work, filling in holes, removing more fire places, as there were three in total. Kayvan had taken one of the doors still waiting to be stripped and written across it 'Kayvan's Office'.
'It seems I am here all the time,' he said, 'so this is my office.' We all giggled when we saw it.
It then became a notice board and we would leave messages for each other on it. It acted as a way of linking us all together. We would all check the door and see if we could spot the latest graffiti or comments. Sometimes it was a silly drawing or maybe a message or often an expression of exasperation! The occasional 'aghhhhhh' could be seen. It made us laugh.
Kayvan can't drive, so he had to walk to the flat every day. I bought a map of the city and marked it with

different routes that he could take to get to the flat. 'Thanks Mom,' he said, 'at least I don't have to see the same things everyday.'

The weather was not the best either even though it was summer time. It was one of the wettest summers I could recall. Maybe it was something to do with global warming, so poor Kayvan would often arrive at the flat soaked to the skin.

One day Kayvan and I were working together in the kitchen whilst James worked away in the bedroom. I noticed Kayvan was very quiet which was not like him, he was normally chatty and full of laughter. I was beginning to think that maybe homesickness was kicking in. I asked him several times throughout the day what was wrong. He just stared at me and said. 'Nothing Mom.'

I was not convinced so I continued the pressure until he crumbled. He admitted that he was a bit down as although he had been in Dundee for some weeks all he had seen was the flat. I could understand how he was feeling, we were all getting sick of the routine of work, flat, eat, and sleeping. He said that he was not used to being cooped up all the time. He loved walking and getting fresh air and a bit of adventure. As it turned out I was meeting Patricia in town later that afternoon so I said.

'Why don't you come with me?'

'Can I,' he said, 'it would be nice not to be here for a while, I know I can't get a job yet but I would like to get away from here if only for a while.'

So I changed my clothes to go and pick Patricia up and said to Kayvan.

'Get changed and come with me.'

He went for a quick wash as he was covered in paint and was changed in a flash. We went to the car and I

drove to town but when I got near the town centre I pulled the car over and said.
'Right young man Patricia and I are going to a store at the other end of town get out and make your way there. We will see you when you get there.'
He looked at me and said.
'Excuse me Mom?'
'Well you wanted a bit of a change, some freedom a bit of adventure well this is the best I can come up with at short notice. Go to the top of this road, turn left and find your way to the store. If you get lost you have a tongue in your head ask someone where to go.'
He jumped out of the car with a grin on his face that went from ear to ear and back again. I put the car into gear and drove off waving to him as I went.
I went to meet Patricia and she said.
'What are you smiling about?'
I told her what I had done to Kayvan and she thought I had gone crazy.
'What if he gets lost?' she said.
'Well he has my mobile number and he will call if he gets in a pickle.' I said.
'Good plan,' she said, 'lets wait and see if he calls then.'
Patricia and I went to a few shops looking for a shirt and tie for Kayvan as they had been invited to a friends wedding, and she wanted him to look smart instead of his usual casual self.
'This will be good for him,' I said, 'going to a British wedding, it will give him an idea of how things are here, then maybe he won't be so nervous about his own wedding.'
My phone rang, it was Kayvan.
'Hello,' I said, 'are you lost?'
'No Mom,' came this cheery voice, 'I am outside the coffee shop beside the store you are in and I am reading the news paper.'

'Good for you,' I said, you made it then.' 'Yeah Mom, it was easy peasy!'
I told Patricia that he was waiting outside and although she never said anything I could see the relief on her face! So shirt and tie in hand we headed off to the coffee shop to find a relaxed and happy Kayvan. He saw me approach and got up, and hugged me.
'Thanks Mom,' he said, 'I needed that.'
It wasn't much but it seemed to do the trick.

The day of the wedding had arrived and they both looked so smart. I had spent hours curling Patricia's long hair and once it was finished I placed a lovely pink fascinator in it to hold back some of the curls off her face. Kayvan was suited and booted and looked so smart.
'What a beautiful couple,' I said, 'so smart.'
Kayvan was a bit apprehensive about the whole thing but was looking forward to it none the less.
'At least you have a day off today,' I said, 'James and I are heading back to your place to get on with more jobs. Off you go and have a ball; you can tell us all about it tomorrow.'
James and I headed off to the flat. We hoped to make good headway today. Next weekend was the stag party so not much would be done then that's for sure.

The wedding went well and Kayvan said it had helped put his mind at rest about weddings in general. He was impressed with the speech part. Although he was not looking forward to speaking in front of people at his own wedding.
'You will be in front of friends,' I said, 'nothing to worry about.
I had been putting James' speech together for the past few weeks, and I was helping Josh with his to as he was to be best man. However, Kayvan wanted to do his

himself, he wanted it to be personal and special so I didn't have to help him. Patricia did not want the traditional speech that father of the bride delivers, so James and I had come up with a speech but with a twist. It started of with the usual 'thank you's' then the rest of it was in rhyme. I can tell you it wasn't easy trying to rhyme Indonesia! Josh's was the key speech. Like most weddings, the best man's speech was the one everyone looked forward to, the one that was funny and full of tales about the groom. However as Josh didn't know Kayvan terribly well we had our work cut out. I gave Josh an outline of the protocol and suggested the 'shape' of it, all he had to do was to beef it up with anecdotes.

The day of the stag day was here. I headed off to the supermarket and bought bottles of water and chocolate to keep their energy up and as each guy left the house to go paint balling they got their supplies. There was a convoy of cars leaving the street, filled with men acting like school kids! The thought of running around in fields getting shot with paint pellets did nothing for me but they were up for it. Once they had gone I did some housework and then started moving beer from the flat to the house. We had kept it in the flat as there was not enough room in my fridge to store the vast amounts that we had bought. I also had food in the freezer there for the BBQ so all that had to be shifted back in time for the guys returning. It was earlier than expected when I got a call to say that they were heading back early as the cost of buying more paint pellets was more than even they wanted to pay. So they would be home in an hour or so. I beat a hasty retreat to the flat as I did not want to be around when they got home. After all a stag do is strictly men only so I was not hanging around! I went to the flat and armed with a pack of peanut M & Ms began to stain another door. Time was passing well when the phone went again. It was James, he said.

'Hey your brother and Gavin want to wear kilts to the wedding, can you come and take them to the shop in the town and get them measured.'

'It is four o'clock on a Saturday afternoon and you want me to take them to get fitted for kilts, the shops close at 5 pm.'

'Yes,' he said, 'they are both adamant about it.'

Nothing unusual there except both my brother and Gavin are English! So I jumped in the car, picked up Paul and Gavin and drove like a demon into town. I dropped them off at the shop and went to park the car. Then I had to run like crazy to get to the shop before it closed. Once there I could do nothing but laugh looking at these two Englishmen in kilts even if they did look smart. Then the climax, in the mad dash they had not brought money so I had to pay the deposits! Then I was fighting time as I had to get them back home then pick up my sister in law then Patricia and then head off to spend the evening with Louise and the boys. All us women were keeping a low profile and letting the guys get on with it .Louise went to the local supermarket and got supplies of chocolate and wine.

'Why should they have all the fun,' she said.

I was driving so no wine for me but the chocolate was good. By 10 pm my phone went and James, who was a bit worst for wear due to too much beer, shouted.

'Hey! Your brother is unconscious!'

I immediately went into a panic.

'What do you mean unconscious?'

'He has passed out. Kayvan made a cocktail and I think it finished him off!'

We could hear the hilarity in the background.

'He is OK isn't he,' I asked.

'Yeah, yeah,' said James, 'he is sleeping on the couch in the lounge.'

More hilarity and laughter screamed down the phone.
'I will be home about midnight,' I said, 'is that OK?'
'Yeah babe,' he said in slurred tones then hung up.
'Well it seems to be a great success,' I said.
My sister-in-law, Patricia and I headed for home to find the front door of the house wide open and a deafening noise coming out. We sauntered in and were welcomed by our partners. Josh looked a bit worse for wear but not nearly as bad as Paul, who was still sound asleep on the couch. I looked around and the guys in the kitchen were having a carry on with chillies. The dare was to eat one raw so Gavin, being daring, said he would do it. Well no sooner was it in his mouth when he darted for the tap and consumed pint after pint of water. Within second of it going down it was up again, he was as sick as a dog. Then of course we had to witness all the war wounds from the paintball. Some were worse than others. Kayvan had a great bruise on his upper arm. Josh had a few on his chest and Gavin had three bruises on his back.
'That was why this was arranged now and not the weekend before the wedding,' I said, 'we don't want photos of the groom covered in bruises!'
Paul surfaced from the couch, had a look around the kitchen and headed back to the couch in a rare old state. That of course encouraged jeers from the rest of the guys calling him a light weight as he couldn't hold his drink! Gradually things began to calm down a bit and people began to go home. I made sure that Josh got a taxi home as he was the last to leave and then I locked the house up.
The next morning I surveyed the damage to the house. There was not nearly as bad as I had expected, it was untidy and the smell of beer would have knocked you sideways, but other than that it was ok. I sat in the kitchen chatting to Paul who looked better than he did when the last time I had seen him.

Then I noticed that my left hand was tingling and the tip of my tongue was as bad. I kept trying to get some life into my hand by wriggling my fingers but it just wasn't getting any better. James came through and asked if I would drive Paul and Gavin up to Josh's house as they had not seen their new house. I looked at James and said.
'Can you do it, I don't feel very well.'
'Oh?' said James, 'what's wrong?'
I told him about my hand and tongue and by now I was feeling sick. He called the emergency doctor. I explained how I felt to the nurse and before I knew where I was there was an ambulance and two paramedics outside the door. They thought I was having a heart attack. I was escorted to the ambulance and the paramedics ran an ECG, it showed that everything was OK but as I was obviously anxious and my blood pressure was raised. They ran another test, this one more in depth. Meanwhile, James, Paul and Gavin where inside wondering what was going on, Kayvan had retreated upstairs and was praying for me. The ECGs were OK nothing wrong with my heart but the paramedics suggested I go and see a doctor. So we went to see the on call doctor who said it was stress and gave me something for the nausea. I went to see my own doctor the next day and he said I had been doing too much and to take time off work. He ran some blood checks just to make sure the paramedics had not missed anything, he was not impressed that they had not taken me to hospital.
James said. 'That is it for you, no more flat work, concentrate on the wedding and nothing else, do you hear me!'
'I have to finish those doors,' I said, 'but I promise I will take it easy.'

He was not impressed with my reply but as I explained there was not much to do now, they just have to be stained and that will be them finished.
So he agreed with me.
'But that and only that,' he said, 'no more, you frightened the life out of me. I have never been so afraid.'
'Ah! Now you know how I have felt all these times when you were sick and in and out of hospital,' I said.
'Bloody hell hun, I thought I had lost you.' The tears welled in his lovely hazel eyes.
'Hey, look I am ok, the doc said it is stress I have just been doing too much, I promise to take things easy.'
We hugged each other close and I felt a tear run down my neck, it had come from James' lovely eyes.

I took a few days to regain my composure after my episode, then I thought it was high time to get the invitations written and posted. Patricia, Kayvan and I started a chain. I would write the invitations and envelopes Kayvan would seal the envelopes and Patricia would put the stamps on. Included with the invitation were the menu options. Everyone was asked to choose what they wanted to eat and return their selections to me. The starters were either Tomato and Basil soup or King Prawns with Garlic and toasted ciabatta. Main courses were either Chicken with Mushroom and Tarragon or Scottish fillet of beef with black peppercorn sauce and dessert was either Sticky Toffee Pudding with vanilla ice cream or a selection of Biscuits and Cheese. There were also vegetarian options and children's meals all angles were covered. Once I got the replies back I would make up menus for each of the guests showing what they had selected. Also included with the invitations were details of the coaches we were running as it was about 40 minutes drive from Dundee. There were to be three coaches, one for the day guests, one for the evening guests and one to get them all back to Dundee at the end of the day. Each invitation was tied together with a beautiful narrow silver ribbon that had been brought from Indonesia.

This took a few days as I wanted to take my time writing them as they had to be perfect. There were invites for day guests and evening guests so it was important to get them right and I wanted my handwriting to be legible. When the invitations were all done I headed to the post office to get them posted off to the guests. Once they had been handed over I gave a sigh, now all we had to do was wait for the RSVPs to arrive. What we didn't know when I posted them was that there was a postal strike! Panic set in! Patricia was getting quite upset about it so I sent emails to everyone telling them that the invites had been posted but due to the strike they may not be delivered or worse... lost. The next few days were a nightmare, waiting to see if the invitations had been received. It turned out that some had been received but some had not, by which time I had received replies to my emails with menu selections. I was then able to design the personal menus. I had bought silver paper and made a watermark with a picture of the hotel where the wedding was to take place. Then I put the guests name on the outer corner and their selection on the inside. Then I scrolled them up and tied them off with white ribbon which had *Patricia and Kayvan 2007* written on it in silver writing. The menu would then double as a place setting.

In between all this were the Hen parties. The spa day was lovely. There were only twelve of us and we spent the day relaxing and being pampered and we had a lovely lunch. We spent our time swimming and getting in and out of the sauna and spa pools. Then we all had massages and our finger nails either manicured and

French polished or manicured and painted in vibrant colours. Most of us went for the French polish but my sister in law went for a metallic purple colour. There was one slight problem, when we were having our massages there were contractors working in another part of the spa doing some repairs. They were anything but quiet so it was not as relaxing as we had hoped. I mentioned this to the manager and we were all given complimentary passes to come again. Once the pampering was over we all had champagne in the lounge as a treat before we went home.

The next event was to be more informal and Patricia had no idea what we had planned for her. My sister-in-law and niece were visiting from England and they decided to go shopping for shoes for the wedding so they dragged Patricia with them. This was our cunning plan to get Patricia out of the house. Once they had left I phoned the bridesmaids and got the scheme under way. They appeared wearing T shirts and jeans. The T shirts had the most ridiculous picture of Patricia on the front and on the back they read 'bridesmaid', whilst mine had 'mother of the bride' emblazed across the back. These had been made by Kaz and we all wore them with pride. Then we put up photographs of her from when she was a little girl to the present day. Needless to say not many of them were flattering. Kayvan had stayed back to help us, he had been sworn to secrecy. We then put balloons up and arranged a load of shot glasses with weird green liquor. My niece kept texting me to find out if we were ready and I had to say, *'no, keep her out for a bit longer'*. I was to let her know when she could bring Patricia home. We had also managed to acquire an old bridal gown from my friend at work and had lots of silly masks and a bouquet made up with flowers from my garden.

Once we were all set I let my niece know and told her they could come home. The three bridesmaids and I were full of giggles knowing what we were about to do. I watched for my sister in law driving up the road and we all took up action stations. The bridesmaids were in the hall waiting for Patricia to walk through the door armed with party poppers. I was primed in the lounge with the dress at the ready. The balloons on the door were designed to let her know that something was afoot. When she walked through the door the bridesmaids showered her with the confetti from the poppers and my sister in law blocked the door so she couldn't make a run for it. They man-handled her into the lounge and I grabbed her and dressed her in the dress, applied make up in a hideous manner with bright red lipstick. Then we made her wear huge black spectacles and a veil that I had made with a net curtain and hair band and gave her the lovely garden bouquet to hold. All the time there were screams of laughter. Poor girl didn't know what had hit her. Then the best part of all ….. we told her that we were going to walk her around all the local pubs in the area!

'No! Not dressed like this,' she said!

'Oh yes,' came the chorus from the hijackers. So we all drank a shot of green liquor and dragged her somewhat unwillingly outside. The bridesmaids led her down the road and me and my two sisters-in-law followed behind. My other sister-in-law had arrived half way through the hijack. It was brilliant, all the cars were tooting at her and children in the street were signing 'here comes the bride'.

We got to the first pub and made her walk in first. The people sitting there were in awe of it all, guys were asking for a kiss from the bride. She was mortified but it added to the hilarity. We all had a drink there and headed off to the next one, meanwhile we made her go

207

into the local off licence and buy another bottle of liquor but this time it was blue!
She asked. 'What do you want me to do that for?'
'All will become clear later,' we said. Then on to the next pub, we decided just to make it the two as her friends were to meet us there at 7 pm and time was running short.
So back up the road to more toots and jeers. At one point Patricia and Louise did a waltz mimicking the first dance at a wedding. I thought I was going to die laughing.
We got to the next pub where some more of her friends were waiting. Unfortunately they had not been able to make it in time to take part in the bridal parade but they did enjoy watching her walk up the road. We stayed there for about an hour and had another couple of drinks, again people were saying how lovely she was…… the sarcasm was running wild.
Other friends were starting to arrive at the house so we left the pub and set off for home. All the girls brought a bottle of something with them as Patricia had 'written bring a bottle' on the invitations. By 8pm the house was full of females and from there on in it just got worse or better depending how you look at it. There was so much alcohol that we could have put the pub out of business! It flowed like water and the girls had made vodka jelly to so there was alcohol in liquid and solid form!
Of course there was also food; we had to use that to absorb the copious amounts of drink. Once Patricia was suitably intoxicated we pulled another trick on her. This is where the bottle of blue liquor came into play. A few days before I had asked Kayvan some questions about himself, for example: his favourite colour, favourite movie, so now Patricia had to answer the questions. We sat her on a chair in the middle of the room and we all sat around her, each armed with a question and a shot of blue liquor! The rules were simple! Someone would

ask her a question; if she got it wrong she had to drink the shot, if she got it right the person asking the question had to drink it. Of course because she had already been plied with alcohol her mind was cloudy, so she ended up drinking 80% of the shots! Then we played Twister! What a riot that turned out to be. I was standing watching the antics and as I watched I noticed that most of the girls who were in contortions on the mat were showing a bit of their bottom, so I decided to drop cold drink on them, the screams were deafening. However when it was my turn they sought revenge and they poured a glass of drink down my jeans and I looked as if I had wet myself! The night went on and they played with a Wii that someone had brought. All the time the music was blaring and people were singing and dancing. Some of them ended up in the garden trying to fit themselves into Cameron's toy car and bouncing on his trampoline. My niece who is a police woman phoned one of her colleagues to come up and pretend to be a stripper! This was the one thing I knew Patricia would not like - she had told me on more than one occasion. However a prank was not out of the question! As it turns out no one was available to help play the prank on her because it was a Saturday night and they are always busy.

Eventually things began to calm down, people were leaving and I was exhausted. Then I heard a shout form the hall, 'what is going on now,' I thought. I went to the door to see a policeman standing there! Oh dear, I was not sure what to do, I was cheeky enough to ask if he was a real police officer or a stripper. I thought maybe one of her friends had arranged it. The officer was not very pleased with me and advised that he was in fact a genuine police officer. I had to explain that it was my niece that had probably called to play a trick on Patricia. Fortunately he took it in good spirit. Phew!

When James and Kayvan came home, having been at James' brother's house for the evening, in order to avoid us mad women, they both took one look at the chaotic scene and retreated to their bedrooms to hide. Not for long as it transpires as Patricia and some of her friends went upstairs and jumped on poor Kayvan who by this time was in bed.

About an hour later people began to leave. When the last one had left, I looked at the place and thought that I would face the clearing up to the next day. One of Patricia's friends, Raquel, was staying overnight. Raquel was a friend that Patricia had made when she first joined the cruise ships and was friends with her and Kayvan. She worked in the spa and was also a beauty therapist. Raquel had offered her services for the wedding and was going to do the make up for Patricia the bridesmaids and me. She refused to take any money, I thought that it was such a kind gesture that James and I told her that we would pay for her to stay at the hotel the night of the wedding as a thank you. So she slept on the floor of the lounge on an airbed, not the best or nicest place to sleep but it was the only thing available. The poor lass, she was surrounded by remnants of party poppers and balloons not to mention photos. I tidied up the food and glasses so at least she wasn't lying on them or surrounded by them! We all went off to bed and agreed that it had been a party to remember.

The next morning was just as expected, there were sore heads and everyone was feeling a bit fragile. The house had to be brought back to normal so armed with clothes and a vacuum cleaner we all got stuck in and sorted the place out and then spent the rest of the day slumped in front of the television.

So that was that, now we had to finish putting the flat in order as Carol and Mick were due to arrive from Canada for the wedding in two weeks. I finished the doors and the last of the painting was done. As I was still off work I spent a day in the flat with Kayvan and waited for the men to arrive to lay the new carpets. That was to be the final touch. Once they were down Patricia and Kayvan could finally move in.

We then started moving furniture in and wedding presents began to arrive and everything got put into its place. Things were now reaching a crescendo.

The flowers had arrived and they looked fantastic. There were buttonholes, Patricia's bouquet and a garland of Jasmine. Patricia had read somewhere that it was an Indonesian tradition that the mother of the bride should welcome the groom to the family by presenting him with a garland of flowers so that was to be my part in the ceremony.

The bridesmaids went to the dressmaker and were measured for any alterations that had to be made to their dresses and of course to have the tulle and the black ribbon removed so all that was left was a red dress. It was amazing that not too much in the way of alterations were needed. Louise's dress was the main one because after having a baby her shape had changed. The problem was that she had just stopped breast feeding Jack so her breasts were engorged and sore. The dressmaker had said that if it was not right she could easily take in another nip or tuck if needed so to try it on again a few days before the wedding just to make sure it fitted properly.

Then Mel and I went to the hairdressers to have a trial style done for the big day. All I knew was that I wanted my hair tied up away from my face, no particular style in mind. Then they were going to see what style would best suit the bridesmaids. Mel's hair was the shortest so that is why she was chosen to go for the trial. No matter what they did to her hair they knew they could do the same for the other two. It turned out that mine was fine but Patricia didn't like what they had done to Mel's hair. The shape was OK but she didn't like the bits that they had left sticking out.

'It makes her look like the Statue of Liberty,' she said. 'If they can do it without the protruding bits then that would be nice.'

A few days later I went through it all again with Patricia. She had seen a style in the Indonesian bridal magazine that she had brought back with her and she wanted to see if the hairdresser could copy it. She had brought back an Indonesian head dress which was simple but stunning. It looked like a hand and each finger of the hand had diamante detail on it, this was on a comb and when placed in her hair the hand would cup the side of her head giving a lovely display of diamonds on one side. The hairdresser commented on the head dress saying *'she had never seen anything like it before.* They tried their best to copy the style but it was impossible. So she ended up with a load of curls, the one thing she didn't want.

'Every bride does that,' she said, 'and I don't want to look like everyone else!'

We also had to go to the registry office and register the marriage. This caused some confusion as Kayvan mother only has one name - not all Indonesians have surnames. She also had to provide his Visa and proof that he was allowed to marry. Back at the car she was so annoyed that she drove home in record time.

'What will it be like on the day?' she said, 'I am going to look hideous,' referring to her hair. 'I don't know if I want them to do my hair on the day.'

'I am afraid we don't have much choice,' I said, 'it is only a small village and there are not many hairdressers there. 'It will be ok.' I said trying to convince her, 'it is only a trial remember!' I thought I had convinced her and that everything was under control, but no, panic setting in.

Things were moving at a pace and I could hardly keep up. Patricia and Kayvan had to go and meet the Registrar and agree on what was to be said and the Registrar had to scrutinise any readings. There was not to be any mention of religion as it was a civil ceremony

Then we all had to go to the hotel and sort out final arrangements. We had decided to take the whole hotel over for the day. That way no one else would be allowed in. The last thing we wanted was for their special day to be invaded by uninvited people. We had all the bedrooms booked and had to allocate people to the ones that were most suitable for their needs. We arranged table decorations and all the small details as this was to be our last visit there before the wedding. The manager had asked if we were going to name the tables so that when guests were looking for their seats they would know what table to go to. In a flash of inspiration I suggested calling the tables after parts of the ship. So we decided that the top table would be called *'The Captain's Table'* the rest were named after the restaurants and decks of the ship that they met on. We had arranged for the DJ, and although he was an older man he seemed to know what he was talking about. He had asked that we send him details of the music we wanted and if there was anything specific so he would have it there.

On our way home we went through everything: dresses, check, rings, check, flowers check, the list continued all the way home. This is when it dawned on us all that the wedding was imminent. One week to go and it would be here.

All we had to do now was to pick Carol and Mick up from the airport the next day.

So James and I went to the airport to meet my sister and her husband. We had a good laugh in the car catching up and telling them all about the arrangements for the wedding.

'Well put it this way,' I said, 'if we have missed something it is too late now'.

The next night we were invited to Patricia and Kayvan's for dinner. Kayvan was going to cook a traditional Indonesian meal for us, but first we had to go to town as Carol and Mick had arranged to pick up a hire car for the duration of their stay. Mick got behind the wheel and said he would follow James and I back home. He had forgotten what it was like to drive a car with a manual gear shift as he only drives automatics in Canada.

'That was eventful,' said Carol as she got out the car. 'A white knuckle ride to say the least.'

'Don't worry,' I said, 'I will be driving tonight when we go out so you will be alright'.

We spent the rest of the afternoon chatting and hearing tales of my nieces, nephew and their children. The time flew by and before we knew it, it was time to go for dinner. It was delicious chicken with noodles and rice and crunchy stir fried vegetables. It was great to have an evening off without running round organising things.

It was now Sunday evening and the wedding was only six days away. On the Monday morning Mick came down stairs and said he wasn't feeling very well. Before I knew what was happening he was as sick as a dog. He spent all day vomiting and by the evening James had joined him. I had to go to the photographer with Patricia and Kayvan as I had to make part of the payment before the big day so I left Carol looking after the men. I told Patricia and Kayvan about Mick and James and Kayvan thought it had been his cooking the night before. However, as it turned out there was a virus doing the rounds and they had fell victim to it.

The next day there was some bad news, my uncle who lived down south had died and the funeral was to be the day before the wedding. Then to add insult to injury Patricia had come down with the virus too and she was being sick. It had been on the news that this virus was a menace and running rife. *That's all we need, the bride and father of the bride down with sickness and diarrhoea,* I just kept my fingers crossed that I wouldn't get it to, and the wedding was to close.

The day after James and Mick began to feel better so it had been decided that James and Carol would go down south on the Thursday evening for the funeral on the Friday then come back home on the Friday evening. Mick said he would stay with me and help me with the wedding arrangements. James had been saying how nervous he was about the speech.
'I know I will cry,' he said, 'I am absolutely dreading it.'
'You know,' said Carol, 'they say that if you rehearse it in front of people then you are not as nervous on the day as whoever listens to it will give you feedback. So if you want Mick and I will be your audience, what do you think?'
They ran the idea past me and I said.
'Sounds like a good idea. I will print if off for you and you can have a trial.'
I printed it off and handed it to James.
'If you don't mind I will leave the room, I want to hear it read for the first time at the wedding.'
So I went to the kitchen and washed some dishes and kept out of the way. About fifteen minutes later I was told that the coast was clear so I returned to the lounge.
'Well, how was it, did you keep your composure?'

'Emm not quite but it was not as bad as I thought I would be.'
Mick and Carol agreed that it was a good speech and heartfelt for sure. 'I have told Mick that if I start to buckle on the day he has to heckle me, that way it will distract me and I won't cry,' said James.
'You know best,' I said, I turned to Mick and said, 'heckle him nicely,' we all laughed.
Thursday came along and James and Carol went away leaving the rest of us with things to do. Fortunately Patricia was feeling better but still looked a bit peaky - talk about cutting it fine!

Josh meanwhile was doing fine. He had been started on Immuno Suppressants for his Crohn's disease and they seemed to be helping. Apparently these drugs are used for people who have had organ transplants and for some reason seemed to help people with Crohn's. His weight had stabilised to so all looking good. I had made sure that he was not really involved with the wedding; I didn't want him running around like the rest of us. All he had to do was put the finishing touches to his speech and that was enough. He sent it to me in an email once it was finished and it was great. Another thing out the way.

That evening Kayvan and I spent the time rolling the menus I had printed into scrolling. To make sure they were all the same size I used my rolling pin from the kitchen. That caused a laugh with all of us. I would roll them around the pin and Kayvan would tie the white ribbon with their names on it around them. Then we placed them carefully in a big Perspex box that I had bought so they didn't get damaged. As he tied them off he would look at the name and say, 'who is this?' He had met all the family by now but there were still lots of names for him to remember, so this was good for him to put descriptions to the names of the people who were going to share in his special day.

Patricia and I then went upstairs to the main computer and we put music onto CD for the ceremony and the first dance. Then she made up a DVD of photographs of Kayvan's family and said.
'They won't be there in person but they will be there spirit.'
Then she added pictures of their life together on the ship, really the story of how they met and fell in love. This was to be played on the DVD in the bar between the ceremony and the meal and looped so that it played all day.
'This will give my family the chance to see his family,' she said.
'What a lovely touch and Kayvan will be pleased.'
She left the room for a few minutes and came back with a CD case and said.
'I got this from Kayvan's friend Gusti when I was there.'
'If it had been possible Gusti would have been Kayvan's best man,' she said, 'but as he can't come he made this.
'I think we should watch it what do you think?'
'OK,' I said, 'load it up'. I will guard the door to make sure no one comes in.'
We watched it in silence, the tears rolled down my cheeks as it was a personal tribute to Kayvan and Patricia and how in love they were. Every word pulled another heart string. Patricia looked up at me and smiled as she saw the tears cascading down my cheeks.
'Lovely,' I said, 'just lovely. We can play that after the meal. All we have to do is get Josh to announce it after his speech; we won't tell Kayvan about it, it will be a nice surprise.'

There were a few things organised to make this wedding special, and the music was part of it. Patricia had said that she wanted people to ask 'what was the significance of that and why is that happening'. So lots of things were being kept very secret. I made a quick call to Josh and told him to add another few lines to his speech.

Patricia and Kayvan's friend Bex arrived from London; she was another friend that they made while on board. As none of Kayvan's family were going to be at the wedding, as it was too expensive they had agreed that some of the friends they had made on the ship that lived in the UK would be invited and that would be his family, as it were. So there was to be Raquel, Bex and Milly, others had been invited but for various reasons couldn't make it. Milly had decided that as she was coming up she would bring her mother with her and treat it as a holiday so we invited her Mum to the wedding too. These collectively were known as the 'shippies'! The table they were to sit at was called 'The Crew Bar' after all that is where they spent most of their time when they had finished their shifts.

Chapter 19

Friday morning - let the fun begin. Mick and I went to the supermarket to buy food and beer for the guys who were staying overnight at our house as us women were going to stay overnight at the hotel so we would be fresh and ready to go to have our hair done in the morning. James was going to drop Carol off on the way back from the funeral. Then we went to pick up the wedding cake and drove home with the precious cargo secured in the boot of the car. I was pointing out any pot holes as one bump could cause chaos. We pulled up outside the house and ever so carefully lifted the two tiers and slowly carried them into the kitchen. By this time Patricia had arrived so she and Mick went to pick up the wedding dress that had been hidden from everyone at my nephew's house. By the time they got back Louise, Mel and Kelly had arrived as we were to go to the hotel later in the afternoon. Mick and Patricia came in carrying her dress which was covered by a protective carrier, so still no one could see it. They had picked up Bex on the way home. The level of excitement was increasing by the minute. We all had a spot of lunch and then made a final check to make sure that we had everything before heading off. Patricia had bought her bridesmaids earrings and necklaces as gifts and as they were not wearing flowers in their hair she had bought diamante hair slides I had put them in nice presentation bags. We also had to take the candles; this is what her bridesmaids were to carry instead of flowers, again another Indonesian tradition. Then of course there were shoes, dresses, the fascinator for my hair which I had made to match the colour of my dress, changes of clothes, CDs, our DVD player, the box of menus and as Patricia and Kayvan were leaving for their honeymoon we had to make sure she had all the stuff they needed for that too. The honeymoon was not to be a fancy affair, anything but, they were going camping on the Isle of Mull, so you can imagine the amount of stuff they needed.

I ran upstairs and got the gifts that we had bought in Spain for the ushers and left them on the table in the kitchen all nicely wrapped in silver paper. I knew they were joining the guys that evening so this was the chance for Kayvan to give the presents to them. I knew Josh was getting a gold chain from Kayvan for being his best man, but that was for him to deal with at the right time. I then went into my bedroom as I had printed of check lists for James so that nothing was left to chance. I could not bear the idea of something being missed, not at this stage. There was not much for them to do really, the list read: kilts, change of clothes, speeches and RINGS!!!!

Then as I knew Kayvan was very nervous I had typed a letter to him explaining the whole event and the timetable of what was about to unfold the next day, I was not sure if Patricia had explained it to him so again I was leaving nothing to chance.

I told him how proud I was to have him as a son in law and that I knew he would take care of our precious daughter. As his Mum would not be there I told him that I would be his second Mum and if he wanted anything I was here for him. I told him how proud I was that he had left his family and country to move here and how he had settled in so well. I left it in his bed so that he would find it before he went to sleep for the last time as a single man.

We loaded up the three cars Mick's, Mel's and Kelly's and made sure that all was in place. I drove with Mick with the dresses in the back and nothing else as we could not afford for anything to damage them. Patricia went with Mel, Patricia nursing one tier of the cake and

Bex nursing the other. Louise went with Kelly to keep her company. Off we went in convoy, one car following the other. We all looked out for each other on the way, making sure no one got lost so that we would all arrive about the same time.

Whilst all this was going on Josh and Kayvan went to pick up the kilts. They were waiting for us to text them to tell them that the coast was clear as the bride and groom were not to see each other now until the wedding!!

We got to the hotel in one piece and went in to be shown our rooms. We had decided that Louise and Patricia would share a room, that way when Josh arrived to stay on the Saturday Patricia would have moved to the bridal suite, Kelly and Mel would share a room and I would share with Carol. Carol would have a room on the Saturday with Mick and James would join me. The rooms are all stunning and they all had everything you could want. Mick made sure everything was OK then went back home. He was looking forward to an evening in with the boys. It had been arranged that they would have drinks there and there was to be about eight of them. James, Mick, Josh and Kayvan were all staying in our house so that no one was left alone. Especially Kayvan who was now a bundle of nerves!

Mel was feeling a bit squeamish so they went off into the village to find a chemist and while they were there they had a look around and see if there was somewhere for us to eat. They found a nice little pub that served meals so we went down and had a drink and waited for Raquel who was driving over from Ayr. We thought it was best to wait for her and we would all eat together, except, of course Carol, who was now on her way back from the funeral with James. We were all so hungry that we couldn't wait for her to arrive.

Raquel arrived soon after us so we ordered a couple of bottles of wine and had a nice meal. It was good to see her again. She was going to do a practice make up trial on Patricia and also do her nails.

After our meal we all went back to the hotel for an evening experimenting with make up. We had just got there when Carol arrived. She was tired and hungry as the journey had taken longer than expected due to the heavy traffic. As we were now in the hotel I ordered her a meal and sat with her while she ate. The girls had all gone upstairs to have the trials done. Carol told me all about the funeral and how my aunt understood why I hadn't gone but was surprised to see that she and James had taken the time out to go down. My brother, sister in law and family were also driving up that night and were staying in Dundee and our friends were following later, but they were staying in the village.

Once she had finished her meal we went upstairs see what was going on. On our way up we were passed by two of the bridesmaids, armed with shoes.
'Where are you off to with them?' I asked.
'We are going to wear them outside,' they said, 'so the soles will be scored. We don't want to slip on shiny soles with all the carpet about.'
'Good thinking girls, don't be long.'
'We have yours too,' and they produced the lovely high heeled golden sandals that I had bought.

When we got to the bedroom that Louise and Kelly were sharing, there were bodies everywhere. Patricia had had her makeup trial done and was pleased with it. Now she was taking the makeup off as Raquel was going to do her eyelash extensions next. Louise and I started wrestling with fake nails. My nails were actually OK but thought what the heck, nice longer nails would be nice so we started gluing the nails on. Unfortunately, we are not experts and it showed. The pair of us giggled our way through the escapade trying to find the right size for each finger, and then we painted them with a nice gold polish to match my lovely sandals.

'Right!' exclaimed Raquel, 'you and Louise over here I am going to tint your eyelashes it is so much better than mascara especially for the mother of the bride as no doubt you will cry buckets!'

So Louise and I took our positions lying on the floor letting Raquel work her magic. We lay there for ages waiting for the tint to work and then afterwards had to remove the surplus tint with cotton wool. Once we were finished it was Patricia's turn, she was having false eyelashes applied and extensions put in too. It was Patricia's turn to take position on the floor. Just as Raquel was about to put the first lash on the lights went out! We were all left in darkness. I went to the hall and it was dark too. The hotel had suffered a power cut! Patricia went to the window and it was not just the hotel but the whole village that was in darkness. Fantastic! What now? No sooner were the words out our mouths and a member of the hotel staff arrived with candles.

'Sorry Patricia I can't do this by candle light,' said Raquel.

So we ended up sitting in the hallway by which time the emergency lighting had kicked in. What a bonny sight, we just laughed about it as there was nothing much else we could do. We ordered a bottle of wine; as Patricia was getting a bit flustered.

She said, 'This is marvellous, now my hair will be a disaster, my dress won't fit properly because I have lost a few pounds with that sickness bug, my eyes won't be done, and I will look hellish.'

'At least your tan is ok,' I said.

I had previously applied a fake tan all over her.

'Look if it means doing things later then so be it, the lights won't be out for long.'

My phone tinkled, it was a message from Kayvan it read just one word……..*'HELP!'* I replied back, *'you ok Kayvan, Have the guys done something to you?'*

I had warned James not to let anything happen to Kayvan, it was usual for the guys to get together and maybe shave off an eyebrow or something, I was in a bit of a panic but had to stay calm so as not to cause Patricia any more anguish.

Too late, I heard an almighty scream of terror. Patricia had got a text form Josh saying that they had hijacked Kayvan to a strip club and now tied him to a lamppost outside the club.

'Mum!!!!!!!!!!!!!!! Do something!'

I rang James' mobile. He answered quickly.

'What the hell is going on there? I warned you not to let anything happen to Kayvan, where are you?'

I was talking so quickly and didn't know if James could even hear me as he was obviously in the club and the music was deafening.

'Hey babe,' he said, 'what's up? What's up?'

'I will give you what's up! Where is Kayvan? What have you done to him? James I swear if you have let things get out of hand tonight of all nights I will drive down right now and personally kill you!'

He began to laugh and the music abated.

'Nothing babe absolutely nothing, we had a bet of £10 to see how long it would take you to phone once you and Patricia got the messages. I won, I said 1 minute 30 seconds. So I am £10 better off!'

'You little sod,' I screamed.

I could here the rest of the boys laughing in the back ground.

'Good wind up eh?' I heard Josh shouting.

'Put Kayvan on the phone.' I ordered.

'Hi Mom,' he laughed down the phone. 'It's OK.'

I told Patricia that he was safe and in the house and told the group, who were still sitting in the hall, of the prank that had just been played.

'How is it going with you guys,' said James, who had now been handed the phone again.

'Are you having fun?'

'Fun is not quite the word we would use, we are sitting in darkness, and the whole village is in the dark.'

Well, that news just added to his laughter. He chuckled down the phone.

'So glad we are here and full of pizza and beer. Not too much beer of course I know the rules no hangovers for tomorrow!'

Just then the lights went back on, there was a cheer from the hall.

'Well got to go, we have so much to do before we go to bed. We still have to finish Patricia's eyes then her nails then we have to go down to see the layout for the ceremony tomorrow and if we don't like it we may have to change things.'

'Better let you get on then,' he said, 'enjoy yourself and we will see you tomorrow. Bye.'

I had to hand it to the guys, that was a cracking wind up. Even Patricia found it funny once she knew Kayvan was alright.

So it was back to beauty treatments, time was against us so Raquel had to make up for lost time. She worked like a demon; she did Patricia's eyes and nails and tidied up eyebrows of the rest of us. She was a marvel.

There was a knock at the door, 'come in,' we all shouted.

It was our friends who had driven up from England.

'Well don't you all look nice,' said Denise, 'we just thought we would pop in to see if you were having fun.'

We chatted for a few minutes and then they left with the parting shot to Patricia.

'See you tomorrow as a blushing bride'! *Reality kicked in, yes tomorrow was the big day and we still had things to do.*

Then Raquel and Bex went to the B&B that they were staying at for a well earned rest. The rest of us went downstairs to meet the manager who was arranging furniture for the ceremony. We decided that as the restaurant area was to be used for the ceremony and the meal that the dance floor should be put in place first then the chairs placed on it for the ceremony. Then after the ceremony it would be set up for the meal, and after the meal the tables would be cleared and the dance floor would then already be in position.

We walked in to find the dance floor in place and the seats arranged, but Louise said.
'There's not enough room between the chairs for the aisle. If your dress has a full skirt you will have to walk down behind your Dad instead of beside him!'
Patricia and Louise had a practice walk down the aisle. There was Patricia imagining that she had her wedding dress on and Louise trying to making herself look bigger width wise as she is somewhat slimmer than James. Sure enough, the chairs were too close. So we got our thinking caps on and tried to resolve the problem. The manager was not best pleased with us as we didn't agree with his plans.
Carol piped up, 'Well it is not your day, is it? So if Patricia is not happy then you will have to change it won't you?'
She said what I was thinking, she is not a lady to be argued with, and so the chairs were moved to make a wider aisle. Then we sorted out where the CD player would be and the speakers so that people could hear the music. I handed over the box with the menus and DVD to the manager who assured me they would be

kept safe in his office. Next was a practice run of walking down the aisle, me first and then standing to the left, followed by Louise standing to the right, Kelly next standing to the left and finally Mel standing to the right. 'Not too fast now, keep it nice and easy, it's not a race,' I said.

With everything in place, we were happy to go back upstairs and try to get some sleep. *We had to look our best for tomorrow, then I realised it was tomorrow, it was 1 am!*

Chapter 20

I got up early and had a shower closely followed by Carol. When she went in the shower I went and knocked on the doors to wake the bridesmaids and of course the bride! They were already awake and full of biz. 'Remember girls, don't wash your hair,' I reminded them.

We had been told not to wash our hair for two days as it was easier to handle when it wasn't shampoo soft.

'We will meet you in the bar for breakfast in an hour; we have to be at the hairdressers at 9 am.'

We met as arranged and had a hearty breakfast we had to make sure our energy levels were up. Louise could hardly eat a thing.

'I am so nervous I don't know how you can eat Patricia,' she said.

Patricia was getting stuck into cereal and a full cooked breakfast. Louise had tea and toast and even that was a struggle for her. The rest of us got stuck in and enjoyed being waited on.

The assistant manager came over to me and asked if she could have a quiet word with me.

'Sure, is there a problem?' I asked.

'No not a problem,' she said.

Firstly she explained that the manager who had been there the night before was not going to be there for the wedding and it had been passed to her to deal with. I felt a moment of panic setting in. *What if she doesn't know all the plans?*

'My name is Denise,' she said, 'now don't worry everything will be fine I have done this many times.'

She showed me to the area where the ceremony was to be and explained that when she had seen it she had not been happy so she had re-arranged it again. She had worked wonders, there was so much room and the dance floor had been made bigger.

'I don't know what he was thinking about when he did that,' she said, 'but I was not letting it go so I hope you don't mind me changing things.'
She was on the ball, my fears allayed.
'Now,' she said, 'did you bring your final figures for the meals?'
'No I gave them to the manager last week.'
'Oh dear, I don't have them,' she said.
'Not a problem.' I picked up the phone and called James.
The details were all held on my PC so all he had to do was print them off and bring them with him, I asked him to bring the seating arrangements too. Nothing was going to go wrong; I had spent too much time on this for it to go wrong on the day. I told her that the details she needed would be here by 12.30 when James, Kayvan, Josh and Mick would arrive.
'Is that enough time,' I said, 'if not he can email it to you.'
'No 12.30 is fine I just want to make sure all goes according to plan.'
She had her finger on the pulse thankfully.
James told me that there was a slight problem there too.
'Oh,' I asked, 'what is wrong?'
'It is Josh,' he said, 'his medication has made his knees lock and he has cramp in his legs.'
'Oh my God, is he ok,' I asked.
'He is fine. Once he got moving it eased off but he is not comfortable.'
'Poor kid, there is nothing we could do about it. I just hope he is alright.'
'Don't worry I am here to look after him.'
'How is Kayvan, is he ok?'
'He is a bit tearful, he got your letter and I think it has brought it all home to him. So I made him phone his Mum and he had a nice long talk with her.'

'Poor soul if only we could have got his Mum here it would have been perfect.'

'I know but as we discussed earlier you had the brain wave too late to give us time to arrange a Visa for her. He will be OK, don't worry.'

'OK, look after the pair of them and I will see you all when you get here.'

After breakfast we went into the hair salon and there was a bevy of hairdressers waiting to tend to us. I was first, we discussed what she was going to do and I was happy to let her do what she thought was best. I explained that I was wearing a fascinator and that I did not want any bits of hair left down, then I let her do her magic. Patricia was sitting beside me and the hairdresser began to put the curls in her hair, pinning sections and curling sections using different sizes of tongs for a better effect. As her hair was so long it took two hairdressers to curl it. The bridesmaids were waiting in turn to be done. There hair was to consist of a bun (with no bits sticking out) but set off centre of their heads, not at the back and the hair slides with the diamante were to sit just above the bun - nothing elaborate, plain and simply elegant.

We took the opportunity to take photos of each person whilst they were having their hair done. My hair was swept up from my face and combed back to give it height, then the back was a mass of pinned curls. I looked dreadful as I had no makeup on and I was pale because of the lack of sleep, but the hair was nice. They were still working on Patricia's hair. As soon as Mel, Louise and I were finished we went back to the hotel where Raquel was waiting with her box of tricks to apply our make up. Again I was first; she spent time choosing the colours for my eyes that would compliment my dress. By the time she had finished I looked amazing, a different person from the one I had just seen in the hairdresser, thankfully.

Then Mel, followed by Louise, by this time Patricia, Kaz and Carol had arrived. Patricia's hair was lovely; one side had been given height then smoothed over to bring a beautiful cascade of curls down her right shoulder. The diamante headdress was placed on the smooth side, giving her a gorgeous sparkle, again simply elegant. She looked absolutely drop dead gorgeous.

Raquel did her makeup and chose smokey colours to compliment the dark shoes that the bridesmaids were going to wear.

Everyone was done, hair and makeup, so now we had to move from one room to another before any guests started to arrive. It was safer and easier to get dressed in the bridal suite, Patricia and I had already hung her dress in there, still not wanting anyone to see it until the last minute. So we moved everything over in relays, making sure that we had all the bits and pieces we needed. Once we were there, there was no going back; no one had to see us before we wanted them to.

'Look at my hair,' said Patricia, 'is it my imagination or are the curls falling. It just looks like one massive curl now.'

'Bloody hell you are right.'

Patricia phoned the hairdresser and explained what had happened.

'OK, I will be there in two minutes,' she said.

I went downstairs and there was the girl who had done Patricia's hair pulling up in her car. She got out and ran up the stairs towards me.

'Thanks,' I said, 'I will take you up to her.'

I turned to find Mel at my back.

'Come on,' she shouted, 'this way'.

So she took the girl upstairs. She was armed with tongs and hairspray.

'It won't move this time,' she said, as she bolted up the stairs.

I took the opportunity to have a cigarette and go and make sure everything was OK with Denise. By the time I had done this the hairdresser had performed a miracle and brought Patricia's hair back to the way it had been previously.

'Thanks again,' I said.

'No problem,' she said, 'all part of the service'

Time was marching on, the ceremony was to start at 1.30 pm, and it was now noon. I got Carol to go and order a bottle of wine, one glass would be nice just to steady nerves but not enough to dull the moment. We spent the next few minutes sipping a nice bottle of Rose, then all of a sudden we heard it....

I had arranged for a friend from work to play the bagpipes for the quests arriving, this was him warming up. We ran to the window to see him. He was wearing a green kilt and jacket. Then we noticed that the two flag poles at the entrance to the hotel were flying The Scottish Saltire on one and the Indonesian flag on the other. I had supplied the flags and was pleased to see that they had not been forgotten. We began to get dressed shortly after that, Patricia was deliberately holding back till the last minute, keeping her dress secret for as long as possible.

James phoned me.

'We are about five minutes away,' he said. 'We have stopped to put ribbons on the car.'

He thought it was best to do it that way instead of driving on the motorway decked with ribbons just in case they came off and obscure Mick's vision, we didn't want any accidents.

'So they are on their way,' I told everyone, 'only 5 minutes away.'

Right enough, a few minutes later we heard a car pull up and we all dashed to the window peeking out so as not to be seen. There they all were and they all looked so handsome in full highland dress.

'Awwwwww,' said Patricia, 'look at Kayvan in his kilt he looks fabulous.'

'Enough,' I said, 'you are not meant to see him until the ceremony.'

I made sure the curtains were closed and told everyone that no one was to near them again.

Louise was dressing now and she looked perplexed. 'Everything ok,' I asked? 'I think I have the wrong dress on as this on is too big at the bust.'

We checked the dresses and found that whilst she did have the right dress, because she stopped feeding Jack her bust had reduced and now it was too big for her.

'What now, I can't go out like this; I will fall out of it!'

I shouted for Carol. I don't know why but I had packed my sewing box so I asked Carol to make a nip and tuck to the dress. She used to be a dressmaker when she was younger. She looked at it and said.

'I don't have time to do it properly, but what I can do is stitch it to your bra Louise.'

So poor Louise was sewn into her dress but at least she was comfortable and the dress looked fine.

I was now dressed and after the panic with Louise I asked Carol to put my fascinator in place.

'Right now that is everything done here I had better go and get myself dressed.'

'OK thanks Carol we would have been lost without you.'

Bex and Raquel left at the same time,

'It is time we got ready too,' they said, and left with the chorus of, 'see you at the alter.'

They were both staying over at the hotel so they didn't have to go far; they had moved all their belongings from the bed and breakfast earlier. Now it was time to dress Patricia. I went to the wardrobe where we had been hiding the dress and carefully brought it into full view. The three bridesmaids gasped as they saw her dress for the first time.

'It is beautiful,' they said in perfect harmony, 'and so are you Patricia.'

'Right girls,' I said, 'as bridesmaids it is up to you to do the finishing touches'.

Just then my phone went again, James said.

'When are you coming down to see me, I have the numbers and seating plans as you asked and I don't know what to do with them.'

'I will be down in a minute.'

I went to the mirror and applied my lipstick. It was the kind that lasts all day so I would not have to worry about applying it again. I topped it off with lip gloss and turned to Patricia who by now was standing in her underwear.

'Mum you look absolutely stunning,' she said with a hint of pride in her voice.

'Thanks sweetheart but I have to dash down stairs and see your Dad, he has paper work for me to deal with.'

I went down stairs to find James; he was in the bar with the ushers, Josh and Kayvan. Luckily he was the only one who saw me. He looked at me in a strange way and walked across the room with a smile from ear to ear.

'Wow! All I can say is Wow! You look absolutely fantastic, and he bent over and placed a sweet kiss on my cheek.'

'Thank you,' I said, 'if you think this is good wait until you see Patricia. You look amazing too, I must say and I am glad you insisted on the plaids, it adds a dash of class. Now come with me and I will introduce you to Denise.'

We headed for the restaurant to find Denise, she was just as I expected looking over the seating and doing final checks.

'Denise,' I said, 'this is James the proud father of the bride and he has brought the figures and seating plan for you.'

He handed them over and she checked to make sure everything was in order.

'That's great,' she said, 'I will get my staff organised now. What do you think of the way I have set things out now?' she asked

'It is just as we want it,' I said. The aisle was wide enough, the table was in place for the registrar and on it were placed four large thick candles and the flames flickered brightly.

'There are meant to be seven candles aren't there?' asked Denise, 'but I was only given four.'

'Yes indeed but it will become clear later,' I said. 'Don't worry it is perfect.'

The table was covered in a lovely crisp linen table cloth and to either side stood pedestals on the tops were beautiful red floral decorations that we had borrowed from the hotel. James gave me another glance and just muttered, 'stunning, just stunning.'

'I have to go now,' I said, 'and see how things are going upstairs.'

'Good timing,' he said, 'the coach has just pulled up with the guests.'

I knew things would be OK as James was overseeing downstairs. The ushers had taken their places and were guiding people to the photographer, and then to the bar for a welcome drink.

James had set up his camera in the entrance as he wanted pictures of everyone sitting in the Scottish seat in the entrance hall.

'This would be so different,' he said, 'so Sean if you can grab people as they pass and take some photos that would be great.'

James' nephew's wife appeared with a helium filled balloon with the words *'Just Married'* written across it.

'I will give this to Patricia and Kayvan later,' she said, 'our daughter insisted we bring it.'

She was first to have the picture taken in the Scottish chair with Neville and the balloon!

Meanwhile I walked to the bridal suite and knocked on the door.

'It's only me,' I cried.

So the door opened and there stood Patricia, with the dress on and she looked amazing. *Oh my goodness, I felt my lip tremble as I saw her for the first time.* I had never seen such a beautiful bride, she was glowing and absolutely radiant. The hair was perfect, the dress beautiful, and the makeup flawless and nails just the right length. She was standing semi profile; it was a picture to behold. Now the bouquet, Mel handed her the flowers made up of lilies, jasmine and thistles and the picture was complete. In the back ground the piper continued to play and it added to the moment.

The ushers were now seating guests in the restaurant in anticipation for the arrival of the bride and groom. My phone rang and James told us that the photographer was ready for the bridesmaids and me; we had to go down and leave Patricia on her own. This was her time to check herself over and prepare for the biggest day in her life. We left her and told her that one of us would call when the photographer was ready for her. Downstairs we were greeted by James who gave us all the once over.

'You all look great,' he said. 'Now off you go and have your photos taken.'

A little voice spoke up and said.

'Hi grandma,' it was Cameron dressed in his kilt and jacket, exactly the same as his Daddy, granddad and Kayvan. He looked so cute.

'Come on,' I said, 'come and have your picture taken with me and Mummy.'

He was more than willing to stand and pose with us which I thought was amazing as he is only two and a half after all.

'Now I need the bride,' said the photographer.

'I will give her a call,' I said and reached into my bag took out my mobile and phoned Patricia.

'Hi honey,' I said, 'this is your moment, come down and meet your Dad in one minute.'

We hurried back into the hotel and I sent James up stairs where he waited on the small landing which was three steps from the top. The bridesmaids, Cameron and I waited patiently at the bottom of the stairs. My eyes were fixed on James as he stood there so proudly waiting for his precious daughter to appear. He looked so gallant in his kilt of Brave Heart tartan, the co-ordinating blue jacket and plaid over his shoulder and the red rouched tie which he did not want to wear, he wanted bow ties but Patricia was adamant that she wanted a more modern look. He fiddled with his sporran and checked his buttonhole of a lily, jasmine and thistle which coordinated with her bouquet, making sure he looked right; he did not want to disappoint Patricia. He had to look perfect for her.

Then I saw the response, a gasp and a smile that would melt ice I knew he had seen Patricia approach. She stood at the top of the stairs and James reached out his hand to take hers and help her down the three stairs. I felt my eyes sting with tears and Kelly handed me a tissue. She was well prepared, she had tissues down the front of her dress and presented us all with one in turn. We dabbed our faces gently making sure not to disturb the make up that Raquel had applied earlier and watched the pair of them descend the staircase. The pair of them were beaming. They went outside and had photos taken. The bridesmaids and I had to prepare the candles that they were to carry and I retrieved the garland that I was going to present to Kayvan. I had put them in an antique dresser that was in the hallway.

I very quietly went to the door and looked at the guests they were sitting patiently and making small talk between themselves. I whispered to Sean, who was standing at the door, that it would not be long now. Sean was in control of the hi-fi system that was going to play the music for the ceremony. In the other entrance to the restaurant stood a white grand piano and placed on top of it stood the wedding cake, Denise had assembled it and there it stood proudly showing the red ribbon and the writing of *'I love you'* in both English and Indonesian – which made it stand out beautifully. Then I looked down the aisle, there was Kayvan and Josh, they looked calm and it looked like they were sharing a joke. They looked so smart and handsome. Things were all in place, I thought to myself. The registrar's assistant came up to me and told me that everyone was waiting and that they had another wedding to go to. We were running ten minutes late. Patricia and James returned and we knew this was it. SHOW TIME!

We were to come in through the hall, then through the hexagonal room and enter by the French doors, that way it was a straight approach to the table where the Registrar was waiting.

I was all set with the garland in my hand, I gave Sean the nod and he pressed the play button on the hi-fi, the

gentle sound of Mariah Carey singing *Thank God I Found You* began to soar. I reached down and asked Cameron for his hand. He was to walk down with me and help present the garland to Kayvan. He froze; he refused point blank to come with me. By this time people had turned round to see the procession. Louise stepped forward and said.
'He can come with me, don't worry, now go on and get this show on the road.'
I turned to a sea of faces; and walked down the aisle. After all my instructions to the bridesmaids I went down the aisle at a gallop as I had been knocked of my guard with Cameron's refusal to budge! I went straight to Kayvan and held his face in my hands kissed him gently on the cheek and welcomed him to my family. I then placed the garland of Jasmine round his neck and then stepped to the right, another mistake it should have been the left! Then came Louise and Cameron, Louise had here candle in one hand and hold of Cameron's hand with the other. He walked down beautifully with her and stood by her as she placed her candle alongside the four already in the table. Kelly came next followed by Mel they both placed their candles, so now there were seven and they formed the shape of an arrow. There was a slight pause and Mariah Carey faded out. Kayvan and Josh stepped forward and waited for Patricia and James to move forward. The music changed this time it was the Indonesian National Anthem that played and James and Patricia started their walk down the aisle. As they approached they looked at the guests and smiled at them all. Kayvan was wiping a tear from his eye, the emotion of seeing his bride and his national anthem playing had jolted him.

James gave Patricia a lovely smile and handed his beloved daughter over to Kayvan. She smiled back at him and turned to face Kayvan. They held each others hands. James looked at me and realised that I was at the wrong side so made me move over so that I could sit beside him. Even that didn't quite work out as I sat beside Josh who had to be nearer the bride and groom as he had to present the rings.

The Registrar began by welcoming everyone and gave details of the ceremony and explained that Kayvan and Patricia would be exchanging rings and the reason for a ring is that it is a symbol of love as it has no beginning and no end. The formalities that by law had to be done were out of the way, and now the ceremony would start.

'We are gathered here today to witness the marriage of Kayvan and Patricia but before I can go on I must ask,' she looked at Kayvan, 'are you Kayvan Augustin....?'
'...Yes,' he replied rapidly.
The guest tittered as the Registrar had not finished. She smiled sweetly at him.
'....are you Kayvan Augustin, residing at 47 Willow Terrace Dundee?'
'Yes,' he replied again.
She turned to Patricia.
'Are you Patricia Gilmore, also residing at 47 Willow Terrace Dundee.'
'Yes I am,' she said in a faint whisper.
Kayvan reached into his pocket and turned away from the guests and wiped tears from his eyes.

Next Bex came forward and read a passage that Kayvan and Patricia had written. There had been a last minute alteration to it as one line read *'they hope and pray'* that they would be together forever but the word 'pray' had to be removed as it had a religious connection. When Bex got to that line she looked at them both and smiled.

They turned again to face each other and they held both hands all the way through the ceremony. First Kayvan had to make his vows. He was worried about that part as he was not confident with his pronunciation, but Patricia held his hands and mouthed the words with him to give him encouragement. He was word perfect and the look of relief when it was all over spoke volumes. Then Patricia made her vows. Josh was then asked to produce the rings. He stepped forward and placed the rings on the table. I noticed that due to his illness that he had lost weight and was finding keeping the plaid in place difficult. He returned to his seat beside me. They exchanged their rings and to make sure that she got the correct hand Patricia stood side by side with Kayvan to work out which one was his left hand. *'She is more nervous than she looks I thought to myself.'*

'Can I have the witnesses now to sign the register?' Josh and I stepped forward. Kayvan signed first followed by Patricia then Josh. As I went to sign it I looked over to Patricia and whispered.

'Dad gave you away and now I am signing you over,' then I gave her a wink.

Then the Registrar said.

'By the powers invested in me I now pronounce you husband and wife.'

There was a ripple of applause from the guests seated behind us.

Time for more photographs, the registrars assistant made an announcement and said.

'It is a traditional Scottish tradition for the bride and groom to have pictures taken of their new wedding rings. So Kayvan, can I ask you to put your hand on top of Patricia's, making sure both rings can be seen.'

Kayvan placed his hand over Patricia's as requested, so that both rings were in view. Then the assistant said.

'Mark my words this will be the first and last time that Kayvan will have the upper hand.'

There was a burst of laughter through the room as all married couples knew he was right! People came up and took photos of them showing their new wedding bands. They then stood up, linked arm in arm and walked back up the aisle smiling at everyone. James and I followed them, then there was Kelly and Mel and finally Louise Josh and Cameron. The music playing was *'You're Just too Good to Be True'* by Andy Williams. This is a song that they used to sing to each other usually when they were parting so it was very appropriate.

We then all went outside for more photographs. Some of the guests had followed us outside and took advantage of the photographer's poses and copied his pictures.

James and I were elated that it was all over, our darling daughter was now married to the man she loved. We could not have been happier; all the worries were now behind us as far as visas etc were concerned. Patricia had married a lovely man and they looked so happy together. The smiles were as wide as I had ever seen. All the upsets they had had in the early days were banished, now they had their lives to live together never to be apart again. James and I were having a celebratory dance in the grounds of the hotel, we stood facing each other and hands gyrating in front and hips swinging. James' kilt was swaying and we must have looked a sight, but I saw the flash of a camera and yes, someone had taken the opportunity of a photograph. 'One for the album,' we said and we laughed out loud. We were called again for more photos but this time in the garden at the rear of the hotel. The bridesmaids were helping Patricia with her dress making sure it did not get dirty as she made her way along the path at the side of the hotel. There were screams of laughter from them all as they made their way to the lovely hedgerow. Guests were enjoying the sights of the bride and groom and sipping wine and eating canapés.

All the men were asked to gather for a photo; all but three men were wearing kilts so it was a spectacular scene. Then the ladies; we all stood in formation with Patricia in the centre. The photographer looking for an informal result asked us all to shout the word 'sex' which we did with great gusto.

Cameron and Jack were at one of the BBQ tables in the garden and Cameron took the opportunity to check what money was in his small sporran. Traditionally people had been generous enough to give them pennies so he was checking them out, not that he hads the faintest idea of money but he liked the look of it all, a typical Scots Man! Meanwhile in the Whiskey bar of the hotel the DVD Patricia had compiled was playing. The photographs of Indonesia and their life on board was a sight to behold. Patricia had said that in the other wedding they been to there had been a bit of a lull at this stage if the proceedings, so this was a great way of entertaining folk and giving them an inkling into Kayvan's life. My niece Nichole had brought her two small daughters to the wedding, they were little angels dressed in red and white, the theme of the day had spread through the guests too.

Cameron was smitten with the elder girl Blaine who is only eleven months his senior. They spent time running around after each other but Blaine was not happy until she had gotten a kiss from him. *Love was in the air without a doubt.*

All the time this was going on, the hotel staff were re-arranging the area that had been used for the ceremony back into a restaurant. I took a moment to sneak away and make sure everything was going to plan. The tables were to be arranged in a certain way and I was overseeing all this whilst the guests was busy elsewhere. The staff seemed to be having problems with the menus so I stepped in and helped put them where they should be, we then placed the candles that had been used in the ceremony as table decorations, spreading the light, as it were, throughout the guests. We put the fans that had been brought from Indonesia on each side plate, and then scattered confetti around each candle. The confetti had been bought specially and was in the shape of thistles, and within the thistles were the initials 'K & P'. Another 'favour' had been given to me by a friend and I was thrilled by her thoughtfulness. They were little bank notes, the stamp of the bank was again the initials 'K & P' and across the top read the words 'Bank of Indonesia'. In the corner was a picture of Patricia and Kayvan. A lovely memento for people to keep, I placed one in each wine glass. The names of the tables were now in place from 'The Captain's Table' to 'Turtle Cove' Patricia had picked this one deliberately for Cameron's table as he looked like a turtle when he was a baby. This was the name of the children's club on the ship they met on! I scrutinised the whole room, it was perfect.

I then returned to the garden to socialise with the guests. Everyone commented on how beautiful Patricia looked and how well Kayvan was coping with everything. 'The worst has yet to come,' I said 'that is the speeches.' All the guys are worried about it. None of them are used to public speaking, James is so worried in case he cries, Kayvan is worried in case no one understands him and Josh is just plain scared. *I am sure they will be ok but we will wait and see.*

I was given a nod from Denise that indicated to me that they were ready to serve our meal. I told the ushers who then announced that they wanted everyone to go inside and be welcomed by the family.

We stood at the entrance of the restaurant in a welcoming line, first was James followed by me then Patricia, Kayvan, Josh, Mel Louise and last but not least Kelly. A few feet in front of us was a board advising guests where their tables were, so all they had to do was check there places and proceed down the line where we were waiting to receive them. The ushers then announced that we were ready and slowly but surely each guest came down the line and shook our hands and kissed us on the cheeks. All the comments were the same, lovely, stunning, beautiful, congratulations. James took the opportunity to tell each man that past that if he buckled through his speech that they were to heckle him. *I had never seen him so nervous.*

Once all the guests were seated, the 'Captain's Table' filed in and stood at our seats. Phil then lifted his spoon, hammered it on the table and announced 'ladies and gentlemen, please be upstanding for the Bride and Groom, I give you Mr and Mrs Augustin.'
The whole room stood up and as they entered the room there was an astounding round of applause. Patricia and Kayvan walked in and acknowledged their guests, they looked so happy. Once seated their guests sat down and began chatting between themselves. Phil again rose to his feet and announced that the wedding party had decided that they would make their speeches

before the meal that way they could enjoy the meal without having to worry about what was to come.

'So ladies and gentlemen I give you the father of the bride.'

Again applause rippled throughout the room. James stood up and removed the speech that we had prepared from his jacket pocket. He gave me a glance and I smiled at him.

'It's OK, I whispered, 'take a deep breath you will be fine.'

He took his glasses out of the case and placed them half way up his nose, peering over the top of them and surveyed the room. It was as if he was looking for them to attack him, he looked petrified.

He braced his shoulders and took a deep breath.

'Hello,' he said and waited for the guests to respond with a hello. 'This may take some time,' he said, 'there are four pages so I hope you are sitting comfortably.'

There was a few titters through the room.

This is the speech in full:

I would like to start by saying welcome to you all, and thank you for coming to share in this special day. A warm welcome to those who have come from far a field, so welcome to Carol and Mick who have come all the way from Canada to be here today and of course to those of you from south of the border. This is a special day indeed to share in the celebrations of our beautiful, lovely daughter and our great new son-in-law as they become husband and wife.

You know I was the first person to see Patricia the day she was born. Such a beautiful baby, brown hair, blue eyes and a wee chubby face. Well the hair and eyes are the same but chubby! Well I have seen more fat on a butcher's pencil!

I remember thinking WOW!! What a responsibility. I have to feed her, clothe her, keep her warm, teach and guide her. But now, my job is done and I hand her willingly over to Kayvan. I know she is in safe hands with you. Anyone who can waken her just after midnight on her birthday, even armed with red roses and birthday cake is a brave and courageous man. For those of you who do not know, Patricia's favourite past time is sleeping. So it is not to be interrupted, except maybe in the event of fire. Even then, unless the flames were licking around her bedroom door I would be reluctant to waken her!

I was told by Patricia to keep this speech short and snappy - not to go on and on about when she was a little girl, so sorry for the baby bit Patricia. I will say this though Patricia, your mother and I are very proud of you, you have achieved so much and travelled 1000s of miles and had a very exciting life and as of today it will get more exciting. Kayvan, Pauline has already welcomed you to the family by way of a garland of Jasmine, so now it is my turn to say welcome, I could not have asked for a nicer man to hand my precious daughter over to.

As you all know Patricia has never been one to follow the crowd, be run-of-the mill as it were, but liked to stand out, be different. So I hope this next bit meets with her approval.

*Patricia was a beautiful baby, so meek, so pure so mild
And even as she got older, was such a well behaved young child….
She never used to say much, in fact, a lot was mime.
But then she found her little voice and to be silent was a crime.*

Then off to school our daughter went, full of dreams, ideals and hope…
And even though she couldn't spell, she found it easy to learn and cope….
Work then beckoned, so off she went to work in Debenham's store…
But then she said, 'I want to see the world, as this job is such a bore.'

So off she went to cruise the seas, to see more of this planet…
Taking in all sights and sounds and eating muffins like a gannet…
The e mails came but with no news of work, was she suffering from Amnesia??
No!! they were all about a certain young man who hailed from Indonesia!

His name was Kayvan Augustin; he was a waiter on the ship…
They spent time in the crew bar having drinks that they would sip….
He has dark eyes and lovely teeth and a crown of jet black hair….
And not long after that she said they were officially a pair!

They got closer and closer and the relationship boomed
But then nearer time for Christmas, their happiness was doomed…
Patricia's time was over, and it was time for her to go
Leaving Kayvan on the quayside with both hearts so full of woe.

The first few days after her return were really not quite nice…

She looked so lost and lonely that she decided to roll the dice…
So back to Debenham's she went to earn a few more pence….
She was saving to go to Indo which to her made perfect sense

Thank goodness for mobile telephones, computers and MSN…
Not to mention the mightiness of the good old ball point pen….
They kept in touch as best they could to stop them feeling glum…
Then one day Patricia said I am off to meet Kayvan's Mum!

So once again they were a couple, travelling around together…
Indonesia is beautiful, as are the people, but not the weather…
Patricia said we are in love and our lives they are to please…
So as soon as they could set it up they went back to sail the seas!

So once again, so far away, a couple they became…
Alas, not for very long, the excuses given were lame…
Patricia was sent home early, and again a broken heart.
It seemed to be that this loving pair was destined to be apart.

Patricia went to find a job, so newspapers she would scan….
I have to get a salary as I have a special day to plan…
So even through the distance the plans were under way
As the 29th of September was to be their wedding day.

Lots to do, lots to see and lots to put in place….
Then when Kayvan got his Visa you should have seen her face….
It really was a picture, as she knew this was the start…
Kayvan here in Scotland and no more being apart!

The plan was to stay with Mum and Dad if only for a time
But the price of property in Dundee was becoming quite a crime…
So, a flat was bought and lots of work to get it nice and bright…..
It was a home for Patricia and Kayvan so it had to be just right.

So now all the drama over, the couple are now as one
Finally Mr and Mrs and their new life has begun…
So here we are all family and friends the special day is here….
So I ask you to raise your glasses and wish them both good cheer.

I give you Mr and Mrs Kayvan Augustin!

James raised his glass and the guests stood and we all toasted the happy couple.

Now James did not perform the speech word perfect by any stretch of the imagination. As soon as he said….
'A warm welcome to those who have come from far a field, so welcome to Carol and Mick who have come all the way from Canada,' he chocked.
That was the start of the emotion kicking in. He tried so hard to keep it together but now and again his lip would tremble and the words stuck in his throat. That was a cue for Mick, he shouted across the room.
'Hey James….. Here's your first heckle!'

That was the best thing that could have happened. The rest of the speech went the same way, every time he showed signs of losing it there would be another heckle from someone. Then it became like an audience participation session. The comments were superb from both sides of the 'Captain's Table' causing laughter throughout the whole place. The best of the lot was when at one point James had said there are another two pages to go and a wee voice from the back of the room piped up.
'OH NO!' It was Cameron, he was actually referring to an incident at the table but it was so appropriate that there was a howl of laughter. James replied simply, 'Thanks Cameron!'
After the toast James sat down and heaved a sigh of relief, mopped his brow with a tissue and whispered 'Thank God that is over.'
I had taken my fan from the red sheath on my side plate, and discreetly held it in front of my mouth and said.
'That was perfect I have never seen anything like that before, it could not have been better.'
We smiled at each other and prepared ourselves for Kayvan and Josh's speeches. Kayvan was next.
He stood up and like James scoured the room, took a deep breath and began.

I thank God for being here, and my father in heaven would be so proud. He died not long ago but he would have loved Patricia.
My wife and I would like to thank James for being the best father of the bride ever. Not only did he give Patricia away instead of locking her in her room but his kind words have also made me feel welcome as the newest member of family. Thank you for your help and your support.

This is the most important day of our lives. Patricia and I are delighted to share it with our closest friends and families. We are also very grateful that so many of you have not only gone to the expense of sharing this day with us but have also bought us presents. Thank you.

I am so delighted to have James and Pauline as my new family. I knew that I'd love them when I fell in love with Patricia, because they helped her to be the person she is. She's so wonderful.

Patricia, you're always beautiful but you have never looked as perfect as my bride I LOVE YOU..!!
Patricia and I would like to say a special thank you to the bridesmaids, who have been a tower of strength throughout the preparation. They've been great.

Ladies and gentlemen please raise your glasses I give you, Mel, Kelly and Louise.

To the bridesmaids!
Thank you very much..!

As he sat down Patricia congratulated him on delivering a lovely speech. As James and I looked around the room throughout the speech we noticed there was hardly a dry eye in the house. The simple sentiment struck a chord with them all. Everyone realised what a big step this was for him, leaving his home and family and starting a new life with a new wife.

Next up was Josh. He stood up, and was more nervous than James and Kayvan put together. He held his speech in front of him and it was visibly obvious to all that he was so nervous as the paper shook violently. He did not prepare like James and Kayvan, he just launched right into it.

Before I start, I have been asked by management to make you all aware that they won't tolerate anyone standing on the tables or chairs for my standing ovation!

I have a few cards here that I would like to read from people who were unable to attend today's ceremony

I would also like to thank Kayvan for toasting the bridesmaids as it saves me having to do it! Only joking, they do look absolutely stunning today.

Well, well! Who would have thought that Patricia would take the plunge? I thought she would travel the world until she reached pension age then maybe settle down. But as always Patricia likes to surprise us and here we are today to celebrate with her and Kayvan on their big day.

Well Kayvan, what can I say about him? That's a Good question? I was at one point beginning to wonder if this guy actually existed! When I was here he wasn't and when he was here I wasn't. Fortunately Louise had met him in the summer last year when he was here and told me I had no worries as he was such a nice guy. Well now that I have met him I have made my own assumptions, and well he's OK …. I suppose!

I finally met Kayvan when he came to Bonny Scotland that is of course, once I returned home from off-shore. By which time I think Kayvan may have also thought that I was an imaginary brother. When we did meet I found it a bit awkward as I didn't know anything about this guy, so I didn't know what to talk to him about, but now I've met him once or twice we get on quite well, especially when the drink is flowing …..he doesn't shut up!

Then there was the flat, this became Kayvan's Office. Every day he would get ready, tidy up Mum and Dads house (never mind Mum there won't be as much mess now Patricia has left) isn't that right Titch? Then he would walk to the flat to start his daily tasks. Quite ironically he had said to Patricia in a phone call from Indonesia 'please don't finish the flat before I get there, leave something for me to do!!!' As he ain't able to work until they are married, well, well! Something to do! The poor bugger didn't know where to start, not by choice though, it was just a bigger task than everyone imagined, eh Dad? So now Kayvan can paint, sand wood, scrape walls, fill holes, cut work tops, put up tiles, so if anyone is needing a hand ... Kayvan is available and at very good rates. But don't tell the tax man...or Mum!!

But in all honesty Kayvan is a great guy, very quiet, very polite and my two boys think he's great! Well anyone that can make motor bikes, cars and hot dogs out of play doh is a winner to me as I can only make snooker balls and sausages. Which is the extent of my creative nature. Kayvan gets down on the floor to play with the boys at every given opportunity, he shows them magic tricks and generally has fun with them and is always making them laugh.

He has also taken up playing basket ball with Shaun which he enjoys. The only thing is that on the first time he went he played solid for nearly 2 hours, no break, so that shows his endurance. Is that right Titch? He was also told that he had to let other folk play as well, and no not with my sister before any rude minds get going!

However I did see a different side to him on his stag do. What a laugh, we went paint balling during the day and as the rest of us were getting pelted with paint balls and screaming obscenities, demanding poor victims to surrender Kayvan was laughing all the time. If he shot someone he laughed, and even if he got shot he laughed, even though the pain was extreme. I'm sure everyone that was there would agree that he was obvious to spot as he was always laughing all the time.

Then of course there was the BBQ. With the sun shining in the back garden we spent the afternoon eating burgers, drinking beer and comparing 'war wounds' and boy were there some wounds to be admired, they made us look like mutants with 3 nipples and not just that but nipples in the most unlikely places! So as the night went on and the beer was going down a treat Kayvan decided to help ease our aches and pains with his own crazy cocktail. He called it INDOSTAG. It would be a bit wrong to say it was tasty, but nevertheless it went town a treat, then he made another one, well that was a mistake. Holy cow!!!! The second batch was mind blowing, It took out more of us than a full round of paint balling, eh Paul!!! What a night that was, Kayvan, just to let you know, the rest of the paint balling gang and I will be getting some payback, so watch out!!!

I would also like to take a moment to say how gorgeous Patricia is looking today, I know she has never heard me say anything nice like that about her before but as they say better late than never. To Patricia!

Now, as you know, unfortunately Kayvan's family could not join us today so unknown to Kayvan there is a special message for him and us in the shape of a DVD which will be running in the whiskey bar. This was made by his best friend Gusti. If it had been possible Gusti would be here making this speech but I have been given the honour and privilege to stand in for him and hope I

255

have done him proud. Although none of Kayvan's family could be here, we do have a few 'token' family members of his here to share this wonderful day with him. They are 'THE SHIPPIES'. So shippies please can you stand up and give us all a wee wave so we know who you are!

Any way, enough of my rambling on, I would like to propose a toast. Can I ask you to raise your glasses and wish Patricia and Kayvan health, wealth, happiness and fun.

I give you MR & MRS Augustin.

During his speech Josh got heckled too. The family realised how nervous he was, it was obvious with the shaking paper. One person shouted.
'It's the paper that's so flimsy, eh Josh?'
He nodded realising people had noticed his shaking hands. Then as he mentioned the paintball someone else shouted.
'What about football? Does he support, Dundee?'
'No!' replied Josh, followed by the expression, 'happy days!'
This went down a storm as the majority, although not all, were Dundee United supporters. When he mentioned the DVD this was the hard bit. He knew he had been given the privilege of best man as Gusti couldn't be here and he choked on the words as he said them.

I was so proud of Josh standing there and speaking in front of all these people and knowing that he was in such pain with his Crohn's and the fact that the pain in his knees was excruciating. He handled it very well. He sat down lay back in his seat and said.
'Thank fuck that is over!'

The applause was phenomenal. They had appreciated every one's speeches, so now they could all relax and enjoy their meals.

'Oh, no, no, no'! said Patricia as she rose to her feet, James and I looked ay each other, we had no idea she had planned a speech too. She stood proud and tall and said.

'I have not prepared a speech but I would like to say thank you to you all but mostly I would like to thank you Mum and Dad, without you none of this would be possible.'
I saw Phil walk across the room carrying flowers and a box, he handed them over to Patricia and winked at her. She turned to look at me and said'
'Mum thank you, you are a legend and we have got you these as a gift to say we love you.'
She handed me the bouquet of flowers and we hugged and kissed each other on the cheeks. I looked down at the flowers and noticed that they were the same kind of flowers that were in her bouquet. There were lilies thistles and jasmine wrapped in cellophane and tied with a lovely bow.
'Dad, what can I say? Thank you so much for everything.'
She handed him the box.
'Now that's it from me so let's eat.'
Then she sat down and held Kayvan's hand. James opened the box; it was a bottle of wine. The label read.
'I can't put into words how much I love you. Love Patricia.' The pair of us stifled our tears.
James said, 'I can't believe she did this, but I am so glad she did.'
It was such a love filled moment and again the place was full of applause and tears.

257

I said to Patricia. 'How did you do that, the flowers are lovely.'

'Easy,' she said. 'I got the email address from your address book and contacted the lady who was doing my flowers and asked if she could do a replica bouquet for you.'

That is when I noticed they were exactly the same as her bouquet not just similar.

'Smarty pants,' I said to her. I was astounded at her thoughtfulness; amongst everything that was going on she had taken the time to do this for her Dad and me.

As soon as the speeches were finished the staff of the hotel began serving the meal. I watched them all moving around the room, knowing exactly who was due to get what, and they were so professional about the whole procedure. The guests were also enjoying the white and red wine that we had put on each table.

I noticed that the sun had come out and was shining brightly through the French windows and over the crowd in front of us. Quite a few people were fanning themselves with the fans that Patricia and Kayvan had brought from Indonesia.

'Great idea,' I said to Patricia, and nodded towards the people just in front of us.

She smiled sweetly and said, 'well at least we know they have been used.'

We finished the starters and began on the main course, I watched Mel who was sitting beside James. She got up half way through the main course and left the restaurant area. A while passed and I realised she had not returned. I wondered what had happened to her so Kelly went to see if she could find her. She went up to her room to find poor Mel vomiting in the bathroom. Oh no! Kelly knew exactly what was going on, poor Mel had

fell victim to the bug that had been going around.
'Please, go back and enjoy your meal, I will stay here for a while and come down as soon as I can.' said Mel.
'OK,' said Kelly, 'I will come and check on you later.'
Kelly came back down in time for dessert and told us what had happened. Then we all remembered that she had been feeling sick when we got to the hotel on the Friday night.

The meal over and we all retired to the bar area, had a few drinks and watched the DVD from Gusti. It went down well, and gave everyone something else to talk about and an understanding of Kayvan's life.
My cousin came over to talk to me.
'You must be so proud,' she said. 'Patricia has done you proud. I could not believe she had the courage to stand up as she did and present those gifts to you and James. It shows you how well you have brought her up and how much she appreciates you both.'
'Thank you,' I said, 'I must admit it tugged at my heart strings and James' too.'

Meanwhile 'Disco Bob' as we had come to name him was setting up his speakers and lighting and the hotel staff were re-positioning the restaurant yet again.
A quick time check and then realised that the guests we had invited for the evening were due to appear in the next few minutes. The day was passing so quickly it was hard to believe that it was now getting dark.

The coach arrived and again Patricia, Kayvan, James and I took our places to welcome the guests. They all said their congratulations and then were served with a glass of wine as they made their way to the bar. Some of them brought wedding presents which were taken by the hotel staff and put away for safe keeping until I was able to transfer them to our bedroom.

Disco Bob started his music and let a few tracks play. No one was dancing yet as they were waiting for Patricia and Kayvan to do the first dance. He had set his decks up at the door leading from the hexagonal room to the restaurant. That way the music flowed forward and the back of the hotel beside the whiskey bar would be quieter should anyone need a quiet spell.

Bob then asked for them to take the floor. They walked on again to cheers and applause. The music began; no one recognised it, as it was from an Indonesian group. They put their arms around each other and began to dance, it was a special moment as it is the first time they had been alone, as it were, all day. A minute or so later James and I joined them followed by Josh and Louise, Phil and Kelly and as if by some sort of miracle Sean and Mel.

James whispered to me. 'You have made this day so special and as far as I can see nothing has gone wrong.'
'A couple of minor hiccups,' I admitted, 'but on the whole it has all gone according to plan.'
We danced and held each other close as if it were us that were the newly weds.
'I love you, monkey,' I said.
'I love you too,' he whispered back to me.
Then a strange thing happened. Talk about stealing the lime light, every one, just everyone, was watching the special dancers, no not Patricia and Kayvan but Cameron and Blaine. They were dancing in perfect harmony to the music and they were oblivious to the stir they had caused. The flashes off the cameras alerted Patricia and Kayvan; they just stopped and looked on with the rest of us. A real show stopper you could say.

The rest of the evening went well; James and I were 'working the room' and now and again we would go outside as some of the guests were sitting at the BBQ benches. We spent the night passing each other with a dance now and then. Mel had to retreat back to the bedroom after the first dance and we didn't see her again for the rest of the night. Kelly was great she went to check up on Mel periodically to make sure was OK. I popped in to see her and all she did was apologise for messing up the day. I told her not to be silly she couldn't help it.

'Please,' she said, 'go and leave me to get on with it, don't stay here you have guests downstairs.'

I left her lying on the bed looking pale and sickly. Poor Mel of all the days to get sick all the build up for her and now this happens.

Josh was sitting most of the night as he was so uncomfortable with the pain in his knees.

He said. 'Mum I can hardly walk never mind dance.'

'Look son, go upstairs and take the kilt off, it weighs a ton and it may make you feel a bit better.'

The next time I saw him he was in his jeans and although still not 100% he was more comfortable. Louise was the star of the night; she danced with everyone in the room never stopping to take breath. By now the disco was in full swing and the drinks were flowing readily.

Millie's mother came across to me and asked if I was Patricia's Mum.

'Yes,' I said, is there a problem.'

'No, no problem at all. I just want to say thank you for inviting me, but mostly I wanted to say what a perfect wedding this has been. I have been to many weddings but this has been perfect. I can't think of another word to describe it.'

I was blown away by her remarks.

'Thank you very much,' I said. I could feel myself blushing. The words reeled in my head; I could not believe that someone I had never met before in my life had given me the biggest compliment ever.

Then another photo opportunity, the cutting of the cake, Again the happy couple stepped forward and this time armed with a lovely silver knife posed for pictures and made the incision into the cake. Then they began to fool around so there is one picture of Patricia holding Kayvan with the knife held at his throat. This caused a few comments as you can imagine. Cameron and Jack were taken away as they were getting tired. Louise's parents were at the wedding so they took them home to their house for the night, leaving Josh and Louise to enjoy themselves and the night at the hotel. They would take them home later the next day. We all got hugs and kisses but they were too tired to be bothered about leaving us behind so they went away quite happy.

Back to the dancing for a while then at 10pm Bob announced that the buffet was ready and that he was going to have a fifteen minute break. People flocked to the buffet and ate the superb food that had been prepared for them. The hotel had been told that under no circumstances should there be pork or ham in the buffet as Kayvan is a Muslim and does not eat pork. They had taken great care therefore to avoid the typical sausage rolls and ham sandwiches and instead presented chicken sate sticks and vegetable samosas and quiche etc. Not a bit of pork to be seen anywhere. Needless to say the wedding cake was part of the spread that was on the table which was covered with beautiful white linen cloths.

Once everyone had eaten it was back to the dancing. This went on until 12.30am as the coach to take the guests back to Dundee was arranged for 1am so this

gave them half an hour to say goodbye, go to the loo or whatever
By this time my feet were aching so I kicked off the high heeled sandals, turned up my skirt so I would not trip and danced the night away. Patricia had also changed from her silver high heeled shoes into little pumps so she could dance.

Kayvan performed all night dancing and dancing and enjoying the whole experience. He did not give in and strip off to stay cool. He did remove his jacket and tie but the kilt remained on all night, James appeared looking more relaxed now too. He had taken off his jacket, tie and shirt and replaced them with a Jacobean type shirt with leather ties criss-crossing below his neck.

I was sitting chatting to Josh when the DJ said.
'Now here is a special request from James.'
My ears pricked up, wondering what he was up to. The DJ announced that this was a special record for me! 'Pauline,' he said, 'James wants to say what a wonderful job you have done today. All the months of planning have paid off and you deserve recognition for it.'
I began to blush again; I felt it move from my face to the tips of my toes. Josh was grinning at me, he nudged me and said.
'Go on Mum this is your dance.'
I looked at the dance floor and there was James with his arms outstretched and beckoning me to dance with him. The music played, the words rang out. *'You're once, twice, three times a lady and I love you.'*
I walked over to James and melted into his arms, my head bowed low into his chest and I cried like a baby. This caused some laughter from James.
'I mean every word you hear,' he said.
Well this just made my tears flow faster. We were left to dance alone as the people looked on, then Patricia and

Kayvan, Josh and Louise joined in. It was great to see Josh dancing with Louise obviously putting the pain to one side, even if only briefly.

The manager of the hotel finally appeared and offered his congratulations to us all. Then asked if every thing had been OK?

'Yes thank you, Denise had been fantastic,' I said, 'you should be very proud of her especially dropping her in it at the last minute.'

'I am glad,' he said, 'that it all went well but I was called away urgently, I offer my apologies.'

He then took me to one side.

'I have had complaints about the music being too loud,' he said. 'Some of the residents living close by are not happy, so I wondered, if it is OK, can I ask your guests to come inside so I can shut the door and contain the music.'

'You must be joking,' I said, 'the music isn't that bad and I am sure the nearby residents have experienced this before. This isn't the first wedding you have ever done.'

I felt myself getting annoyed. If Denise had asked I would not have minded but this guy appears late in the proceedings and tells me we have to keep the noise down. The cheek of it! James asked what was wrong; he could see I was less than pleased. I explained the complication and he said.

'Well it is getting late and cold so maybe a good idea to bring everyone inside.'

'Well, I suppose so.' I agreed and left the manager to advise the people outside to come in.

Later on I bumped into Denise and told her I was less then pleased, but she informed me of a somewhat embarrassing predicament. It appeared that some of the guests had been sneaking beer from their car to the reception and it had been seen on the security cameras. I was mortified that someone would be that forward.

In keeping with tradition the bride was thrown up into the air and caught by the ladies, followed by the groom being caught by the men. Kayvan was shocked with this. I just hoped he had on underwear and not listened to James and Josh who had let it slip that men don't wear anything under their kilts!

The disco was brought to a close by signing 'Auld Lang Syne' and that was it……over.

It was hard to believe that the months of preparation had now finished. The wedding done and it appears everyone had enjoyed it.

My neighbour who had kindly agreed to organise the coach to get people home safely checked her list and made sure everyone that should be departing was organised and on the coach ready for its departure at 1 am.
The guests that were staying overnight retired to the whiskey bar. Close family and friends shared a drink and relaxed together. Not long after that we all turned in for the night. It had been a fantastic day and even if I do say so myself it had been perfect.

James and I went upstairs to our room and he just stared at me……
'Wow, what a day, huh. It was fantastic; I loved every minute of it.'
'Me too,' I said, as I removed all the makeup Raquel had applied earlier.
'What will you do with your time now?' said James.
'I don't know,' I said, 'but people have warned me of the wedding anti-climax. They say that after all the time

spent preparing and organising that the weeks that follow are dreadful. So the answer to your question is I really don't know.'

We went to bed and cuddled together. For weeks now I had been going to the doctor and getting pills for anxiety and been told to relax as I was stressed, but now I was so happy and relaxed.

I relived the day over and over before I finally drifted off into sleep.............

Postscript

……..the next morning James and I showered and went down for breakfast.
'I doubt if anyone else is up yet,' he said, 'but I can't wait I am so hungry.'
We went outside to have a cigarette, from where we stood we could see that there were people in the bar already.
'Who has beaten us to it,' James said, as we peered through the window.
'I think it is Josh and Louise,' I said.
'Never!' exclaimed James, 'surely they would take the advantage of a long lie-in, seeing as the boys are not here.'
We went into the breakfast area to find it was Josh and Louise sitting drinking tea they had already finished breakfast.
'You two are up early,' we said.
Louise looked up at me and said. 'Josh isn't feeling very well. The pains in his knees appear to be getting worse.'
She looked concerned to say the least.
'What's up Josh?'
'Man I have been awake most of the night with the pain. Nothing I do seems to ease it,' he said.
He looked awful; the grimace on his face and his grey complexion told the whole story.
'Look,' I said, 'I will try and get someone to take you home early and I suggest you go and see the emergency doctor.'
'No Mum,' he said, 'it's alright, I am not going to spoil things.'
I got angry with him, 'do as you are told young man. You are not spoiling anything, the wedding is over. I am worried about you and so is Louise. Look at her face. Louise looked tired and scared.

'See I told you your Mum would be annoyed with you,' said Louise anxiously.

James and I sat down for breakfast, all the time I kept an eye on Josh. The rest of the family started to filter down and we all sat chatting while they waited for the waitress to bring their food. My brother and his family arrived,
'Blaine has been sick this morning,' he said.
'Not another one,' I said. 'I hope Mel hasn't past her bug around.'
'Probably too much excitement yesterday,' he said.
'Maybe but we will keep an eye on her.'
'Still no sign of Patricia and Kayvan,' said Josh.
'I know, I suppose they are exhausted, it was a busy day for them.'
'It was their wedding night Mum,' he said and winked at James.
'I know what you are hinting at!' I said and the place was in an uproar.

Blaine sat down to eat her cereal and no sooner had she swallowed a mouthful then it was up again. That was the start; she vomited continuously from there on in. I stood in front of her trying to shield the rest of the family who were now eating bacon and eggs. The last thing anyone wants to see whilst eating is someone being sick. Denise arrived right on cue to deal with the situation. She took Blaine to the bathroom with her Mum so she could help tidy her up. Once she was gone the waitress came along and cleaned up the mess.
My brother looked at me and said.
'I think we will just head home after this. I know we had arranged to go to your house but I don't think it is a good idea now.'
'Maybe not,' I said, 'the poor wee soul should go home'.
Just then Phil and his wife Susan arrived.

'Just thought we would call in before we head off home,' he said, 'see how you all are today'
'Well could be better,' I said, 'Josh isn't feeling well and Blaine is in the loos being sick.'
'Oh dear,' he said, 'that's not good.'
'Did you say you were heading home now?' I said.
'Yes we just popped in for a minute.'
'Can you do me a big favour then, this will be the last I ask of you.'
'Can you take Josh and Louise home please?'
'Yeah, sure,' he said, 'not a problem.'
'Right, you two get your things and Phil will take you home and as soon as you get there phone the doctor. I will check on you as soon as I can.'
A few minutes later they had gone.

One problem solved only to be faced with another. Mel and Kelly arrived only to be told that Kelly had been sick all night too. I couldn't believe my ears, I suppose it was an obvious outcome, seeing as Kelly had looked after Mel all evening. The pair of them said. 'Would you mind if we don't have breakfast but just go home?'
'Not at all,' said James and I, 'we have already packed Josh and Louise away home.'
Just as they turned to leave, Patricia and Kayvan came in.
'What's up?' said Patricia.
I told her what was going on and she couldn't believe it either. 'Hope it wasn't the food,' she said.
'I doubt it, I am afraid the bug is taking its toll all round'

At least the bride and groom had escaped it, was the general consensus of opinion.
We spent the next couple of hours saying goodbye to our family. Then we had to pack our cars with the candles, DVD player clothes etc and leave Patricia and Kayvan behind. We thought it would be nice for them to

spend another night there before they went on honeymoon to stay in a tent!

All packed up it was time so say goodbye to our lovely daughter and new son-in-law. The four of us stood outside the door of the hotel and hugged and kissed each other.
'Thanks for everything,' they said, 'it was a brilliant wedding. It couldn't have been better if we had paid someone to do it.'
'Glad you liked it,' we said, 'and I think we gave everyone nice memories to take away and lots to talk about. There won't be at another wedding like this one that's for sure.'
'Unless, of course, someone else marries and Indonesian,' said Kayvan, then chuckled loudly.
'We are off now then. Carol and Mick are waiting in the car.'
Another kiss and hug then we turned and walked down the steps towards the car.
'I will be back tomorrow,' said James, about 8 o'clock so be ready.'
The pair of them chorused, 'OK Dad'! They stood and waved at the car until we drove out of sight. *I wanted to cry but Carol kept talking to me, which was good. I didn't really want to shed anymore tears.*

The four of us arrived home and I put the kettle on for tea and coffee then tried to phone Josh but there was no answer. I then got a strange phone call from a doctor. It was the emergency doctor trying to get hold of Josh.
'I am afraid he isn't here,' I said. 'What is going on?'
'I was trying to get a message to him that he should come down to the surgery so I can have a look at him,' the doctor said.

Then I realised what had happened, Josh had not changed his phone number with the surgery when he moved house to live with Louise. So when they looked at his notes they phoned my number instead of his. I explained the situation and told him I would call Josh and get him to go to the surgery as soon as possible. I phoned Josh and this time Louise answered. I told her what had happened and to tell Josh he had to go to the doctors now and once he had been seen to let us know what was happening.

Then James' phone went. It was a text message from Patricia. I didn't know what it said but I knew it wasn't good as I heard James take a sharp intake of breath followed by a stifled sob,
'Oh my God James what is wrong?' I asked'
He handed the phone to me the message read. 'I feel such a bitch, 'cos I didn't give you a kiss when you gave me away. Sorry!'
'What is all that about?' he said. 'I am going to phone her. He took the phone back and dialled her number.
'Hi babe, what is that text all about?'
She answered, 'when you gave me away I was meant to give you a kiss and I didn't, I feel such a bitch.'
'Don't be silly,' he said, 'you gave me a smile which spoke volumes. I didn't need a kiss.'
'You don't understand Dad,' she said, 'I wanted to and I didn't. I feel awful.'
By this time James had a tear running down his cheek which made me cry to. I went into the lounge where Carol and Mick were sitting.
'What the hell is wrong with you?' said Carol. I explained about the text message and the conversation that James and Patricia were having.
'Hey, it was a great day and everything went well, surely she can give him a kiss when he picks her up tomorrow.'

'I suppose so, but it is not the same is it?'
She obviously had the vision in her head and now she is gutted because she forgot.
Then I realised what had happened, James walked her down the aisle and handed her over to Kayvan, but he was never asked, 'who is it that gives this woman?' The usual occasion for a bride to kiss her father.
'There is nothing we can do, we can't retrieve the moment and the pair of them are hurting.'

I went back into the kitchen to find James holding the phone close to his chest and weeping.
'What a girl she is,' he mumbled, 'she is all upset because she never gave me a kiss, what a compliment.'
'Never mind,' I sighed, 'you can kiss her tomorrow when you pick them up to take them to the bus station.'
'Yes I will without a doubt,' said James, then regained his composure.
'What an afternoon,' I said, 'it never rains but it pours in this house.'

Louise called shortly after that.
'The doctor said that the problem with Josh's knees is being caused by his medication, so you were right. The doctor has given him stronger painkillers and he has to rest. This should sort him out.'
'OK, thanks for phoning Louise,' I said, 'I will let the rest of them know. Have you got the boys yet?'
'No,' she said, 'I have left them with my Mum and Dad for now, I will go and get them later on once Josh feels a bit better.'
'Sounds like a good idea, maybe if he takes the tablets and has a sleep he will feel more like himself. Bye for now, I will call again later to see how things are going.'

The rest of the afternoon was spent looking at photos that we had taken and going over the wedding bit by bit.

I sent an email to family and friends and asked them to send me any photos they had either on disc or just in an email.

I had had an idea. What I wanted to do was put the pictures in order and then make a DVD of pictures, and at the appropriate time put the correct music over it, so it all flowed like it did on the day.

After dinner the four of us relaxed in front of the TV and then Carol and Mick went off to bed. I went and cleaned the kitchen and when I got back into the lounge I saw the sweetest thing I had seen in ages. James had fallen asleep on the couch with his feet resting on the coffee table and he was holding the balloon which read. 'Just Married'. He looked so relaxed, happy and contented, I reached for my camera and snapped a photo, that will be one for the DVD I thought.

'Come on sleepy head,' I said as I woke James from his slumber, 'let's go to bed it has been a hectic weekend and you have an early start tomorrow.'

The next morning James went to the hotel to pick up Patricia and Kayvan, not to mention all the gear they needed for their camping honeymoon. There were no buses available from the hotel to Perth early enough to get them there in time for the bus to Mull so James was more than keen to go and get them. He wasn't away very long only a couple of hours. On his return I asked if he got his kiss.
'No,' he said! 'I got two'!
And a broad smile covered his face.
'You look like the cat that got the cream,' I said and the pair of us agreed.

'They got there in plenty of time,' he said, 'so now they have hours on a bus then a ferry to catch. They won't be there until early evening.'
'So what are we up to today then,' James asked us all.
'Well I will make coffee and you guys can decide what you want to do.'
There were no ideas when I got back with the coffee. James was speaking to Mick about our house and how he wanted to move.
'Not that old story again,' I said, 'we tried and failed remember?'
'I know,' said James, 'but I feel now that both the kids have left home that maybe we should look for something smaller, a new start for us, just you and me.'
'I will be back in a minute,' I said.
I went upstairs and checked what houses were up for sale on a web site I had used before. There was one, it was in an area we had looked at last time and the asking price was within our budget. Armed with the details I had printed off I put it on the table and said.
'There you go. How about we make an appointment to view this one.'
The three of them poured over the schedule for the house.
'It looks nice,' they said.
OK, full of bravado I picked up the phone and arranged to go and view the house.
'Problem solved about what we are doing today,' I laughed. 'We are all going to look at that house.'
James' jaw dropped, 'are you joking?'
'Nope, we have an appointment at noon, so get your skates on.'
I was obviously still in organising mode!
So as good as my word at noon we walked up the path to the property and as we approached the owner came to the door.
'Hello,' he said. 'I wasn't expecting four people.'

James explained that Carol and Mick were visiting from Canada and were having a nosey. We were shown around the house room by room. Mick and the owner were getting on famously, talking about old Dundee and trying to find out if they had any mutual friends. The house was great, just what we would have been looking for should we be looking to buy. As it happens we weren't, but Mr Starling the owner didn't know that! He did say that the house had been on the market for a month and so far no one had put in an offer or even a note of interest!

We left the house and we went for a look around the shops and again for coffee. All the time James kept on about the house.

'Look,' I said, 'it was just something to do, our house is not even on the market.'

'Yes I know all that, but I love it Pauline. I really love it. I think we should put an offer in on it and see what happens.'

I was gob smacked to say the least, what turned out to be a passing of time has taken a strange twist. James couldn't wait to get home so he could phone our solicitor. He called him and told him to put an offer in on the house. He told him that there had not been any previous offers and the solicitor said that that could be in our favour.

'I will put your offer in and let you know if and when I hear anything.'

He called back in less than an hour and told us that our offer had been rejected but if we would offer another £5K Mr Starling would accept. James looked at me with a quizzical look on his face.

'No,' I said, 'I am not prepared to go another £5,000. Increase our offer by £3,000 and tell him this is the final offer. If Mr Starling is wise he will accept.'

So the new offer went in and we just sat back and waited. We knew we wouldn't hear any more today as it was now 4.30 pm and most offices close at 5 pm.

'Let's just wait and see what tomorrow brings.'

The rest of the evening was spent discussing the house. Mick and Carol were as smitten as James. I was much more reserved about the whole procedure. We had been there before and been disappointed so many times that I had learned my lesson, not to build my hopes up. Besides, we would have to get this place sold too and there was a little bit of work to be done.

'Patience is a virtue, que cera cera,' I was coming out with all these crazy sayings and driving the rest of them up the wall.

Patricia texted me to let me know that they had arrived at the camp site and that the place was lovely. I replied to tell her that we were glad they were OK and by the way we may have bought a house! The reply was just, 'WHAT'!

The next day brought the news they had all been waiting for, our offer had been accepted!

'So now we have to put this place on the market,' said James.

I was actually delighted as I loved the house too and now I could get caught up in the drama.

The rest of the week was a whirlwind preparing and organising. Carol and Mick were as bad as us. Mick had even decided where we should build a garage!

Before we knew where we were it was time to pick up Patricia and Kayvan. James again went through for them and took them home. They were going to come around later for tea as Carol and Mick were heading back to Canada the next day and they wanted to see them before they left.

Carol and Mick finished their packing and had everything in place for their departure tomorrow. Patricia and James came around and we had a meal and looked at the photos again.

'You know,' said Patricia. 'I can't remember anything. It is all a blur.'

'Don't worry,' I said, 'we have lots of pictures and there were four video cameras running so that will jog your memory. Speaking of pictures, do you have any from your honeymoon?'

'I have brought my camera,' said Patricia, 'I will hook it up to the laptop so Carol and Mick can see them before they go.'

We poured over the photos and laughed as we saw the tent that they had been living in for the past few days.

'Certainly not luxury then,' we said.

'No, but it was a laugh. We had a toilet and shower, so it was luxury by tent standards,' she laughed.

They had been to Oban and Iona so most of the pictures were of scenery or ones of the pair of them jumping in puddles or sheltering from the rain.

'Weather not so good then?' asked Mick.

'No, not really, but it added to the charisma and romance,' she giggled.

One photo in particular caught my eye, it was similar to one the photographer had taken with their hands on top of each other showing their wedding rings the difference was it had been taken with their hands over the side of the ferry and below the water was crashing.

'I like this one,' I said, 'it is your hands across the sea again but without the distance between you!'

'I thought you would like that one,' said Patricia, 'but now our hands are together forever.'

Then she said. 'So what's all this about a house?'

So we told them the whole story and how quickly it happened.

'So you finally did it then Dad?' she said.

'Yes I can't believe it myself to be honest.'

They didn't stay late and said their goodbyes to Carol and Mick.
'We hope to see you again soon,' said Kayvan. 'It has been a pleasure meeting you.'
'You never know,' said Carol, 'we may come for Josh and Louise's wedding next year. Not very likely though as it is expensive but you just never know'.

We took Carol and Mick to the airport and had a nice lunch which Mick paid for.
'Well, I have to get rid of this funny money,' he said.
Then again it was time for goodbyes. Carol knows I hate them so she made it short and sweet. She gave me a quick hug and just said
'See ya!'
Mick hugged me and said. 'Look after yourself and your fantastic family. It has been great.'
He shook hands with James and said. 'Look after her.'
James just nodded back at him then they made their way to the departure lounge.

Back home and then the silence fell. It was strange, No kids, no grandkids, no visitors just James and I.
'Is this what it is going to be like then,' I said to James, 'quiet and tranquil.'
'Hardly,' he said, 'we have a house to sell.'
Never a truer word has been spoken.
'Let's just enjoy what is left of the weekend. Josh and Louise will be over tomorrow with the kids so enjoy the peace while we have it.'

Sunday was nice the kids entertained us as always. Cameron is such a comic and Jack is an angel. The pair of them light up the room and certainly our lives. Josh seemed better and not in as much pain as far as his knees was concerned but his gut was playing up.

'No surprise there,' I said, 'you are full of pills they are bound to make you feel a bit off. Once the immuno suppressants take control you will feel better.'

'Yeah, no doubt I just have to take it as it comes, I suppose. I just hope they kick in sometime soon.'

'We all hope that for you son, you know if I could cut off my arm to make you better I would.'

'I know Mum,' he said.

'I think you should go home now,' I said to Josh, 'get the kids to bed and you should follow soon after, get some rest.'

'Good thinking,' said Louise. She bundled the kids and Josh into the car and went home.

James and I were alone again; we tidied up once more and sat down to enjoy the peace.

James said, 'well it is back to work for me tomorrow so I am going to have a dram of whiskey and watch TV then head off to bed myself.'

'I will have a Bacardi and coke then,' I said, 'we may as well enjoy ourselves.'

A couple of hours later we went to bed ready to start a new week. I had lots to do to the house as we had told the solicitor that we would be ready for viewers by Tuesday.

Monday morning and now things were back to as near a normal routine. I was still off work but was due to see the doctor on Wednesday, James left the house at his usual time and I got out of bed to wave goodbye to him. Once the car was out of sight I went to make myself a cup of coffee. I sat there in solitude enjoying the nothingness. I hadn't even put the radio on which is not like me. I sat and planned my day in my head. First a shower then dress, then I will start in the bathroom and clean it top to bottom. After that I will strip the beds and maybe do some ironing. Yes that sounded like a good days work.

I did deviate a little from my plan, before it even started as I had another cup of coffee. But after that I showered and dressed then cleaned the bathroom. I stripped my bed and as I wrestled with the duvet the phone rang.

'Hi,' said Louise, 'are you busy today, can you take the boys.'

'Sure,' I said, 'the beds and ironing can wait, have you and Josh got something planned.'

'No, not exactly,' then her tone changed. 'It's Josh he is in a lot of pain and he can't see the doctor until 1pm but I am not prepared for him to wait that long so I am taking him to the hospital.'

'That bad?' I asked'

'I think so,' she said. 'Well put it this way I am not waiting.'

'OK,' is said. 'I will watch at the window for you, don't come in I will come out for the boys.'

'I will be there in about twenty minutes.'

As soon as I hung up I dialled James' number. James I said. 'How busy are you at work today?'

'What a crazy question,' he said, 'things are manic here as it always is when I have been away for a week or so, why do you ask?'

I told him what Louise had said and without thinking twice he said.

'I will meet them there.'

'Thanks babe,' I said. 'I am just waiting for the boys now. Let me know what's going on as soon as you find out.'

'Of course, catch you later.'

I sat at the window and waited for the car to pull up. I didn't have to wait for long as the car screamed to a halt. I ran out and grabbed Jack, and Louise brought

Cameron around the side of the car. I had a quick peek at Josh. He looked hellish.
'Go Louise, just go, James will be there to meet you.'
'Keep me posted.'
She jumped back in the car and with a quick wave to her boys she drove off.

It was hard work trying to keep two children happy when I was so worried about my own child, *no matter how old he is, he is still my boy, I kept thinking,* Jack must have picked up on the tension as he just would not settle. I tried everything but nothing would console him. I ended up putting the television on for Cameron so he could watch the kid's programmes. That always stopped him in his tracks. Now I could focus on Jack. The only thing that calmed him was if I stood and rocked him back and forth. He is heavy and my arms were getting sore holding him, but worst of all my legs were like jelly.
'I am going to have to sit down Jack,' I said, 'cos if I don't I am going to drop you for sure and we don't want that.'
I knew that my anxiety was taking over and I couldn't stop it.
'What a pair we are Jack the pair of us are up to 99.' I whispered in his little ear.
Cameron continued to be transfixed with the television so that was a God-send. As soon as I sat down Jack screamed again. I was getting quite concerned as I had not heard from the hospital. The more concerned I got the more my legs turned to jelly.
Come on phone ring will you I kept thinking.
Then it did eventually, James said.
'Listen to me carefully.'
I couldn't hear a word he was saying for Jack screaming.
'Speak up,' I said. 'I can't hear you.'

'Look!' The command was urgent. 'Put Jack on the floor and listen to what I am saying.'
'He is crying,' I said.
'Put him on the floor and listen.'
This time the command was sharper.
I put Jack on the floor and listened to James.
'Josh has to have surgery,' he said.
My heart skipped a beat.
'Surgery! For what?' I asked almost afraid of the answer.
'His bowel has ruptured and he has to have surgery to correct it. They are going to try keyhole surgery but they don't know if it will work.'
I was dumbstruck.
'Speak to me,' James said, 'did you hear what I said?'
'Yes.' I whispered. The thought of my boy going through surgery sent my head spinning.
'I am on my way home now then you can go up and see him.'
I picked Jack up off the floor and cuddled him, the poor wee soul was so upset. Cameron was oblivious to what was going on he was too involved in 'Bob the Builder'.
James arrived and told me more details. It seems that the rupture was to the rear of his bowel which apparently is good.
'But they may have to cut him and remove the bowel if worst comes to worst.'
'Right I am off to buy him toiletries and pyjamas etc. I will be back soon, then I will go to the hospital.'
'Will you be ok with the boys?' I said.
He looked at me as if to say: I am a Dad you know!
'I will be fine'.
I drove down to the shop and bought nappies, pyjamas for the boys as they would have to stay with us tonight then a dressing gown, slippers and pyjamas for Josh. I wasn't there long but when I pulled up outside the door James ran out and said.

'Don't come in Josh is going for surgery in the next half an hour. So get your backside up there and see him before he goes in. Patricia is on her way too, she will see you there.'

'Here,' I said, 'nappies and pjs for the boys,'

I threw them at him and then made a bee-line for the hospital.

When I got to the ward I was shocked to see Josh lying there with an oxygen mask and an intravenous infusion running. His colour was so bad, he was grey, cold and clammy. At least I had made it before he left for theatre. Fortunately he was we sedated for the pain but I didn't like the look of him. Louise and I nodded at each other we didn't have to speak the look in our eyes was enough.

I broke the silence. 'What's going on now then?'

'He is meant to be going to theatre in the next couple of minutes' she said.

'Right, yeah, OK,' ... 'Hi son,' I said as I leaned over his bed and stroked his face. I felt myself recoil as I felt his cold clammy skin. I sat by his bed and just stared at him, willing him to get better and muttering prayers in my head. A while later Patricia arrived.

'I thought he was going to theatre ages ago,' she said.

'We are just waiting for a slot to become available.'

She had just finished work and came straight up.

'Look,' I said. 'I will go and get some sandwiches and drinks, you must be hungry and Louise has been here all day.'

I left the pair of them while I went to find somewhere still open that sold food. I bought sandwiches and coke: enough to keep us going for a while as who knew how long we were going to be there.

While I was out of the ward I took the chance to phone James and give him an update and check on the boys.

'I am OK,' he said, 'and the boys are in bed, Jack settled eventually it took my touch to sort him out,' he laughed weakly down the phone.

'Ged is here with me,' he said. 'He didn't want me to be here alone.'

'That's nice of him,' I said.

'He has been keeping me going with details of what he wants to do to the house so he is keeping my mind occupied.'

'I had better go sweetheart,' I said, 'as soon as I have more info I will let you know.'

I hurried back to the ward fearing I had missed Josh going away. But he was still there.

An hour or so later the porters came to take him down to the theatre. The surgeon that was going to do the operation was with them.

'Hello Louise,' said the surgeon, 'is this 'your' Josh?'

'Hello there,' said Louise, 'are you doing the operation?'

'Yes,' she said.

She sat and explained that she was going to do.

'I will try keyhole first and if that works great, if not I will have to cut him and see what is needed. I will try and do it without leaving a stoma but that is the worst case scenario. If I do have to do that it should only be temporary.'

'OK,' said Louise, 'do whatever you have to, to make him better.'

She took the words right out of my mouth which was good because I couldn't speak.

They checked Josh's identity then when they were satisfied he was the right patient they wheeled him away. Louise leaned over the bed and kissed him gently,

'Love you,' she whispered and even in his dozy state he said. 'I love you too.'

'How long will it take?' Louise asked the surgeon.

'About an hour for keyhole surgery, but up to three or four hours if I have to cut him,' she said.
It was now 9pm.
'We could be in for a long night,' I said.
'How do you know the surgeon, Louise?' I asked.
'I used to look after her little boy,' she said. 'I know she has a good reputation as a surgeon so he is in good hands.'
'Always a bonus when you know the doctor,' I smiled.
The three of us went up to the main concourse and ate our sandwiches.
'Mine is tasteless,' I said and the others said the same. 'It fills a hole though and will keep us going until we get home.'
We paced the floor for a while and then went back to the ward to see if there was any information.
'Nothing yet,' said the nurse, 'he must still be in theatre.'
We all looked at our watches, it had been an hour and a half, and we feared the worse. We sat in the ward waiting room and watched TV. Patricia was great; cracking jokes and reading silly articles out of a magazine she had picked up. Another hour passed.
'I am going to ask the nurse if there is any news yet,' said Louise.
She got up and left the room, I followed and stood by the door way. I watched her walk back up the ward. She saw me standing and just shook her head. She started to cry.
'Its OK,' I said trying to comfort her,
'I wish I was strong like you,' she said.
'I am not strong Louise. I feel the same as you. If I started crying now I wouldn't stop and that is no good for anyone. Look he is obviously in for the long haul. Why don't we go home and phone in a while? Remember you also have two boys to think about.'
'I can't!' she said. 'I can't leave until I know what has happened'.

'Well lets wait some more, it can't be much longer now.'

Then, at 1am after what seemed like forever, the nurse came down and told us that Josh was out of theatre.

'Thank God!' I said, 'no matter what they have done he has come out of surgery. I will go and let James know.'
I went outside and phoned James.
'I don't know what they have done yet but he is out of theatre,' I said.
'Oh thank God, I was really getting worried it has taken so long.'
'We should be home in a little while. Louise is hoping to see him before she leaves.'
'OK babe see you soon.'
As I was walking back to the ward I saw Patricia approaching.
'Louise is away down to the theatre. You missed the surgeon; she came down to speak to Louise. Apparently they did have to cut him but there is no bag. She cut away the part of the bowel that ruptured and also all the bowel that was affected with Crohn's. She said he was a lucky boy, if Louise had not acted as she did it might be a different story.'

Louise appeared about ten minutes later.
'How is he?'
'Drowsy obviously but his colour is better and he told me he loves me.'
'Great, now let's go home.'
I dropped Patricia off first then took Louise back to my house. We filled James in on the situation over tea then went to bed.

The next day we went up to visit Josh, he was looking a million times better than when we had seen him last. He was on a morphine shunt so that when the pain was too bad he could give himself a shot. He was not allowed to eat either. That did not go down well! He had a tube up his nose draining the bile from his stomach and the intravenous infusion in his arm was keeping him hydrated. They had moved him into a side room in the ward as he was young and the rest of the patients in the ward were elderly. They thought that he would appreciate a room to himself with his own washroom and the bonus of a television.

The fasting and IV went on for a week or so as they had to rest his bowel to ensure it healed properly. He was making good progress, he was up on his feet and able to get to the phone in the dayroom to call Louise dragging his IV with him. Then the doctor recommended they commence on a light diet. If he could tolerate this they would remove the tube and the IV from his nose.

We could not believe the difference in him. He was looking more like his old self every day.
He tolerated the diet of clear soup and jelly so the tube was removed, however they monitored him closely because if he began to feel sick then the tube would have to be reinserted. He managed beautifully so his diet was increased to solid food.
'Happy days,' he said. It was becoming a catch phrase. 'The doctor said that if I manage this then they will let me home in a couple of days.'

Louise called.
'Josh is getting home today,' she said.
It had been hard for her; she was keen to get Josh home. She had visited him every day but still had little Cameron and Jack to look after.
I was so pleased to hear the news.
'That's great Louise I bet you are glad?'

'Oh yes, now I can look after him. I am going to pick him up from the hospital this afternoon.'
'OK, tell him I will phone him tonight to check up on him.'
I put down the phone and heaved a sigh of relief.

I got to thinking, what a year it had been, the ups and downs, the good times and bad, a new grandson, the wedding, the flat, my anxiety attack, Josh's illness and a new house to move into.

As for what people had said about the anti climax of the wedding................well I am still waiting!!

THE END

Hands across the sea!!